MATTERHORN THE BRAVE™
ADVENTURES THROUGH TIME

TWO BOOKS IN ONE

THE SWORD AND THE FLUTE

TALIS HUNTERS

Mike Hamel

Matterhorn the Brave™ Series: Book 1

The Sword and the Flute

Talis Hunters

Copyright © 2016 by Mike Hamel
Published by EMT Communications
Colorado Springs, CO 80923

Matterhorn the Brave is a trademark of EMT Communications.
Cover, Interior design and typesetting by John Besmehn
Edited and proofread by John & Leo Schulte

Printed in USA

ISBN-13: 979-8-9911301-7-2

The stories and characters in this series exist
because of Susan,
who made them all possible.

THE SWORD AND THE FLUTE

Mike Hamel

Contents

Introduction

A sad thing happens to most people when they grow up. As their bodies get bigger, their imaginations get smaller. In time, their imaginations become so tiny and timid that they are afraid to go out alone. That's why kids have always been the greatest explorers. And among the greatest of them all are Matterhorn the Brave and his friends.

Matterhorn is a brave knight, when he isn't busy being a twelve-year-old boy.

Few people have heard of him, which isn't surprising, for most of his adventures happened in other times and places. And like all who know how to travel, he has learned to do so without drawing attention to himself. He and his friends have been around the globe, under the earth and over the moon. Not bad for kids who don't even have driver's licenses.

The books in this series don't reveal everything about this remarkable boy and his amazing companions. But herein are some of their greatest exploits for kids of all ages to enjoy. For Matterhorn is, after all, a twelve-year-old boy.

When he isn't busy being a brave knight.

Emerald Isle

Aaron the Baron hit the ground like a paratrooper, bending his knees and keeping his balance.

Matterhorn landed like a 210-pound sack of dirt.

His stomach arrived a few seconds later.

He straightened his six-foot-four frame into a sitting position. In the noonday sun he saw they were near the edge of a sloping meadow. The velvet grass was dotted with purple and yellow flowers. Azaleas bloomed in rainbows around the green expanse. The black-faced sheep mowing the far end of the field paid no attention to the new arrivals.

"Are you okay?" the Baron asked. He looked as if he'd just stepped out of a Marine recruiting poster. "We'll have to work on your landing technique."

"How about warning me when we're going somewhere," Matterhorn grumbled.

The Baron helped him up and checked his pack to make sure nothing was damaged. He scanned the landscape in all directions from beneath the brim of his red corduroy baseball cap. "It makes no difference which way we go," he said at last. "The horses will find us."

"What horses?"

"The horses that will take us to the one we came to see," the Baron answered.

"Are you always this vague or do you just not know what you're doing?"

"I don't know much, but I suspect this is somebody's field. We don't want to be caught trespassing. Let's go."

They left the meadow, walking single file through the tall azaleas up a narrow valley. Thorny bushes with loud yellow blossoms crowded the trail next to a clear brook. Pushing one of the prickly plants away, Matterhorn asked, "Do you know what these are?"

"Gorse, of course," the Baron said without turning.

"Never heard of it."

"Then I guess you haven't been to Ireland before."

"Ireland," Matterhorn repeated. "My great-grandfather came from Ireland."

"Your great-grandfather won't be born for centuries yet."

Matterhorn stepped over a tangle of exposed roots and said, "What do you mean?"

"I mean we're in medieval Ireland, not modern Ireland."

"How can that be?" Matterhorn cried, stopping in his tracks. "How can I be alive before my great-grandfather?"

The Baron shrugged. "That's one of the paradoxes of time travel. No one's been able to figure them all out. You're welcome to try, but while you're at it, keep a lookout for the horses."

Matterhorn soon gave up on paradoxes and became absorbed in the paradise around him. The colors were so alive they hurt his eyes. He wished for a pair of sunglasses. Above the garish gorse he saw broom bushes and pine trees growing to the ridge where spectacular golden oaks crowned the slopes. Bird songs whistled from the trees' massive branches into the warm air. Small animals whispered in the underbrush, while larger game watched the strangers from a distance.

The country flattened out and, at times, they glimpsed stone houses over the tops of hedgerows. They steered clear of these and any other signs of civilization. In a few hours, they reached the spring that fed the brook they had been following. They stopped to rest and wash.

That's where the horses found them.

Five strikingly handsome animals they were. The leader came from ancient and noble stock. He stood a proud seventeen hands high—five foot eight inches—at the shoulders. He had a classic Roman face with a white star on his wide forehead that matched the white socks on his forelegs. His straight back, sturdy body and broad hindquarters suggested both power and speed. A rich coppery mane and tail complemented his sleek, chestnut coat.

The Baron held out an apple to the magnificent male, but he showed no interest in the fruit or the man. Neither did the second horse. The third, a dappled stallion, took the apple and let the Baron pet his nose.

"These horses are free," the Baron said as he stroked the stallion's neck. "They choose their riders, which is as it should be. Grab an apple and find your mount."

While Matterhorn searched for some fruit, the leader sauntered over and tried to stick his big nose into Matterhorn's pack. When Matterhorn produced an apple, the horse pushed it aside and kept sniffing.

Did he want carrots, Matterhorn wondered? How about the peanut butter sandwich? Not until he produced a pocket-size candy bar did the horse whinny and nod his approval.

The Baron chuckled as Matterhorn peeled the bar and watched it disappear in a loud slurp. "That one's got a sweet tooth," he said.

The three other horses wandered off while the Baron and Matterhorn figured out how to secure their packs to the two that remained. "I take it we're riding without saddles or bridles," Matterhorn said. This made him nervous, as he had been on horseback only once before.

"Bridles aren't necessary," Aaron the Baron explained. "Just hold on to his mane and stay centered." He boosted Matterhorn onto his mount. "The horses have been sent for us. They'll make sure we get to where we need to go."

As they set off, Matterhorn grabbed two handfuls of long mane from the crest of the horse's neck. He relaxed when he realized the horse was carrying him as carefully as if a carton of eggs were balanced on his back. Sitting upright, he said, "Hey, Baron! Check out this birthmark." He rubbed a dark knot of tufted hair on the chestnut's right shoulder. "It looks like a piece of broccoli. I'm going to call him Broc."

"Call him what you want," the Baron said, "but you can't name him. The Maker gives the animals their names. A name is like a label: it tells you what's on the inside. Only the Maker knows that."

Much later, and miles farther into the gentle hills, they made camp in a lea near a tangle of beech trees. "You get some wood," the Baron said, "while I make a fire pit." He loosened a piece of hollow

5

tubing from the side of his pack and gave it a sharp twirl. Two flanges unrolled outward and clicked into place to form the blade of a short spade. Next, he pulled off the top section and stuck it back on at a ninety-degree angle to make a handle.

Matterhorn whistled. "Cool!"

"Cool is what we'll be if you don't get going."

Matterhorn hurried into the forest. He was thankful to be alone for the first time since becoming an adult, something that had happened in an instant earlier that day. Seizing a branch, he did a dozen chin-ups then dropped and did fifty push-ups and a hundred sit-ups.

Afterward he rested against a tree trunk and encircled his right thigh with both hands. His fingertips didn't touch. Reaching farther down, he squeezed a rock-hard calf muscle.

All this bulk was new to him, yet it didn't feel strange. This was his body, grown up and fully developed. Flesh of his flesh; bone of his bone. Even hair of his hair, he thought, as he combed his fingers through the thick red ponytail.

He took the Sword hilt from his hip. The diamond blade extended and caught the late afternoon sun in a dazzling flash. This mysterious weapon was the reason he was looking for firewood in an Irish forest instead of sitting in the library at David R. Sanford Middle School.

The Call

The Sword of Truth had called Matthew Horn on a Friday afternoon.

As usual, he had finished his class work early and had gone to the library. Miss Tull the librarian (everyone else called her Miss Dull) glanced up from her book, pleased to see him. Matt spent a lot of time down here reading or drawing or just sitting, his green eyes half closed under a shock of unruly hair. He didn't have as many freckles as most redheads, but enough to give his full face some character.

Matt was big for his age, an early bloomer nearing six feet tall. The growth spurt made him a bit clumsy, but who isn't at twelve? His friends called him Big Red. His teachers called him "precocious," which means too smart, too young. They talked about him skipping a grade next year. Fine with Matt. That would put him a year closer to high school and a shot at their powerhouse soccer and wrestling teams. His older brother Victor was an All-State wrestling champ who always practiced on Matt. As a result, Matt could pin much larger and older opponents. He was anxious to follow in his brother's footsteps, now that Vic had gone off to college.

The library was Matt's favorite part of David R. Sanford Middle School. Located in the basement underneath the cafeteria, the huge room smelled of old books and cold pizza. Solid oak tables with initials scarred into their faces and petrified gum caked onto their bellies lounged around the main room. Gray metal bookshelves poked out in all directions, each ending in a study carrel. Matt's favorite happened to be in the farthest corner from the librarian's desk.

He dropped his backpack by his chair and rummaged through it in search of *A Connecticut Yankee in King Arthur's Court*. Like most of the books Mrs. Williams assigned, this one was good enough to read a second time. What he pulled out instead was *A Study in Scarlet*, the book that had introduced him, and the world, to Sherlock Holmes.

Replacing the dog-eared volume, he felt the tiny bottle of insanity sauce he used to spice up the school lunches. The potent seasoning had gotten him into trouble a few weeks earlier when he let a curious buddy try some. The poor kid howled loud enough to bring the principal.

In most cases Mr. Hatcher would have tossed the sauce—end of story. But he realized the incident had been an accident. He also had a taste for the fiery, and he admitted that the tired menu needed serious help. He returned the hot sauce on condition that Matt never share it with mere mortals again.

Matt's gaze wandered over to Mr. Rickets. Mr. Rickets was an antique bookshelf donated to the school years ago when the town library had been remodeled. He came stocked with several strange and curious volumes. Since Miss Tull never met a book she didn't like, she refused to throw any of them away. Those that were too old or odd to associate with the other books, she left with Mr. Rickets.

Some old furniture is warm and friendly like a favorite uncle. Mr. Rickets was weird and decrepit like a hobo. Cobweb hair sprouted from his top shelf. A musty smell clung to him like cheap cologne. His sagging shelves held tired books suffering from bad backs and loose joints. One volume stuck out from the center shelf, its shiny gold lettering out of place on the wrinkled leather skin.

Why hadn't he noticed that one before, Matt wondered? He walked over and tried to hip the book back into place.

It wouldn't budge.

Matt had strong legs. His goalie kicks often sailed past midfield. He pushed harder.

Nothing happened.

He bent down and shoved, putting his shoulder into it. Still the book wouldn't go in.

The harder he pushed the madder he got. Swatting the stubborn hardback in frustration, he saw it jiggle forward. If it won't go in, maybe it would come out. He yanked it free—and promptly dropped it on the floor, creating a small cloud of dust.

The book was thick as a brick and heavier than Matt expected. He lugged it to his carrel, anxious to find out what made it so weighty. Blowing off the remaining dust, he opened the cover.

The words on the title page matched those on the spine.

The Sword and the Flute.

No author.

No publisher.

No copyright date.

No other information appeared on any page. It seemed completely blank.

Matt tugged at the hair behind his left ear, a sign that his brain had gone into overdrive. Next in motion were his feet, as he went to ask Miss Tull about the peculiar book. She wasn't at her desk, so he checked the computer and the old card catalog. The Sword and the Flute wasn't listed.

It was five minutes until three when he returned to his carrel and began flipping through the blank pages. Although thin as regular paper, they had the weight of hammered metal. Their gilded edges cast slivers of light as they pranced from right to left.

Matt stopped in the exact middle of the book. On the left-hand page was a black dot the size of a period. As he stared, it seemed to be coming toward him like the snout of a slow-moving train. The sound of a distant wind grew with the optical illusion.

He squirmed in his seat as the oncoming mystery reached half a page in size. The 3-D effect gave the sensation of staring into a bottomless well. He could now see that the void was whirring, spiraling inward. Air whistled by his ears and down the hole.

It made him think of the black holes his Uncle Al often spoke about.

Some physicists thought black holes might be wormholes in space, through which matter could travel to distant parts of the universe. Of course, this couldn't be a real black hole because its enormous gravity would have swallowed him, the school, and the whole town without so much as a burp.

Matt rubbed his eyes. This couldn't be happening! He was just tired from the long practices for the Park District soccer championship this weekend. His eyes and ears were playing tricks: his fingers would tell the truth, though. Cautiously he reached for the black circle.

As he touched the page his hand disappeared, followed by his arm. He felt like a lump of dough being stretched into molecule-thin spaghetti. There was no pain, just a fizzing sensation as his body dissolved.

His vision blurred and faded to black.

His pulse raced, then froze.

Static.

Silence.

First Realm

he next thing Matt knew he was skittering across the floor of a dimly lit room about the size of the school gym. The echoing in his ears resolved itself into a persistent "here ... ere ... re."

"Herere."

"Here."

"Come here."

When Matt's eyes adjusted, he saw a young woman seated on a stage about ten yards away. Everything from the crown on her head to the throne on which she sat said she was royalty!

"I do not bite," the woman said. "Come here."

He rose slowly and obeyed.

A quick smile crossed her face but didn't seem to reach her light brown eyes, which took his measure. A gold crown studded with fire opals floated on layers of milk chocolate hair. Her blue satin gown spilled over her shoulders like a waterfall. The fabric was a shade lighter than the large sapphire sparkling at her neck. A lion-headed charm bracelet encircled her left wrist, from which dangled a half dozen elegantly carved animals. She was the very picture of calm beauty.

Except for the Sword in her lap.

Matt's jaw dropped at the sight of the blade. It was made of a single diamond, three feet long. In its center glowed a thread of light like a frozen sunbeam.

"Beautiful, is it not?" the woman said. "It is the Sword of Truth. You are the knight it has called. I am Queen Bea of First Realm. What is your name?"

Matt was speechless.

"We do not have all day," Bea said.

"I'm Matthew Horn," he finally managed.

When he spoke, a pulse flashed through the blade. The stabbing brightness filled his vision with pinwheels and made his eyes water.

"Welcome to First Realm, Matterhorn," Bea said, running his name together.

Matt scanned his memory for any reference to First Realm while he squinted into the gloom for clues to his whereabouts. There were no windows offering an outside view, no doors, no clocks, no pictures. The library smell was gone, replaced by a hint of peppermint.

"I've never heard of First Realm," Matt said at last, taking a cautious step toward the seated woman.

"There is much you humans have never heard of," Bea said, pushing the footstool away from the throne. "Your race is quite ignorant when it comes to traveling."

"You humans," Matt repeated to himself. What did that make her?

"So few of you bother to go beyond," Bea continued. "The curious among you become philosophers or mystics or physicists. Yet, even they seldom travel."

"We travel a lot," Matt countered. "We've got cars and planes and ships. We've even been to the moon. But you'd know that if you were from Earth, which," he added carefully, "I take it you're not."

"No I am not," Bea replied.

"Are you an alien?"

"Actually, you are the alien here."

"Where is here?"

"The Propylon in First Realm."

How had he gone from the library at school to someplace he'd never heard of? Then it came to him: he must be daydreaming. This royal fantasy sprang from his recent reading. In *A Connecticut Yankee*, Hank Morgan had been transported to Camelot by a blow on the head. Matt reached up to check his forehead—and stared at the forearm in front of his face.

It was hairy and muscular.

Looking down, he saw a different body from the one he had taken to school that morning. His eyes were four inches higher from the floor. His arms and legs were bigger, thicker. Even his jeans and sweatshirt had grown. His hair had stretched into a ponytail resting between his shoulder blades. The journey here had aged him to adulthood. He had hyper-jumped over puberty, pimples and the prom.

"In the place where you live," Bea explained, "life unfolds gradually. A tree has to mature before you can eat its fruit. A rose must bloom before you can enjoy its fragrance. This process does not apply when you become a Traveler. What you will become, you already are."

The drastic change scared and excited Matt at the same time. He sensed the latent strength in his new muscles. He flexed his biceps and felt the bulge under his sleeve. If only he could take this body to the wrestling mat, or the soccer pitch and try it out!

"You will be able to use your new muscles soon enough," Bea said. "More importantly, you will have the chance to use this." Rising with the Sword in both hands, she glided forward, preceded by the scent of jasmine. The hem of her gown swept the purple carpet as she strode between the sleek alabaster urns by the stairs.

"When the Maker created First Realm," she said from an arm's length away, "He established a royal family to teach His law, administer His justice, and preserve His peace."

"Sounds like you're talking about God," Matt said. "Why do you call him the Maker?"

"Because that is what He is. Your word 'God' is an empty noun. It needs definition. But 'Maker' comes from an active verb, full of meaning. It describes the One who expanded time-space and created energy-matter. He is Lord of the past, the present and the possible.

"The Sword of Truth is one of the Ten Talis, which the Maker has fashioned to help us rule," Bea said with a nod to the diamond shaft. "They are tokens of His nature, reminders of who He is. Each has power in keeping with what it represents. The Sword symbolizes the Maker's truthfulness. Its light exposes deception."

"Fascinating," Matt said, not taking his eyes from the Sword. "But I still don't know what all this has to do with me."

"You'll find out soon enough," said the stranger who appeared in a doorway to Matt's left.

The Baron

he six-foot-three newcomer wore faded jeans and a light gray T-shirt. A red corduroy baseball cap rested on buzz-cut hair the color of toast. His piercing, blue-gray eyes seemed to take in everything at once. A square chin gave a confident cast to his tanned face. His wide shoulders tapered to a slim waist.

Now this is the kind of man who could handle the Sword, Matt thought as the stranger approached. My being here is a mistake.

Bea made the introductions. "Matterhorn, this is Aaron the Baron. He is also a Traveler and a friend of the Realm."

"Yell-O," Matt said in his personal slang. "And it's Matthew Horn, not Matterhorn." He stuck out his hand, but Aaron the Baron ignored it and put his left hand on Matt's left shoulder by way of greeting.

Turning to the Queen, he asked, "Where's Princess Jewel?"

"I have not been able to reach her," Bea said. "While I was trying, the Sword summoned Matterhorn. He will have to do."

Matt had no idea why he was here, but he didn't appreciate being talked about like leftover meat loaf. "Do for what?" he demanded.

"To help in the Lost and Found Department," the Baron said, as if that explained everything.

As daydreams go, this one was getting ever weirder. School should be over by now. Why hadn't the bell awakened him? Matt pointed to Bea. "She thinks I'm a knight, but I'm not."

"Knight or no, it is time to go," Bea said, smiling at her rhyme. "The Baron can fill you in on the details."

"Leave!" Matt protested. "I just got here. What did you call this place, the Propy-what?"

"Propylon," Bea said. "Also known as the Hall of Portals. Think of it as an airport. Travelers use it to go wherever they want."

"Airports are a lot busier than this," Matt said, glancing around.

"Well, more like a private jet port," Bea said. "Few people have access to the Propylon. It is the most important place in First Realm. There are many portals through time-space, but this is the only portal hub in the multiverse. You can visit almost anywhere from here, including the past."

As she spoke, the Queen made a slight gesture with one hand and the lighting in the room went up. So did Matt's eyebrows. Rich tapestries of burgundy and gold and hunter green covered the walls from floor to vaulted ceiling. Potted trees and ferns flourished everywhere, giving the place the texture of an indoor garden. A miniature forest of peppermint plants accounted for the air's freshness.

The platform beneath the Queen's throne was a circular slab of rose quartz three feet high. The throne itself rested on four eagle claws, each grasping a different colored gem the size of a softball. Crisp reds and cerulean blues danced inside the opals studding its arms and legs. Plush crimson cushions padded the seat and back.

"This is the Royal Chamber," Bea said with a sweep of her arm. "It is one of the Propylon's many rooms."

A dozen questions tried to bungee jump off Matt's tongue. Before any of them got past his lips, Aaron the Baron said, "I can explain more on the way. Grab the Sword and let's go. We have to see a horse about a man."

Matt hesitated. "Do I have a choice?" he asked.

"Yes, Matterhorn," Bea said. "Those who serve the Maker do so of their own free will." She pointed at the wall behind him. Through a circular opening, Matt could see the school library and the bookshelves near his carrel.

"Return to your world if you wish," Bea offered. "The Sword will summon another worthy to wield it." Then, with a challenge in her voice, she added, "Or, you can follow your destiny."

Dream or no, it was decision time. Return to being Matt the Kid, or go forward as Matterhorn the Knight— at least for a few minutes. How could he go back when he had the chance to go exploring!

With a shiver of excitement he said, "I'll take that Sword now."

Queen Bea extended the weapon. "This is different from any sword you have used before."

"You can say that again," Matt muttered. The most lethal weapon he owned was a pocketknife.

"Let me show you something," Bea said, handing him the Sword.

Matt was surprised at how light, yet solid, it felt. The red leather hilt adjusted to his hand and seemed to be gripping him instead of the other way around. He felt a slight pulsing. Cautiously he swished the blade from side to side.

"How old are you?" Bea asked casually.

"Twelve," Matt answered, fighting off an invisible attacker.

"Are you an honest young man? Do you always tell the truth?"

"Yes, ma'am," Matt said. A brilliant pain zinged up his right arm as if he'd stuck the tip of the Sword into a light socket. He dropped the weapon and yelped. The unexpected jolt almost knocked him off his feet.

You weren't supposed to feel pain in dreams, Matt thought.

"Pick up the Sword," Bea said. It was a command, not a request. "Never forget, this is the Sword of Truth. You cannot hold it and speak a lie. You do not have to be perfect to use it—only its Maker is perfect—but you do need to be honest."

Matt gingerly retrieved the Sword. He noticed something engraved in flowing script on the silver crosspiece: Truth is a Blade sharp as Light.

"A moment ago, I said you had a choice," Bea continued. "Always remember that it is a second choice, for the Maker has first chosen you. It is a high calling. If you serve well, you will serve long."

"Why me?" Matt wanted to know.

Queen Bea sighed. "I am not sure. This has never happened before, a Talis summoning a human. But I can tell you this: there must be something special about you that suits the Sword. Are you prepared to swear allegiance to its Maker?"

A half hour ago, Matthew Horn had never heard of First Realm or the Sword of Truth. Now these things seemed as real as anything he had ever experienced. He read the hope on the Queen's face and the questions in the Baron's eyes. He felt the mystery and power of this unusual weapon. The thought of where it might take him filled him with energy—and dread.

Tightening his grip on the hilt with both hands, he said, "I'm ready."

Sword Sworn

ueen Bea nodded. "Do you solemnly swear to follow where the Sword of Truth leads and to faithfully serve its Maker?"

"I do," Matterhorn replied.

"To the death?" the Queen asked.

Matterhorn paused. What was he getting himself into? He glanced back at the school library through the circular opening in the wall. He looked down at the Sword. This was a weapon in his hands, not a violin bow. And his body was now big enough to do some serious damage with it if he had to. But "to the death" seemed over the top.

The Queen waited for his answer.

"I'll do my best," was all Matterhorn could manage.

The blade flashed, sealing the bargain between man and Talis. Queen Bea smiled. "Good enough. Have faith in the Sword and stay close to the Baron. To both you can trust your life." Under her breath she added, "As you may soon discover."

Turning to Aaron the Baron, she said, "These are desperate times. It is important that you find what you seek. Be careful with your toys. And do not teach the locals anything they should not know. You must limit the changes you cause."

"I know, Your Majesty," the Baron replied. In a quieter tone he added, "Sorry about your father."

The Queen's shoulders stiffened and she closed her eyes for a long moment. When she opened them she asked, "Are you two still here?"

"Just leaving," the Baron said with a bow.

"Will I see you again?" Matterhorn asked.

"I hope so. Serve well."

"Serve long," Aaron the Baron replied. He led Matterhorn through the doorway that opened onto a narrow corridor with off-white walls and light blue carpeting. "We have to stop by my place for a few things," he explained, veering right at the end of the hall.

Matterhorn followed the red baseball cap into a larger passageway. As they hurried along, he noticed doors of varying shapes and sizes. Some were guarded by granite-faced men. The air around them crackled with such power that the hair all over Matterhorn's body came to attention. The tall figures wore loose-fitting cassocks belted with different colored sashes. None carried weapons; yet they had the unmistakable aura of being dangerous.

The Baron paused to speak with one silver-sashed guard. "Any word about your captain, Trayko?"

"No," Trayko replied.

"Any idea what happened?"

Trayko looked at Matterhorn and didn't answer.

"Next time," the Baron said and started walking.

"What was that about?" Matterhorn asked when they were out of earshot.

"Realm business," he answered mysteriously.

"What's behind all these doors?"

"I've only been in a few rooms myself, but I assume they're full of portals like the one you came through." Pointing right with his chin, the Baron said, "The Earth Room is that way." Then he took a sharp left down an empty hallway, halting in front of a normal-looking door. "This is where I stay when I'm here," he said, placing his right hand on a palm reader. "It's my shop."

As the door swung open, Matterhorn saw workbenches sticking out of three walls like fat tongues from pimply, pegboard faces. Piles of old magazines and technical journals were crammed beneath the benches. The hum of computers and the purr of electrical motors created a soothing background music.

On the workbench opposite the door sat a laptop computer hooked to an oversized flat screen monitor. Cables snaked everywhere among the odd assortment of devices. Stacks of storage discs formed a skyline to the techno-scape. Electronic gear, scopes and small machines crowded the other benches, along with tools and a few dirty plates. A thin smell of oil coated the air.

"Where'd you get all this stuff?" Matterhorn asked the back of the Baron's head as he followed his host upstairs.

"Brought most of it from home, picked up the rest on my travels. A lot of the scopes I built myself. I like to tinker around and make things. If you're hungry," he said, changing the subject, "you can make us some macaroni and cheese while I finish packing." He steered Matterhorn to a cozy kitchen. "But be quick, for we need to leave soon."

Mac-and-cheese wasn't high on Matterhorn's list of favorite foods, but he was hungry. Waiting for the water to boil, he watched Aaron the Baron cram two old backpacks full of foodstuffs, antique cooking utensils, bedrolls and other supplies, including a first-aid kit stenciled with a red cross. The fabric packs had no frames, just sturdy shoulder straps. Along their tops and sides ran strips of shiny metallic tape. A rubbery yellow lining covered their backsides.

"Come and get it!" Matterhorn shouted when the food was ready.

The Baron walked into the kitchen holding a couple of square patches.

"What are those?"

"Scritch pads. I developed the material myself."

"They look like Velcro."

"Same idea, but these are much stronger."

"What are they for?"

"You can't walk around with that Sword in your hand all the time. You're liable to cut somebody's ear off, and I don't want it to be mine." Using goop from a tiny tube, he stuck one pad to Matterhorn's belt and the other to the Sword hilt.

"Very clever," Matterhorn said. "But what about a sheath for the blade?"

"What blade?" the Baron asked, giving the handle back to Matterhorn.

The diamond shaft was gone. The crosspiece had also retracted into the hilt. "What happened?" Matterhorn asked.

"Travel mode," the Baron said.

Matterhorn stared at the red hilt with its silver pommel. "It's like a light saber."

"Far from it," the Baron replied. "The blade's not made of energy, but of the hardest substance in the universe. Besides, light sabers aren't real: the Sword of Truth is." He pointed to the pad and said, "Stick the hilt on your belt."

Matterhorn did so.

"Now try to pull it off."

He couldn't. Even with his adult strength he was unable to separate the two pieces of scritch.

Aaron smiled. "Here's the secret of scritch. Pull downward from the right to the left like peeling a banana."

Matterhorn tried it and the patches came apart with a soft, scritching sound.

"Hence, the name," the Baron said, obviously pleased with himself. "Now, let's eat."

Costume Party

etween bites of macaroni, the Baron asked Matterhorn how he had gotten to the Propylon.

"I wish I knew," Matterhorn replied, and he explained what had happened.

The Baron nodded knowingly. "You were digitized and posted."

"What's that mean?"

"You were broken down into energy packets, sent here, and reassembled."

Matterhorn scowled.

"Do you know much about the Internet?"

"Some."

"The Propylon is like a router on the Net," the Baron mumbled through a mouthful of food. "It's a node in the zero-point energy field of time-space."

"Time-space?"

"The fabric of the multiverse," the Baron said. "Anyway, information can move through the Propylon trans-dimensionally. All matter, including us, is made of energy and energy can be zipped around like Email."

"People aren't Email!"

"Energy is energy."

"What you're implying is impossible."

Aaron the Baron reached over and poked Matterhorn in the arm with his fork.

"Ouch!" Matterhorn cried. "Why'd you do that?"

"To prove this isn't a dream, which is what you've been telling yourself."

Just then, a mechanical voice squawked from the laptop on the bench below. "Incoming. Incoming."

"That's a priority Email," the Baron said. He jumped from the table and descended the stairs, three at a time, to his workbench.

"You can get Email here?" Matterhorn asked as he trailed along at a more cautious pace.

"I figured a way to keep a virtual link open to my home computer," Aaron said, pulling up a chair and sitting on it backward.

Matterhorn looked over the Baron's shoulder. The Email read:

Hi Baron, I wish I could come with you, but my mom isn't doing well. She starts another round of chemotherapy tomorrow, and I can't leave her. I realize time is relative when traveling, and I wouldn't be gone that long. But you and I both know the possibility of not returning from these trips. I can't risk that now. I hope you understand. Maybe next time.

— Jewel

"That's disappointing," the Baron said. "We could use her help, but family comes first."

"Is this the princess that you and the Queen were talking about?"

"Yeah. Want to see her picture?" He double-clicked a file on the desktop.

The first features Matterhorn noticed, as the pixels arranged themselves into a female face, were the liquid brown eyes. Innocent and open, they beamed from an oval face as smooth as satin. The young woman had a cinnamon complexion and brunette hair that poured over her right shoulder in a thick braid. Her perfectly matched teeth were framed by full lips.

"She's pretty," Matterhorn said. "What did she mean about not returning?"

"Traveling is risky business," the Baron replied. "No telling what kind of mess we might land in."

"Could we be hurt?"

The Baron nodded as he closed the file.

"Killed?"

"Yeah. Still want to go?"

Matterhorn was having second thoughts.

"You don't have anything to worry about," Aaron reassured him, "as long as you've got the Sword."

"I'm not sure how much good it will do me," Matterhorn said, drawing the hilt with difficulty from his belt. The diamond blade extended. "I don't know the first thing about using a sword."

The Baron crossed to the other side of the room. He pulled a Chinese throwing star from a pocket on his thigh and flung the deadly disk at Matterhorn's head.

Quicker than Matterhorn could think, the Sword sliced upward to deflect the star. The second and third stars came just as fast, but fared no better.

The Baron walked over and picked up the lethal weapons.

Matterhorn shivered, and shook the instant sweat from his brow. Those mini saw blades could have ripped his face open. The clang of them bouncing off the Sword still rang in his ears.

"Don't take it personally," the Baron said. "I'm fast, but nothing can get past that blade. You're safer with that in your hands than if you were inside a tank."

"Why didn't you warn me!" Matterhorn almost screamed.

"And miss the expression on your face?" Aaron opened a closet beneath the stairway and rummaged among hangers of old clothes. "Put these on," he said, tossing Matterhorn a pair of woolen pants and a linen shirt with full sleeves. Neither article had buttons or zippers.

Matterhorn removed his shirt, pulled the linen one over his head, and laced the neckties. He changed pants and threaded his belt through the loops in the waistband. Then he reattached the hilt to the scritch pad. Lastly, he shifted the contents of his pockets to his new clothes.

He carried two items at all times. The first was a small blue notebook with a yellow golf pencil stabbed through its wire spine. He wrote down memorable sayings he had read or heard in this quote book until he could transfer them to his computer. The second item was a harmonica he'd taught himself to play.

Aaron changed into similar clothes, except that his pants had more pockets. He handed Matterhorn a fleece vest and a pair of supple leather boots. "These are the biggest shoes I have, size twelve. See if they'll work."

Matterhorn sat in the hammock chair suspended in the corner and tried them on. They were a bit tight, but soft enough that they might stretch. "They'll do," he said as he stood. "Why the costumes?"

Handing Matterhorn a pack, the Baron replied, "For the same reason we're using these old things instead of modern gear. To blend in. Travelers must never draw attention to themselves. Put your clothes in your pack. With any luck, you won't be returning here."

Matterhorn obeyed. "You still haven't told me where we're going."

Aaron the Baron smiled. "I'll show you. Come here."

Matterhorn stepped closer and studied the rounded object in the Baron's left hand. It looked like an old-fashioned Rubik's Cube with partially melted sides. Each facet was a different gemstone. The glimmering colors swirled together in a bizarre way that made Matterhorn dizzy when he tried to focus on it.

The Baron carefully placed his fingers around the deformed globe like a pitcher searching for the seams before throwing a fastball. After a final adjustment he gave the gizmo a sharp twist.

The floor disappeared and the duo dropped into a field in Ireland.

Pint-Sized Potentate

And that was how Matterhorn came to be where he was now, looking for firewood in a forest so overgrown and snarled that it took him a while to fill his arms with sticks. He had a pretty good sense of direction, but he could see how someone might easily get lost in this place. Retracing his steps, he found Aaron tending a small fire in a shallow, rock-rimmed circle.

"What took you so long?" the Baron asked.

"Daydreaming," Matterhorn replied. He glanced around the clearing and asked uneasily, "Where are the horses?"

"Relax. They'll be back if we need them. Let's eat."

Dinner turned out to be the low point of Matterhorn's day. The Baron's stew was thin and murky as pond water. Whatever meat and vegetables had been used were boiled beyond recognition. The toasted cheese sandwiches tasted like pieces of charcoal glued together with orange paste. This fare was worse than anything Matterhorn had eaten at the school cafeteria. If only he had some insanity sauce to spice things up.

After supper the Baron threw wispy clumps of moss into the fire. The resulting smoke stung Matterhorn's eyes. "What'd you do that for?" he asked.

"It keeps the bugs away," the Baron said, sipping on a tin mug of steaming cocoa.

Matterhorn moved back a few feet and took out his harmonica. It looked so small in his large hands. He had been twelve years old the last time he'd played it—only one day ago! He moistened his lips and started into a Dixieland riff. Soon his foot was tapping with the tune and his worries were dissolving in the one-two rhythm.

Several songs later, he finished playing, but the music didn't stop. A vocal descant floated in on the evening breeze. The answering tune grew louder until the singer followed his melody into the clearing.

Clad in a pine green coat, earth-tone britches and pointy shoes, a man about eighteen inches tall appeared out of the dusk. The startled campers leapt to their feet. The Baron touched his forehead and bowed.

The visitor touched his hat with his stout walking stick and nodded back. "Are ye the Tall Ones I'm to be expectin'?" he said in a high-pitched voice.

This squeaky stranger sounded like he'd been breathing helium, and Matterhorn stifled a laugh. A moment later he struggled not to cry out when the man thwacked him on the shins with the blackthorn walking stick that doubled as a weapon.

"Wow, that hurt!" Matterhorn hopped around rubbing one leg, then the other. He could feel dents in his shinbones.

"Great snort!" the little man bellowed. "Where be yer manners, ye lout?" Anger flushed the chubby cheeks on either side of his bulbous nose. Fiery green eyes flashed beneath shaggy brows.

"Your pardon," Aaron the Baron said. "This is our first time in Ireland. Would you be Ian, king of the leprechauns?"

"In the province of Connacht, I'd be," the stranger answered.

"Leprechauns!" Matterhorn cried. "You mean the fairy tales and legends are true?"

"Legends are the cotton candy that gets spun around a stick of truth," Aaron quipped.

That's a good quote for my book, Matterhorn thought.

"Ian is a direct descendant of the Sidhe
, of the race Tuatha," the Baron added.

"And worthy of a wee bit of respect," the pint-sized potentate said, folding his arms across his chest. The king's ears stuck through his curly sideburns and matched the color of his red felt cap. His skin was bunched and wrinkled as though there was too much of it to fit on his face. Above his right eye bloomed a large purple mole sprouting a single gray hair.

Matterhorn tried not to stare. "I'm sorry, Your Highness," he apologized. "I meant no disrespect."

28

"Highness!" the leprechaun screeched. "Do I look like a Highness?" He raised his stick and Matterhorn twisted sideways to avoid another blow.

That's when Ian saw the Sword. The blade had extended and a thin sliver of light glowed through its center. The leprechaun lowered his staff.

"Forgive me temper, sir. I see from the Sword that ye be the Queen's knight. She said you'd come."

The Baron's forehead wrinkled at this. "The Queen's been here?"

"In a dream, sir. The day after me flute was stolen."

"Have a seat and tell us what happened," the Baron invited. "Would you like some hot chocolate?"

The mini monarch perched on a rock near the fire. He laid his staff, known as a shillelagh, across his lap. "What kind of spirits be hot chocolate?" he asked warily.

"It's not spirits, Your High—, I mean Your Grace."

Good recovery, Matterhorn thought, still rubbing his shins.

"Chocolate is a confection," the Baron said. "A flavor. It makes a great drink. Here, try some." He handed Ian the battered tin cup, which the leprechaun took by the rim so as not to burn his fingers. After a big sniff he tried a small sip. His eyebrows wiggled in delight. He took another swig, then another, until the dark liquid was gone.

"'Great Peep, 'tis delightful!" he exclaimed. "Might I have another draft?"

Aaron refilled Ian's cup. He noticed the age spots on the leprechaun's hands and the white hair around the bracelet of amber beads and wondered how old Ian was. "What can you tell us about your flute?" he asked.

The king put down his cocoa to let it cool. He drew a smooth stick on a leather cord from around his neck. "The Flute's been in me family for generations," he explained. "I got it from me father on his deathbed. He got it from me grandfather, who got it from his. A few weeks ago, I woke to find this in its place. A piece of wood where the silver rod had been."

"Is that why someone's stolen it?" Matterhorn interrupted. "Because it's silver?"

The Baron answered before Ian could. "Probably not. It's far more valuable than the metal it's made of. Like the Sword you carry, Ian's Flute is a Talis from First Realm. It was entrusted to the leprechauns for safekeeping."

Ian nodded at the Baron's words and kept his head down in shame at having failed his sacred duty.

Matterhorn laid more wood on the fire. After an awkward silence, he asked, "Is the Flute named after you?"

Ian retrieved his chocolate and took a loud swig. "I'm named fer the Flute," he replied, "not t' other way round. The Tall Ones hereabouts call it the Pixie Piccolo, but the gentleman who gave it t' me ancestors called it Ian's Flute. Said 'twas named after the greatest musician ever to play it."

"The Queen told me the Talis have special powers," Matterhorn went on. "What does the Flute do?"

Bonehand

King Ian took a pipe from his coat pocket. He stuffed shredded leaves into the bowl carved from a giant acorn and scratched a match on his boot heel. He blew blackberry-scented smoke rings into the night and, with a faraway look, began his story.

"If I had the Flute t' play now, ye'd hear nothin' more than if I blew on this pipe," he said. "Only the rarest and shyest creatures can hear the music. And when they hear it, oh, they can't help but come to the sonorous sound, so transported with joy that they'll do whate'er the player asks.

"I've played the Flute fer unicorns and watched those wondrous creatures dance on moonbeams. I've played it on the coast and seen the pleasure of the white dolphins caperin' in the surf. What a joy 'tis to give joy."

"Why would anyone want to steal it?" Matterhorn wondered aloud.

"Because of its pow'r," Ian said, surprised the lad didn't grasp the obvious. "In the wrong hands, it'll do great harm. Unicorns could be lured into traps! Their horns cut off and ground into sorcerer's potions! White dolphins could be drawn into nets and filleted alive. Their flesh is a great delicacy.

"But that's not why the Flute was snatched," the king continued, his eyelids dropping to half-mast. "I fear something worse. Something ye may be too late t' stop." His concern hung wreathed in a cloud of gloomy smoke.

"We'll do all we can to find the Flute," the Baron spoke up.

As if in agreement, the Sword at Matterhorn's side pulsed brightly. Then the blade retracted. Matterhorn wondered what Sherlock Holmes would do with a case like this. Look for a trail of clues, no doubt. But where to begin?

Ian puffed through his acorn of tobacco and refilled his pipe. "I've had me people goin' through these woods like bees through an orchard," he continued. "We've got nothin' t' show fer our trouble. I'm afraid all I can tell ye is the thief's name."

"You know who stole the Flute!" the Baron cried, spilling his chocolate.

"That I do," Ian sighed. "He used t' be me friend. His name is Bonehand."

"What kind of name is Bonehand?"

"Well, it ain't his given name," Ian admitted, "but 'tis what everyone calls him now. Walk a bit and I'll tell ye the story, fer I must be on me way." He tapped out his pipe and put it away, then pulled himself up with his shillelagh.

The Baron and Matterhorn accompanied Ian along a winding path southward from the clearing. The sun had grown tired of eavesdropping and had fallen asleep behind the heather hills. The moon peeked over the east horizon, not sure it was safe to rise and shine.

"Ye must be wary of Bonehand," Ian warned his long-legged companions. "But ye should also know that he wasn't always bad. Life's dealt him many a cruel blow. His parents died in a fire when he weren't no bigger 'n me. The lad hid in the woods to keep from being sent t' his auntie in England. The Tall Ones searched fer days and never found him. They gave 'im up fer dead.

"But he was a survivor, that boy. Only had to see a thing done once t' figure out how t' do it himself. He became wiser in the ways of nature than most animals. We met in the forest while he was still a youth. We often sat by the fire and talked. I watched him grow up bear-strong and fox-sly."

The king's voice held a tone of respect as he told his tale. But there was also a raw edge of pain caused by Bonehand's suspected betrayal.

Ian stopped walking, but kept talking. "Bonehand never returned t' his people. Instead, he made himself the Warden of the Woods that stretch from the hills t' the sea. He loves the animals and has become their protector. One spring a few years ago, some soldiers came. They killed many animals fer sport, leaving carcasses t' rot in the sun. They set fire t' the trees just t' watch 'em burn. They made a game of racing the flames on their swift steeds. But they couldn't outrun the Warden. None of 'em made it out of the woods alive."

The leprechaun shivered with the memory and began moving again. "The Warden saved many an animal that day, including a stag trapped under a flaming tree. In the process his right hand was so badly burned he should ha' lost it. Yet he scraped away the dead flesh and left the bones and tendons. In time, he taught himself t' use that hand again. 'Tis the scariest thing ye ne'er want t' see.

"The fire changed the man in other ways," Ian went on. "His mood became darker than the black cowl he wears. He shuns all company, humans and leprechauns. He distrusts all outsiders. He treats this land like his private property. If he smells a whiff of trouble, he'll act first and never bother t' ask questions. Ye be strangers and he won't take kindly t' yer presence. Be careful."

"We will," the Baron replied. "The fire explains Bonehand's name, but not why he would steal the Flute, especially if he's your friend."

"The Flute brings joy t' the animals called by it," Ian replied. "But it also put 'em under the control of whoever's playin'. They become like innocent children who do whatever they're asked, even if it's bad fer 'em. I told me friend about the Flute—even showed him its power once. He got real upset. Said it shouldn't be used t' control free creatures, even if it did make 'em happy. He wanted me t' get rid of it so it wouldn't fall into the wrong hands. But I said I couldn't just throw away somethin' I'd been charged t' protect. We argued about it a lot."

Matterhorn scratched the hair behind his left ear as he listened. There were valuable clues in these details that needed ferreting out.

"I was away at the time of the fire," Ian continued. "When I got back and heard of the tragedy, I tried t' console me friend. He wouldn't have it. Blamed the whole mess on me, he did. Said the soldiers had come lookin' fer the Flute and that more would follow. I didn't see him again till the day before me Flute disappeared. He refused t' share me fire, but he saw where I was camped. I think he came later that night and took the Flute. I doubt the instrument can be destroyed. Still, if

Bonehand has enough time, he'll hide the Flute where it'll never be found."

The king's eyes grew moist. "Do what ye can. And if it's gold ye be wantin' in return I've a pot or two I can spare."

"That won't be necessary," the Baron said.

Ian gave a shudder of relief. Then he pulled himself to his full height, raised his right hand toward the Travelers and gave them his blessing. "May the sun warm yer face, the wind cool yer back, and the Maker guide yer way." With that, he walked into the forest.

Questions in the Dark

Back at camp, Matterhorn wrote down what the Baron had said about truth, while the author of that clever phrase rinsed their dishes. The moon was so bright and the stars so numerous that he didn't need the firelight. But he was still in the dark about why the Sword had selected him and sent him to Ireland via First Realm. He was smart, but no genius. He was a good athlete, but years away from his full potential. He liked adventure, but hadn't found much in his young life. Surely there were thousands of adults better suited to finding the missing Flute.

The fire crackled and spat a chunk of smoldering ash into Matterhorn's lap. He swatted at the orange ember while Aaron laughed and splashed him with water.

"What did you think of Ian?" the Baron asked.

Matterhorn put away his quote book and said, "I thought leprechauns were fairy-like creatures. Ian was taller, and, well, more earthy, than I would have expected."

"You mean he was dirty and smelled funny. That's the difference between books and real life."

"Did Queen Bea tell you why the Flute was given to the leprechauns?" Matterhorn wondered. "If the Talis was made for First Realm, what's it doing here?"

The Baron dried his hands and propped himself against a tree. "She didn't tell me much about Ian," he replied, "just that his family had been entrusted with the Flute and that it had been stolen. Several of the Ten Talis have recently been hidden on Earth because of the trouble brewing in the Realm."

"Recently?" Matterhorn repeated. "Ian's story made it sound like it's been in his family for generations."

"And that's true, from an earthly perspective," the Baron said. "But First Realm's timeline is different from ours."

"Do you know what sort of problems they're having?" was Matterhorn's next question.

Aaron shrugged. He did know, yet wasn't sure how much to burden Matterhorn with on his first night. "The Queen's been pretty tight-lipped about it all. You'd better ask Her Majesty next time you see her."

"When will that be?"

"That depends on how long it takes us to find the Flute." The Baron got up and untied the bedroll from the bottom of his pack. He kicked a pile of leaves into a makeshift mattress and made his bed.

Matterhorn did likewise. The bedroll on his pack had a foil lining that reminded him of the space blanket his dad kept in the car for emergencies. This was the first time he'd thought of his family since this adventure began. His parents must be worried sick. His sister would have walked home alone from school. Victor would be there by now. They would all be upset by his disappearance. Dad would call the police. They would search the library and find the book at his carrel. But would they be able to follow him through the portal?

Seeing the book in his mind's eye sent a chill through his body. Slowly he spoke the title aloud. "The Sword and the Flute."

"What did you say?" Aaron asked.

"The Sword and the Flute. That's the name of the book I got sucked into. I know what it means now." But he didn't know how the volume had found its way onto Mr. Rickets' shelves. Questions piled up in his brain until he reached mental gridlock. He quit thinking about them and hoped everything would make more sense in the morning. Lying on his back with his arms crossed over his chest, Matterhorn searched the indigo sky until he spotted some familiar constellations.

Sleeping under the stars was not a new or frightening experience. The Horns spent their summers camping across America. Matterhorn's dad was a freelance writer and could set his own schedule. His mom taught psychology at the community college and refused to teach during summer term.

Matterhorn had been as low as Death Valley and as high as Pikes Peak. He'd been fossil hunting in the Badlands, bird watching in the Everglades, salmon fishing in the Pacific Northwest, and backpacking along the Appalachian Trail. He'd gone swimming in both oceans and several lakes in between. His favorite was Echo Lake in Montana. He had traveled to a lot of places in his short life and he could now add Ireland to the list—except no one would believe him.

His thoughts returned home. The district championship match would be over by now. Who had started in goal in his place? Not Rusby. But there wasn't anyone else to fill in ... they would have lost for sure. He wondered how the coach and the other kids felt about his disappearance. Had he been declared a missing person yet?

Matterhorn played with his ponytail as he mused. He liked the look and feel of it and thought about letting his hair grow when he got home. Since he would no doubt revert to his twelve-year-old self, he would have to start from scratch.

The prospect startled him. If his body returned to adolescence, what about his mind? Would he remember any of this: Queen Bea, First Realm, the Sword of Truth, Aaron the Baron? What about Ireland, Broc and Ian?

Maybe his memory would be erased so he couldn't reveal the activities of Travelers or the existence of First Realm.

A still more frightening possibility suddenly occurred to him.

What if he never made it home?

Matterhorn awoke dazed and confused. The first thing he saw was a straggle of red chest hair sticking out from under a folded pair of brawny arms. What in the—. Then he remembered that he had been super-sized. He felt the stubble on his chin with hands that looked too big to be his. But they responded to commands from his brain, so they had to belong to him.

His appetite had also grown and he hoped breakfast would be better than supper.

The horses returned while the Baron and Matterhorn were erasing all evidence of their campsite. Matterhorn walked over to Broc, patted his neck and rubbed the peculiar birthmark. But the animal remained stiff until Matterhorn produced a candy bar.

"What a break!" Aaron exclaimed, approaching his own mount. "Yesterday they came to take us to Ian. I didn't expect them to show up today. But I never turn down a free ride."

"Do you think they know where we need to go?" Matterhorn asked, wiping the horse slobber off his palm and onto his pants.

"Only one way to find out." They loaded up their packs and climbed aboard, where they sat for a pair of minutes while nothing happened. "I guess we're driving today," the Baron said at last.

Heading their mounts north from the spring, they eventually ran into a large stream, which they crossed and followed west.

Echo Lake moved to the number two spot on Matterhorn's list that afternoon when he and Aaron topped a piney ridge and discovered the valley of the lake. From their vantage point it looked like an immense earthen funnel filled with melted glass. The transparent edges sparkled with sunlight and its center plunged to sapphire depths.

Matterhorn was glad to dismount. His back and rear were sore from a second day on horseback. The insides of his legs felt raw and his knees throbbed. Broc looked as fresh as he had that morning, despite having hauled a heavy passenger up and down the hilly terrain.

"You could at least have the decency to sweat," Matterhorn complained as he rubbed Broc's neck. The horse tossed his mane and went off in search of tender shoots for supper. Matterhorn opted for a soak in the crisp, clear water to soothe his aching muscles. Swarms of dragonflies played tag among the marsh marigolds and water lilies where he floated.

The Baron, meanwhile, found a few fallen trees and decided to make a raft. Using his survival saw—a cutting band between two rings—he trimmed the limbs off three logs and lashed them together. He had Matterhorn scratch in the mud for worms while he rigged the tackle. Then they made for deep water and began fishing with lines tied to their fingers.

This secluded lake seldom had visitors, so the native stock grew to unusual size. Matterhorn saw an enormous old-timer drift into their shadow. It was by far the biggest fish he'd ever seen in the wild, measuring seven feet from nose to tail.

The hungry sturgeon took Matterhorn's bait on the way by, dragging him off the raft. Matterhorn grabbed for the line to keep from losing his finger. The Baron jumped in and thrashed around with his knife until he cut the monster loose.

As they clung to the raft, the Baron's laugh rolled across the valley. "I didn't realize fishing here would be so dangerous."

"I'm glad that one got away," Matterhorn gasped. He bit the loop from his finger and soaked the sore digit in the water.

That evening they pitched camp high on the eastern slope in the last swatch of daylight. They ate dried food and watched the steady stream of animals coming to drink: Sika deer, red foxes and skittish rabbits. At one point, Matterhorn glimpsed a small white horse cresting the ridge across the way, but the animal disappeared before he could get a second look. Had there been a horn on the creature's head?

Matterhorn's aches and pains made it hard to sleep. Rolling onto his stomach, he propped his chin on his hands and stared at Aaron, resting a few feet away. "Are you asleep?" he asked.

"I'm working on it," came a faint reply.

"Can you answer a question first?"

"Fire away."

"How did we travel back in time?"

The Baron sighed and leaned up on an elbow. This was going to take a while. "Picture the multiverse like a balloon being blown up by the Maker." He mimed inflating a balloon. "Time-space is like the skin on the balloon. Saying "when" something happened, such as your birthday or the first moon landing, is just pointing out the place on the balloon where that event occurred.

"When we came here," the Baron patted the ground, "we traveled to a specific address in time-space. Since it happens to be farther down the balloon from where you live, you think of it as in the past, but that depends on your point of view. Ever hear of superstring theory?"

Matterhorn nodded, remembering the time Uncle Al had tried to explain it to him. He knew it had something to do with gravity, yet most of the details had flown over his head and out the window.

"Current superstring theory, also known as M theory, says there are at least eleven dimensions," the Baron explained. "Actually there are more. Most of these extra dimensions are quantum-sized, meaning they're incredibly tiny. But if you know how to uncurl them, you can move around time-space on your own miniature subway system."

"If time travel is possible," Matterhorn protested, "why haven't I read about it?"

"You have. Only you didn't realize it because there are all kinds of ways to get into portals. You can be sucked into one like Dorothy in *The Wizard of Oz*. Or fall into one as Alice did in *Wonderland*. Or accidentally walk into one like Peter and Susan and Edmund and Lucy did in *The Chronicles of Narnia*. Portals adapt to the time in which they open."

"But those are just stories," Matterhorn protested.

"The best fiction is often based on fact," the Baron countered. "Sometimes it's hard to tell the difference."

Indeed, the book Matterhorn had been reading only yesterday—*A Connecticut Yankee in King Arthur's Court*—underscored the Baron's point. The recollection brought another question to mind. "The Hall of Portals where we met," he asked, "was that in the past or the future?"

"Neither and both."

"Now you're really confusing me."

"Well, then, let me throw more light on the subject."

The Baron got up to put another branch on the fire. The next second, a heavy object fell from the sky and stuck in the ground where his head had been.

UFO

he UFO—unidentified falling object—looked like a large bone. It was stark white and thick as a man's forearm. Its sharpened point had been driven into the soft ground by its speed and mass.

"Someone must have a bone to pick with us," the Baron said, glancing over at the still-quivering stake.

Matterhorn wasn't as calm. He had almost done something he hadn't done in years—wet his bed. He sat up and said in a shaky voice, "Wh-where did that come from?"

Staring into the night, the Baron replied, "I'm not sure how it got here, but I'll give you three guesses who sent it, and the first two don't count."

The surrounding dark became more threatening than it had been a minute before. "What do we do now?" Matterhorn bleated.

"Let's scoot under those trees to protect ourselves from any more bone bombs," Aaron said. He pulled his bedroll near the base of a large Douglas fir. Matterhorn did likewise.

"As for a ground attack ..." The Baron drew from his pack what appeared to be three metal toothbrushes. Tiny red buds stuck out where the bristles should have been. From Matterhorn's pack he removed three disks the size of hockey pucks that had been attached to the lining. He put a brush in each puck and placed them in a triangle around the camp.

When the Baron finished and crawled beneath the tree, Matterhorn asked, "Are those some kind of motion detectors?"

"They're electric eyes."

"Like the ones that open automatic doors?"

"Not quite. The ion-battery bases generate an electric current that flows between the poles. Anyone crossing the beam is in for quite a shock."

"From those tiny things?" Matterhorn said skeptically.

The Baron pointed to their packs. "See those metallic strips on the top and sides? Those are accelerated solar collectors. They've been charging the batteries since we arrived. Each one contains a day's worth of sunlight, more than enough to disable any prowlers. By the way," he added, snuggling down into his bedding, "be careful if you get up before me. I don't like the smell of burnt skin."

Matterhorn felt slightly safer as he lay down on the fragrant boughs.

The next thing he knew the sun was poking him in the face. He sat up and rubbed the sleep from his eyes. A thin layer of dew glazed the buttercup and clover countryside. The fear he felt the night before didn't survive the dawn. He heard Aaron snoring softly a few feet away.

When he glanced over at his partner, he realized their security system had a flaw. Anything on two—or four—legs would have had trouble sneaking into camp. But a creature with no legs, such as the one curled up on the Baron's chest, had no problem paying them a visit.

"Aaron," Matterhorn whispered urgently. "Aaron."

The Baron stirred and opened his eyes. When his new hood ornament came into focus, he stiffened like a corpse. Except for his eyes, which quickly outgrew their sockets. Not many things frightened him, but one of them sat coiled twelve inches from his nose.

Matterhorn knew there was good reason to be scared. Having recently done a science project on poisonous snakes, he recognized the zigzag black markings of a European viper. He also knew there weren't supposed to be any snakes in Ireland. According to legend, Saint Patrick had driven them all away in the fifth century.

He liked snakes, even poisonous ones. You just had to be careful around them, that's all. He would have had a pet snake if his sister weren't deathly afraid of them. Without knowing where the idea came from, he knew what to do. Taking the Sword hilt quietly from his belt, he willed the blade to extend. Slowly he laid it between the serpent's head and the Baron's. Then he slid it carefully under the snake, whose tongue began flicking in and out.

The Baron's eyes got wider by the flick.

At this point, Matterhorn raised the temperature of the Sword with his mind. He wasn't sure how he knew he could do this, he simply did it. He felt the warmth in contrast to the morning chill. So did the viper, and it stretched full-length along the blade until its head almost touched Matterhorn's hand.

What an elegant creature, Matterhorn thought. He saw intelligence in those reptilian eyes. He wished his slinky friend well as he lifted the blade and put it on the ground on his other side. Then he willed the shaft to cool. The snake disliked the change and slithered off into the bushes.

Aaron's bedroll, which had been rigid as a bar of silver, deflated as its occupant exhaled. "Whew! I owe you one!"

"In that case," Matterhorn replied as he laid back and clasped his hands behind his head, "I'll have breakfast in bed. Anything except burnt cheese sandwiches."

After serving powdered eggs on toast, the Baron took the security system apart while Matterhorn studied the bone that had almost orphaned him in Ireland. He scrutinized it for clues, wishing he had the powerful microscope from his chemistry set at home. Yet even with his naked eye, Matterhorn learned a lot in a few minutes.

"This thing is fossilized," he said when the Baron wandered over. "That explains why it's so heavy. It must be from a large animal that got caught in a bog and got petrified. What's interesting is how the end was sharpened. Run your finger along this edge."

"It feels smooth."

"And that tells us—"

"That the point was made by a grinding wheel," the Baron said, "not a sword or axe."

"Elementary, my dear Watson!" Matterhorn cried. "And these gray streaks?"

"Friction burns," the Baron replied. "And don't call me dear."

Matterhorn got to his feet. "Since electricity hasn't been harnessed yet, the grinding wheel must be water driven. That would require a stream moving fast enough to turn a mill wheel. Like the one we crossed our first day here."

"Then that's the place to pick up the trail," the Baron concluded. "Thank you, Mr. Bonehand!" he shouted skyward. "You have given us our first clue."

hey backtracked to the stream they had followed earlier and traced it west. Matterhorn daydreamed while they trotted along its green-carpeted banks. The gurgling river and Broc's gentle gait rocked him to the brink of sleep.

The Baron, on the other horse, sat wide awake, straining to get a fix on whoever had been trailing them all morning. The tracker was good, but he'd made one or two tiny mistakes—a twig snap here, a careless footfall there—enough for the Baron to guess his presence. In the past, he would have been as clueless as Matterhorn about their unseen tail. But not now, not since his adventure with the greatest tracker of all. The Queen had told him some fantastic stories about this other Traveler, an Aboriginal known as Nate the Great. After one trip with him, the Baron realized the Queen had been somewhat mistaken.

The man was even better than the myth.

Nate the Great had tracked every kind of animal, yet he never killed for sport. Built like a log with legs, he could still fold himself into the tiniest hiding places. He could walk on snow without leaving tracks. He could smell bacon cooking a mile away and tell you which side of the pig it came from. The only way you knew Nate was around was if he walked up and shook your hand. Otherwise, forget it.

Nate had shown Aaron how to check suspicious sounds on the trail by varying his pace. Twice that morning the Baron had let Matterhorn and Broc get a few yards ahead and then halted. Both times he heard telltale noises.

When the sun reached high noon, the Baron decided to do some tracking of his own. "Let's give the animals a rest," he said in a loud voice.

They parked their mounts beside a natural windbreak of poplars. Matterhorn knelt on moss as soft as mouse fur and stuck his face in the

47

river for a long drink. The Baron leaned his pack against a tree and squatted on a rock. Cupping the refreshing water to his lips, he said between sips, "You shouldn't drink that way: it leaves you vulnerable."

"Vulnerable to what?" Matterhorn asked, wiping his chin on his sleeve.

"To an attack from behind. We're being followed. Don't turn around."

Matterhorn stared straight ahead and lowered his voice. "We are? By whom?"

"That's what I intend to find out," the Baron said. "Wait here. And whatever you do, don't leave. The last thing we need is to get separated." With a wink and a smile he slipped between the poplars and vanished.

The Baron wiggled stealthily through a tangle of underbrush until he came to a game trail hedged by waist-high ferns. When the path widened into a clearing, he skirted the fringe to stay hidden. Off to the right he heard a whooshing noise and spun in time to see a rope tied to three rocks coming in low and fast. The weapon wrapped around his legs, tripping him forward.

Before he could get to his knees, a hood came down over his head. It was tied off so that he could barely breathe, much less scream for help. Strong hands jerked his arms back and bound his wrists. His ankles got the same treatment. Then he was flipped onto a litter tied to the south end of a northbound animal, which began picking its way through the trees, dragging its heavy wooden tail.

The whole episode took less than a minute.

As the Baron lay on the litter, stunned but unhurt, he tried to piece together what had just happened. He couldn't see anything, but he kept his ears open for clues. It was no use: his captors were quiet as poachers. They didn't want him dead, the Baron reasoned, or else he would be. They hadn't searched him for valuables either. That meant kidnapping must be their aim.

But who were "they"?

The pace of the pack animal convinced the Baron he was attached to a donkey, not a horse. The stretcher turned out to be several inches shorter than its passenger, so he had to bend his knees upward to prevent the ground from pulling off his boots. To keep his muscles from cramping he did isometric exercises and abdominal crunches.

He couldn't move his arms, but his fingers could just reach his belt. As time passed he was able to work it around his body until he touched the slim buckle. He pressed the silver stud holding it to the leather. This activated the receiver in his backpack. The homing device had an eight-mile radius. He hoped Matterhorn would figure out what the beeping meant before the donkey clopped out of range.

A razor blade lay hidden along the bottom edge of the belt. If his kidnappers shifted him around when they stopped for the night, he might be able to cut his ropes and escape. The tracking stud and cutting blade were only two of the many tools on the Baron. He also wore a thin nylon pouch around his stomach that held several useful items including the fixings for a powerful bomb. The detonators were stored in the hollow heel of his left boot. The heel of his right boot contained a mini survival kit of fishing line and hooks, a miniature magnifying glass for starting fires and some penicillin capsules in case of infection.

"Be prepared for everything," his mother always said, "and you'll be prepared for anything." As the only child of a single parent, the Baron was very close to his mom. His father had abandoned them years ago. His mom worked two jobs and did her best to be both parents. By her simple words and daily example, she taught Aaron to be resourceful and to never give up.

Although his situation was desperate, the Baron refused to believe he would die in Ireland. He had learned in his travels that all things, including the unexpected and the painful, worked together for good when one served the Maker.

He hoped that applied to being kidnapped.

The afternoon plodded along as slowly as the donkey. Aaron tried to keep a cool head, but it was impossible inside the black hood, which smelled like dirty socks. Sticky sweat crawled over his face and oozed down his neck. The wetness made him realize how parched he was. If only he'd taken a bigger drink at the stream.

Hours later, the one-donkey parade finally stopped. The Baron was dumped on the hard ground. He rolled over and stretched. To his left he heard the snapping of branches, followed by the crackling of a fire. Next came the sizzle of frying meat. Rabbit, by the smell of it. The bag loosened around his neck and a callused hand with dirty fingernails shoved a slice of something greasy into his mouth. He chewed greedily and was thankful for the squirt of water he got before the bag cinched closed for the night.

In a few hours he would try to escape. For now he would make himself comfortable and get some sleep. He wondered if Matterhorn had figured out the homing signal. If so, what would he do about it?

The Baron would soon find out. And his kidnappers would soon learn that they had made not one, but two strategic mistakes that day.

The first was grabbing the Baron.

The second was not grabbing Matterhorn.

hile the Baron was being bagged, tagged and dragged away, Matterhorn sat waiting by the stream.

And waiting.

And waiting.

Ten minutes passed.

Then twenty.

Matterhorn fretted about the Baron. He leaned against a soft rock and considered the possibilities. Maybe Aaron couldn't find anyone because no one was out there. Maybe he'd gotten lost. The Baron wasn't in trouble, Matterhorn reassured himself, or he would have yelled for help.

Matterhorn sat very still and listened hard for unusual noises.

All was quiet. Too quiet.

The next thing he knew, he felt a wet nose nuzzling him awake and looked up to see Broc standing over him.

He'd fallen asleep!

A wave of hot panic lifted him to his feet. How could he have dozed off? How long had he been asleep? How long had the Baron been gone?

He felt ashamed at his laziness. Regardless of the Baron's command to stay put, he had to do something. And he wasn't the only one in turmoil. The Baron's horse nickered and fidgeted from foot to foot to foot to foot. Did he know his rider wasn't coming back?

"You can leave if you want," Matterhorn said to the animal.

The stallion nodded and took off.

Matterhorn shifted his gaze to Broc, who stood still as a stone horse in a park. Only his ears moved, tilting forward.

"Do you want to go, too?"

The horse shook his head and gave an angry snort.

Relieved, Matterhorn asked, "What do we do now, Broc?"

Just a few days earlier, Matterhorn had been minding his own business in the library at school. Now he was lost and alone in medieval Ireland. Someone tried to kill his partner last night. Had they succeeded today?

While the situation around Matterhorn unraveled, the clouds above him knit themselves into a woolly gray blanket. The unfamiliar landscape grew somber and the scent of rain seeped through the sultry afternoon. Thunderclouds gathered on the horizon and flung lightning bolts at each other.

Matterhorn's mood should have been as gloomy as the weather. Instead, he chose to get excited. The courage of the called and committed surged through him. The peril was overwhelming for a twelve-year-old boy, but he no longer thought of himself as a kid. The Sword of Truth had called him to be a knight—that's what the Queen had told him. And the Sword couldn't lie: he was ready to believe that. It would guide and protect him as he searched for the Baron: he was ready to believe that, too.

Now, if he only knew what to do! Being a novice in the hero business, he wondered how to proceed. His mind raced. His heart pounded.

Boom! Boom! Boom!

Beep! Beep! Beep!

Boom! Boom! Beep! Beep!

Wait a minute. Did hearts beep?

The noise was coming from the Baron's pack. Matterhorn fished out a slim metal box with a radar-like screen. A dim green light flashed near its edge in time with the beeps.

Probably a homing device, Matterhorn guessed, as he saw the words "HOMING DEVICE" stenciled under the screen. The Baron must have activated a tracking signal, which meant he was still alive!

Matterhorn had to move fast, and he now had two packs to carry. Did he have the right to involve Broc in a risky rescue?

Broc began snorting, nodding, and pawing the ground, making it clear he wasn't about to be left behind.

"Are you with me?" Matterhorn asked.

Another fierce flurry of nods.

"Then let's go."

The kidnappers hadn't bothered to hide their trail. Matterhorn didn't need the Baron's beeper and switched it off. Broc steamed down the parallel tracks left by the litter. Horse and rider rushed past massive oaks whose intertwined arms shielded them from most of the rain. Hanging ivy, tree ferns and wild strawberry plants formed the sides of the verdant tunnel through which they churned.

They caught up to the kidnappers by nightfall. From a safe distance, Matterhorn surveyed the sprawling meadow where they had stopped. He watched the six short men pitch camp. These were dwarfs—twice as tall as leprechauns and twice as thick. Their heads were screwed tight to their broad shoulders. They had full mustaches and bushy beards grown down to their barrel chests. Their powerful limbs made them look like a troop of miniature Turkish weightlifters.

Three of the six wore red kerchiefs. All had flat metal chains on the outside of their rough cotton shirts and deerskin vests. Black leather boots matched their wide leather belts, which sported ornate iron buckles. The belts also held an assortment of short-handled axes and knives.

These were not Snow White's dwarfs.

Matterhorn spied the Baron near the fire, hooded like a cat about to be drowned. He was in no shape to help with his rescue. Matterhorn would be on his own. He had the cover of darkness, the element of surprise and the Sword of Truth. Now all he needed was a plan.

He spoke quietly to Broc. The more time they spent together, the more he realized this was one smart horse. "What do you think, Broc? Option A: we can leave the Baron where he is and follow the group. Perhaps they'll lead us to Bonehand and the Flute."

Broc tossed his head from side to side.

"How about Option B?" Matterhorn said. "You create a diversion to draw some dwarfs away while I overpower the rest and free the Baron." He was twice their size: maybe he could handle two or three.

Another flurry of no-nods. Broc tilted his head to the right and looked down his long nose as if to imply, "Is that the best you can do?"

Matterhorn reddened at the visual rebuke. "Okay," he blurted. "Option C: I wait till everyone's asleep, sneak in, cut the Baron loose, and we run for it. I doubt the dwarfs will post a guard. They didn't bother to cover their tracks, so they're not expecting to be followed. Maybe they thought I'd hightail it for home." Like I know how to get there, Matterhorn thought.

He agonized over these possibilities for a minute until Broc chose Option D. He put his muzzle in the middle of Matterhorn's back and shoved him toward the fire.

Twelve steely eyes focused on Matterhorn as he stumbled into view. In his panic, he recalled a quote from Aesop he'd written in his quote book not long ago: "It is easy to be brave from a safe distance." Now he had to be brave up close.

He scritched the Sword of Truth from his belt and said as gruffly as he could, "You guys are in a lot of trouble."

Teamwork

If this show of boldness was supposed to intimidate the kidnappers, it failed completely. At six to one, they liked their odds against this tall redhead. Even if he did have a mean-looking sword, he would never get close enough to use it. The nearest dwarf noted the flush of fear on Matterhorn's face and the way his hands trembled. With a sneer he plugged one nostril with his thumb and blew out the contents of the other in Matterhorn's direction. Then he reached for the rock-and-rope weapon he'd used on the Baron and hurled it in one smooth motion.

The Sword sliced downward on its own, cutting the rope like dental floss. The stones flew by on either side. Matterhorn was amazed that he'd managed to hang on to the hilt.

Another dwarf yanked a short axe from his belt and charged. No sooner did he have the weapon raised than Matterhorn lunged—or was pulled—forward. He turned the axe into a stick by chopping off its metal head. A lightning backswing reduced the stick to a stub. Holding the tip of the now-glowing blade an inch from the attacker's chest, Matterhorn heard himself bark, "Sit!"

The stunned man dropped so fast his beard flew up into his face.

All this commotion scared the donkey that had been loosely tied to a sapling. The frightened beast jerked free and raced across the clearing. Matterhorn dodged the runaway, which gave another dwarf the chance to slink up behind and grab him, pinning his arms to his sides and making him drop the Sword.

Though a bit awkward with weapons, Matterhorn understood wrestling. Instinctively he responded to this bear hug by stepping forward on his outside foot, lowering his center of gravity and dipping his left shoulder. When the dwarf shifted to maintain his hold,

Matterhorn back-stepped and jerked an arm free. But when he spun to throw a headlock, his elbow sailed over his stocky opponent's head.

The dwarf tightened his grip and arched his back. Matterhorn was about to be pile-driven face first into the dirt when a rock zinged in and clocked the dwarf. His face went slack, so did his grip, and he slid down the back of Matterhorn's legs.

Forty feet away, Aaron the Baron picked up another stone with his left hand. While his captors had been focusing on Matterhorn, he'd cut his ropes on the belt blade and removed the hood. He had no trouble hitting his target with the baseball-sized rock. After all, he had hurled hundreds of strikes from a pitcher's mound, and he knew how to dust a batter who hugged the plate. This guy had definitely been hugging.

Now the odds weren't so good and the remaining dwarfs bolted for the forest. Another beaner from the Baron dropped the slowest runner before he reached the trees. The others disappeared, but not for long. They came shooting back into the clearing, stubby legs pumping, a few feet ahead of Broc's thundering hooves. The horse snorted in triumph as he corralled the fugitives.

"Good job, Broc!" Matterhorn cried. The shout tightened a ring of pain around his chest. He must have a couple of bruised ribs. He gingerly picked up his Sword and walked over to the Baron. "Are you okay?"

"I'm stiff," the Baron replied, rubbing the blood back into his wrists, "but I'll be fine. You did a brave thing taking on those dwarfs. Thanks for coming after me."

Matterhorn blushed at the compliment.

Ten minutes later they had a six-pack of sullen dwarfs tied with their own ropes and stewing in their own juices. The rancid sweat was so overpowering that Matterhorn and the Baron moved to a breathable distance and plopped down to rest.

"So you're a southpaw," Matterhorn said. "Where'd you learn to throw like that?"

"Little League."

"How long ago did you play baseball?" Matterhorn asked in surprise.

"Last month I pitched a one-hitter in the city playoffs." The Baron grinned. "I don't travel all the time you know."

It suddenly dawned on Matterhorn that Aaron's story might be similar to his own.

"How old are you in the real world?"

"All worlds are real," the Baron said. "Back home I'm thirteen."

"You're just a year older than me," Matterhorn said. "How long have you been traveling? Where are you from? Do your parents know you're in Ireland? Do they worry about you when you're gone? Do you—"

The Baron raised a hand. "Slow down, slow down. I've been traveling since I was nine. I'm from the good ol' U. S. of A. My parents don't worry about me. At least my dad doesn't. He left when I was three. My mom doesn't know I travel."

"How can that be?" Matterhorn interrupted.

"You'll see when you get back. Now, are you going to keep grilling me or can we ask my kidnappers a few questions?"

They approached the dwarfs. The Baron stood, hands on hips, and scanned the six stony faces. "Who wants to explain what you were up to? Am I so ugly that you felt the need to stick a bag on my head and drag me away from civilization?"

"You're not that ugly," Matterhorn said.

The captors-turned-captives remained mute.

"If you won't talk," Matterhorn said, breaking the long silence, "I'll have to read your minds."

Six jaws tightened in unison.

"You don't think I can do it?" Matterhorn asked. "You're a tough crowd. However, with the help of my faithful assistant, Aaron the Baron, I will mystify one and all."

"Ready when you are, Sir Matterhorn," the Baron said. He had absolutely no idea what was going on.

"Very well," Matterhorn said. "I will now select my first victim, er, subject." He moved in front of the second dwarf from the left. This was the one the Baron had beaned. He had a nasty purple bruise spreading from his right temple down his cheek. He might be more likely to talk.

"Anything you want to say before we begin?"

The stark silence matched the dwarf's hard stare.

"Since our volunteer has lost his voice, I will read his thoughts using my mind—and my Sword," Matterhorn announced. He laid the blade in the startled man's lap and placed his hands on the dwarf's head.

Matterhorn had pieced together an idea, but he wasn't sure it would work. He recalled the shock the Sword had given him in the Hall of Portals when he had lied. He also remembered how he commanded the blade to heat up when he saved the Baron from the snake. If he could just combine those two experiences....

"Ask him his name, Baron, and I'll answer for him," Matterhorn said.

"What's your name?" the Baron said, a slow grin sliding across his face. Now he got it.

A moment later so did the unfortunate dwarf when Matterhorn answered in a loud voice, "My name is Amos!"

The jolt knocked the little man over, straightening his frizzy beard and curling his eyelashes at the same time.

Matterhorn sat the dazed dwarf upright as if resetting a bowling pin. He winced at the pain in his ribs and stifled a yelp. Putting the Sword in place, he rested his hands like before. "Guess I'm a bit rusty," he said. "Shall we try again?"

The dwarf sucked in his upper lip, bit his mustache, and said nothing.

"What's your name?" the Baron asked again.

"Bob," Matterhorn said, willing the Sword to shock once more.

Zap!

Over toppled the dwarf.

Reset.

Matterhorn held the blade above the man's quivering knees and stared into his watery eyes. "This is the Sword of Truth," Matterhorn said. "You can tell me your name—or I can guess my way through the alphabet."

The dwarf fainted.

"His name's Zeke," said the dwarf sitting next in line. "And before you use that thing on me, the name's Diller. What else you wanna know?"

Clean Shave

he dwarf who spoke up was the one who had used the throwing rocks on the Baron and had tried to use them on Matterhorn.

"Who's in charge of this band of brigands?" Matterhorn asked.

"I am," Diller said in a baritone voice. A missing front tooth gave him a slight lisp. "But we ain't brigands. We're smithies by trade."

"Kidnapping is strange work for blacksmiths," the Baron said.

"We wouldn't have taken the job, only we was desperate. Few travelers come this way since the fire. Work's been hard to find."

"Who hired you?"

"Don't know," Diller replied. "Karn told us a man was lookin' for some muscle to get rid of a couple of nosy strangers. Promised us a bag of gold if we made you disappear."

"Who's Karn?" the Baron pressed.

"He's the lep what runs the tradin' post where we get our supplies."

"Lep?"

"You know, leprechaun," Diller said.

"Where were you taking me?"

"To an island off the coast."

"Then what?"

"Then we was gonna let you go. Honest. Karn just told us to get rid of you. He didn't say we had to kill you. That ain't our way. So we decided to grab one of you—didn't matter which one—and take you to this island we know.

"We left a trail what the other fella could follow," he explained. "We didn't expect you to be so quick about it." He glared at Matterhorn. "Once we stranded one of you, we thought it'd take the other guy a while to rescue his friend. That would give us time to collect our gold."

"Sorry to spoil your plans," Matterhorn said, "but we have plans of our own." He tossed some wood on the fire and said to Broc, "Keep an eye on this bunch while the Baron and I take a walk."

The horse reared and stomped the ground near the dwarf's bound feet. They scrunched closer together and tried to pull their legs into their chests.

"These guys are a few pepperonis short of a good pizza," Matterhorn said when they got out of earshot. "What shall we do with them?"

"We'll have to let them go," Aaron said.

"How can we keep them from following us and causing more trouble?"

"Leave that to me. But first, let's see what else we can learn."

Back at the fire, Aaron sat on his heels in front of Diller. "Tell us what we want to know and we'll cut you loose," he promised.

"But we don't know nothin'," Diller started to protest.

"I'm not talking about who hired you. I want to know if there's a mill around here."

Puzzled, Diller said, "It's about ten miles downriver from where we snatched you."

"How about this Karn fellow? Where's his trading post?"

"Right next to the mill," Diller said. "It's not far from the main road. That all you wanna know?"

"No," Aaron answered. "Have you ever heard of Ian's Flute?"

Diller cleared his throat. "We heard of it, sure."

"Did you know it's been stolen?"

"Heard that, too, and that the leps been goin' crazy lookin' for it."

"Any idea who took it?"

"Nope."

Matterhorn stepped forward with the Sword of Truth, but the dwarf didn't flinch.

"Use that if you want," Diller said, "but I'm tellin' the truth."

Matterhorn believed him.

"One more question," the Baron said, getting to his feet. "Does the name 'Bonehand' mean anything to you?"

A sudden shudder rippled through the group. "That man's gone evil," said the dwarf on the far right. "Dresses all in black and slinks around like a ghost. Don't talk no more, just watches everythin'. People say he caught the soldiers what started the fire that ruin't his hand. None of them's ever been found."

"That fire turned his heart coal black and diamond hard," piped in another dwarf. "He ain't a man to mess with."

"Did you ever stop to think he might be the one you're working for?" the Baron asked.

The dwarfs looked stunned. "If this is Bonehand's business," Diller said slowly, "then we're even sorrier we got involved."

"You'll be sorrier still if you follow us," the Baron said. "Give us your word that you won't bother us again."

After the dwarfs followed their leader in making the promise, the Baron cut their ropes and handed Diller back his knife. He took it with stumpy fingers that ended in the black crescents of dirty fingernails. The lines on his calloused palms looked like they'd been tattooed there with black ink.

"Now use it to shave your beard," the Baron ordered.

Diller looked as though the big man had slapped him. "Do what?" he bellowed.

"You heard me. All of you will shave—or else."

"Or else what?" Diller shot back.

Matterhorn drew his Sword and Broc stamped the ground.

"Or else we'll tie you to the trees and let the animals see to you. Or maybe Bonehand will come by to check on his flunkies."

"I can't show my naked face back home," Diller moaned. "I'd die of shame. I've had my whiskers since I was fourteen."

The Baron shrugged. "Then I guess you'll have to stay in the woods till they grow back. It shouldn't take long for hairy guys like you to get presentable."

The dwarfs fussed and fumed, but in the end they each took the knife and did the deed. The look in Broc's eyes and the otherworldly light in the Sword made it unavoidable. Afterwards, they gathered their shorn locks and fed them to the flames. The terrible stink was a fitting expression of their grief.

They didn't stay sad for long, though. Their shame was soon lightened with laughter at the discovery that Diller and another dwarf named Peat had deep clefts in their chins.

"Where'd you get that crease?" howled Zeke, who had recovered from his shock treatment. "Your chin looks like a baby's butt!"

"Feels like one too," Diller replied as he scratched his tender jaw. "But at least I ain't as pig-ugly as the rest of you."

The youngest of them, a fellow called Red Flint because of his ruddy features and sharp nose, decided to shave his whole head.

"Young 'uns," Diller said disapprovingly.

Matterhorn returned the dwarfs' other weapons so they could hunt for food while waiting for their beards to grow back. Touched by the gesture, Diller said, "You're honorable men. I'm glad you came by no harm."

It was well after midnight when Matterhorn, the Baron and Broc began retracing the drag marks to where this whole misadventure had begun. High overhead a stealthy bird watched them go. Even at night its beady eyes could see the fleas on a rat's back from a half mile up.

Another set of eyes followed them at ground level. This tracker was much more skilled than the dwarfs, and more than content to stay in the shadows.

For now.

Karn the Lep

he weary Travelers made it back to the stream by dawn and caught a few Zs before going in search of Karn. They had little trouble with the dwarfs' directions, and late that afternoon Matterhorn and the Baron were crouched in the heather a hundred feet from Karn's Trading Post. Broc eyed the establishment and gave a dismissive whinny.

The squat log building had an overhanging sod roof that gave it the appearance of a giant mushroom. Rough wooden crates and iron-hooped barrels cluttered the wraparound porch. Black pots and cast-iron skillets hung from ceiling hooks. Burlap sacks lounged against the walls. Strips of jerky festooned the open windows, attracting flies by the swarm. A pod of plump pickles swam in a brine vat near the door.

Except for a few skinny chickens and a tethered goat, the compound looked deserted.

"Let's go," the Baron said, slapping Matterhorn on the back. As they approached, they heard a wooden mill wheel paddling a spirited stream. The smell of dill filled the air.

"What's a leprechaun doing running a trading post?" Matterhorn asked. "I thought they were solitary creatures who avoided humans and hoarded gold."

"They will end up that way because of how people treated them," the Baron answered. "The big always take advantage of the small, and the small either adapt or perish. When Ireland becomes more populated, the leprechauns will learn they have to hide to survive."

Speaking of leprechauns, one came out of the door holding a shoe in one hand and a cobbler's hammer in the other. The rat-faced little man was a few inches shorter than Ian. He had pinched features and BB eyes. Shy wisps of corn silk hair poked out from his narrow-brim derby hat. His large ears stuck to his scalp at the top and flapped loose at the bottom. He had a black olive mouth between his pointy nose and hairless chin.

Broc lowered his head and looked the leprechaun up and down. He took a few steps closer and gave the fellow a thorough sniffing. Then he swung his neck around and pushed Matterhorn back the way they had come.

Matterhorn resisted and said, "Calm down, Broc. We just want to ask the man a few questions."

Broc snorted and swished Matterhorn with his tail before trotting off.

The leprechaun ignored the snub and said in a reedy voice, "Ye must be Matterhorn and the Baron. I've been expectin' ye."

The Baron and Matterhorn looked at each other in surprise. Had the dwarfs double-crossed them and sent word of their escape? They didn't know what to say.

The leprechaun came to the edge of the porch. "My uncle said ye might show up. He told me to help ye any way I could. Name's Karn." When he spoke, the little man's rancid breath pushed the visitors back.

Matterhorn coughed out a, "Yell-O."

"Likewise," the Baron managed. "King Ian is the only leprechaun we've met since we've been here. Is he your uncle?"

Karn nodded.

"Doesn't that make you some sort of royalty?" Matterhorn said.

"If it did, I wouldn't be a shopkeeper," Karn spat out. The knuckles on his hammer hand went white.

"Do you own that mill?" the Baron asked, hitching his thumb toward the river.

"The farmers round here built it. I manage it."

"Does it have a grinding wheel?"

"Aye, there's a wheel next to the large millstones. The farmers use it to sharpen their tools."

"That's not all it's been used to sharpen," Matterhorn said. He untied the bone bomb from his pack and handed it to Karn, who put down his shoe and hammer.

"I've never seen the like of it," Karn said. "Where'd ye get it?"

"It came special delivery," the Baron said. "Airborne. Any idea who might have sent it?"

"No," the leprechaun said, almost dropping the bone. He gave it back to Matterhorn and began wiping his hands on his apron, his slender fingers a blur of motion.

The gesture reminded Matterhorn of Sherlock Holmes' number one rule of criminal detection, "Always look at the hands first, Watson." Karn was definitely nervous about something.

"Have there been any strangers around?" the Baron pressed. "Like the one who told you to set a pack of dwarfs on our trail. I don't think that's what your uncle had in mind when he said to help us."

Karn stepped back, stumbled, and caught his balance. His sharp gaze flitted from one tall outlander to the other. "It was just a business deal," he stammered. "I didn't want no part of it, but I couldn't afford to anger a man like—" he stopped and glanced around.

"Like who?" Matterhorn demanded.

"Like Bonehand."

"We've had about enough of this Bonehand character," the Baron said in disgust. "We've got a score to settle with this one-handed menace and some stolen property to recover. Do you know where we can find him?"

"He keeps to himself," Karn said. "But he comes here sometimes to buy supplies. Ye can wait till he shows up if ye want."

"And when might that be?"

"Don't know. But you'll never be findin' him in these woods." Sweeping his arm in a circle, Karn said, " 'Tis his front yard and most of the animals act like his pets. They pretty much do what he tells 'em."

I wonder if that applies to birds, Matterhorn thought. Especially ones large enough to carry deadly cargo.

Low thundering in the distance drew the Baron's attention to the graying horizon. The threat of rain caused him to ask Karn about a dry place to bed down for the night.

"There's a storage building by the mill," Karn offered.

"We'll take it."

A bevy of white swans graced the millpond where Matterhorn and the Baron fished for their supper. They enjoyed spit-roasted trout garnished with onions and fresh greens from Karn's garden, thanks to Matterhorn taking over the cooking after the Baron burnt the first two fish to cinders.

They enjoyed a stream-bath before heading to the storage building. The tall, two-story structure was built of stone blocks that were stained moss green on the outside and wheat-dust yellow on the inside. The ground floor served as a stable—a fact Karn had failed to mention—so the guests decided to sleep upstairs.

The stalls were empty, but the place was not completely deserted. Reddish brown insects with yellow stripes buzzed around a giant gray spitball wadded above the large double doors. Pointing to the hornets' nest, the Baron said, "Those things don't lose their stingers when they attack. They can pop you like a nail gun."

The tremor in his voice made Matterhorn ask, "Are you speaking from experience?"

"A near-death experience," Aaron said as he slipped back outside.

Lofty Dream

atterhorn did not want to spend another night on the cold ground. "What are you afraid of?" he asked Aaron.

Slamming the door behind them, Aaron said, "I spend my summers at my grandpa's ranch. I love the place and everything about the country." He rubbed his shoulder and added, "Well, almost everything. Grandma hangs the wash on a clothesline in the yard to dry. One morning I climbed into my jeans and found they were already occupied. The hornet stung me eight times before I could de-pants myself."

Matterhorn chuckled as he pictured Aaron hopping around wildly swatting himself.

"You laugh," the Baron scolded, "but I had an allergic reaction and almost died. The last thing I need is to get stung out here in the boonies."

"Getting stung in the boonies sounds painful," Matterhorn quipped.

"Stick a few of those buzzers in your britches and see for yourself."

"No, thanks," Matterhorn declined. "For a great adventurer you don't seem very comfortable with nature," he teased.

"I can hold my own," the Baron retorted. "I just don't like creatures that bite or sting."

"Tell you what, we can use the side door and not disturb the residents." This they did, making their way carefully to the stout ladder, watching both the ground and the air for surprises. They climbed to a spacious loft strewn with freshly cut hay. The delicious smell of yellow sunshine and green fields wafted from the straw as they mounded it into fluffy mattresses.

The hayloft was occupied by a family of field mice who lived beyond the reach of Karn's cat. The feline security guard refused to climb and left them alone. The mice didn't mind the human company and Matterhorn soon had one of them eating out of his hand. The fuzzy creature reminded him of Reepicheep, his pet hooded rat. Reepicheep lived in a complex of plastic boxes and tubes that sprawled under Matterhorn's bed and into his closet. Matterhorn hoped someone was feeding Reep while he was gone.

Thinking of his room with its carpet-patch floor and poster-plastered walls made him homesick. Closing his eyes he could imagine his bass guitar propped by the cinder-block-and-pine bookshelves across from his bed. The top plank held his stereo, CDs and several harmonicas. The second shelf hosted the works of Sir Arthur Conan Doyle, including his four novels and fifty-six short stories about Sherlock Holmes. Holmes was Matterhorn's favorite character in all fiction.

The remaining shelves boasted books on everything from astronomy to zoology.

Ever since he was eight, Matterhorn had made it a rule to read one book a week. In the summers he read more. He found the people in books far more interesting than the ones on TV. His comic book collection, given to him by his dad, rested in neat piles underneath the bottom shelf. Its most valuable pieces were still cocooned in plastic.

A list of famous redheads was pinned above his desk to inspire him. The list included several presidents such as George Washington and Thomas Jefferson. Writers like Shakespeare and Mark Twain. World-changers like Galileo and Christopher Columbus and Napoleon.

So, what was this redhead doing lying on a pile of scratchy hay centuries from his soft bed? His sore ribs made it hard to get comfortable and reminded him that traveling was dangerous business. He glanced over at the Baron, who was picking his teeth with a twig. "What would've happened to me if those dwarfs had killed you?" he asked.

"Ever thought of being a farmer?"

"No. Would I have been stuck here the rest of my life?"

The Baron laughed. "Queen Bea would send someone to look for us if we didn't return. It might have taken a while to find you, though. How about shepherding? Do you like being outdoors?"

"I like being home," Matterhorn said. "We do get to go home once this is over, don't we?"

"After we accomplish our mission."

"Will we remember everything?"

"Yes."

That was a relief to Matterhorn. "Can you teach me to use that Cube of yours just in case?" he asked.

"It's pretty complicated," the Baron said, holding up the misshapen device. "First you have to triangulate the nearest portal with your desired time-space coordinates and then—"

"Never mind," Matterhorn said as the Baron's fingers flew around the gem-studded globe too fast to follow. "Just don't get yourself killed."

"It's nice to know you care."

"How did you get started with time travel in the first place?" Matterhorn asked. "Did you get sucked into it like me?"

Laying the Cube on his chest and folding his hands behind his neck, Aaron said, "I was recruited through a video game. It was the summer I got stung by the hornet. I always stayed at the ranch when mom had to go back to the city. Grandpa let me follow him around during the day. He taught me about machinery and how to fix things. At night we played video games together. He was pretty good for an old guy.

"One Saturday it was raining and I was bored. Grandpa had to go to town for feed, but before he left he handed me a game called Travelers. I'd never seen it before. You had to find these hidden portals and use them to collect artifacts from different time periods without getting caught. I got pretty good at it. Learned a lot about history along the way. Anyway, one day I got the bright idea there might be deeper levels to the game."

Matterhorn guessed where the story was headed but didn't interrupt.

"I thought the portals might be connected somehow," Aaron continued with a hint of pride. "I went looking for a hub and found it several nights later. And when my character stepped into the Hall of Portals, I became him."

"Were you as shocked as I was?" Matterhorn asked.

"I suppose so," the Baron replied. "Particularly about becoming an adult. That took some getting used to. I didn't meet the Queen until a few trips later. One of the Praetorians, those are the guardians you saw in the Propylon, explained traveling to me and I signed on."

"What do you know about First Realm?" Matterhorn asked.

"Not much," the Baron said. I've never been outside the Propylon. The Praetorians tell me Earth is a mirror world of First Realm. That's why we're so similar."

They talked a bit longer until last night's lack of sleep caught up to them and pulled them under. A few hours later, Matterhorn was enjoying a family camping trip in a lucid dream. His dad sat against a tree reading a book. Christy, his dog, chased butterflies across a mountain meadow. Matterhorn played catch with his older brother, Vic, and threw pinecones at his younger sister, Louise.

The weather in his dream warmed from balmy to blazing and Matterhorn kicked off his blanket. Sweat began pouring down his face. He watched in horror as his family melted like wax candles. The evergreens turned brown and burst into flames. Smoke stung his eyes and throat.

Above the snap-crackling inferno he heard a woman's voice cry, "You are in grave danger!"

The shrill warning shattered his nightmare and startled Matterhorn awake. He sat up into a dense cloud of acrid smoke; then fell back in a fit of coughing.

The loft was on fire!

Fire Escape

Matterhorn's loud hacking woke the Baron. "We've got trouble!" he coughed. Together they crawled to the edge of the loft and peered down. Bales of hay had been stacked beneath their perch and set ablaze. Wild orange flames cackled up at them. Intense heat slapped their faces and answered their unspoken question.

There was no way down.

No way out.

Whoever planned this barbecue had done a good job of trapping them on the grill.

"Follow the water to its source!" said the female voice that had awakened Matterhorn. They both heard it this time, but neither saw the speaker. A streamlet of water flowed through the straw toward them and poured over the edge to be vaporized by the heat. Matterhorn obeyed and moved into the wet with the Baron on his heels. They snagged their packs and boots as they slithered to the back of the loft.

By now their eyes were smoked shut. Matterhorn banged his head into the wall. A good thing he had thick hair to pad the blow. He squinted up to discover water pouring down from the window eight feet above. It was their only way out—if they could reach it.

Aaron the Baron also saw the opening. Filling his lungs with what little air he could find near the floor he knelt and made a stirrup. He motioned for Matterhorn to step up and then hoisted him to the broad windowsill. Next, he tossed up the packs before hauling himself up Matterhorn's down-stretched arm.

The strain on Matterhorn's ribs was almost more than he could bear.

They were on the river side of the building, and, despite gravity, there was a reverse waterfall climbing up the stones. Matterhorn braced himself and squeezed his eyes shut. He was afraid of heights and the twenty-foot drop made him dizzy. The Baron had no such qualms; he launched Matterhorn into space and followed him down.

Their clothes hissed when they landed in the water. Upon surfacing, they saw the one who had saved their lives. An exquisite young woman hovered in the mist above the churning mill wheel. Shoulder-length tawny hair outlined a porcelain doll face with blue eyes, soft cheeks and a delicate chin. Moonlight glimmered off the aqua gown draping her trim figure. A shell-pink pearl dangled from each ear and an even larger bead hung around her throat on a strand of gold. She had pearl rings on several fingers and nail polish that matched her dress.

"Are you all right?" she asked in her silvery voice.

"Yeah, thanks to you!" shouted Matterhorn above the din. "We owe you our lives."

"So you do," she said. A coy smile played across her thin lips. Then her petite frame melted into the mist and her pearls plunked into the water.

Matterhorn tried to grab one and missed. "Who was that?" he asked the Baron.

"A naiad."

"What's a naiad?"

"A water nymph," the Baron answered as he tied his boots to his pack strap. He kicked away from the burning building into midstream.

Matterhorn followed. "So water nymphs are real here, too."

"They're real everywhere. They just don't show themselves very often. A good thing for us this one did." He scanned what could be seen of the riverbank in the firelight. Other than the fleeting outline of a small horse, nothing else moved. Whoever had set the fire hadn't waited around to see the outcome.

"Let's float downriver," the Baron said, "then circle back when things cool off to search for clues."

Although a strong swimmer, Matterhorn had trouble with his heavy pack until the Baron said, "See this tab?" He pointed to a small square on the pack's yellow rubber liner. "Pull it." With an inrush of air the backside of the pack expanded. "I attached a self-inflating airbag in the unlikely event of a water landing."

This guy is ready for anything, Matterhorn thought. And, for the first time since the fire, he remembered the one piece of equipment he was responsible for—the Sword! He felt for the hilt at his side and was relieved to find that the jump hadn't torn it off. It was stuck to the scritch pad on his belt. Relieved, he rolled onto his back and rested his head on the pack. As the current carried him along, he looked back at the burning building blowing smoke rings into the night sky. "Lucky for us the water nymph came by," he said at last.

"I don't believe in luck," the Baron proclaimed from a few feet away. "Nothing happens by chance. The Maker sees to that."

"We would've been shrimps on the barbie without the naiad," Matterhorn went on. "How did she do that? Get water up through the window and all?"

"Naiads can do anything with water," the Baron said. "It's what they're made of."

"How can someone be made of water?" Matterhorn scooped up a handful of river and let it run through his fingers.

"It's not so unusual. Our bodies are mostly water."

"That may be true," Matterhorn agreed, "but this body is ready to be dry again."

They had floated a fair distance by now and when the Baron spotted a red glow on the far shore he said: "Race you to that campfire."

"What if that's the arsonist?" Matterhorn said.

The Baron's eyes narrowed. "Then we'll teach him not to play with matches."

Helping Hand

Aaron won the race to shore because of Matterhorn's sore chest. Together they shivered their way toward the stranger sitting with his back to the water and his face to the fire. The man had a dark woolen cloak draped over his large frame. The hood was down and a ponytail hung over his shoulder. He spoke without turning. "Do you always swim in your clothes?"

"Just doing our laundry," The Baron joked, shaking himself like a dog. "Can you spare some heat?"

The man nodded at the fire.

The Baron and Matterhorn approached and dropped their packs. They turned themselves slowly in the warmth while their host studied them with cat-green eyes.

Matterhorn stared back at the open, clean-shaven face unwrinkled by laugh lines. The man was well groomed compared to the dwarfs and leprechauns they had met so far. He had the lean features and musky odor of someone who lived outdoors. Matterhorn was good at guessing people's ages; he pegged this guy in his late twenties.

The pastel scent of chamomile spluttered from a teapot whistling to itself in the coals. Observing the code of the road, the man said in a gravelly voice: "Help yourselves. Meat, too, if you're hungry." He pointed with his chin to a line of sausages sizzling in a frying pan.

"Thanks," the Baron said. He dug two tin cups from his gear and held them while Matterhorn used the tail of his shirt as a potholder and poured. "Rather late for supper, isn't it?" he commented.

"I'm a night person. This is breakfast."

While waiting for his tea to cool, the Baron found a stick and stabbed a sausage. He offered it to Matterhorn; then speared one for himself. "Umm, these are good," he mumbled. "Crunchy on the outside and chewy on the inside. Is this venison or pork?"

"Caterpillar," the man said.

Aaron spat out what he hadn't swallowed and rinsed his mouth with scalding tea. Matterhorn laughed so hard that he almost choked. When he regained control he said to the cook, "These are pretty good. They need a little salt, though, and maybe a dab of horseradish."

Where food was concerned, Matterhorn would try anything once. His parents had taught him to treat food with an open mind and a discerning palate. He'd eaten everything from sushi to chocolate-covered grasshoppers.

While the Baron scraped his tongue with his front teeth, Matterhorn reached for another crispy critter. "These remind me of calamari," he said.

"What's that?" the man asked.

"Squid. You should try it next time you get to the coast. I assume you're not a local or you wouldn't be out here. Where are you from?"

"Around," said the caped figure. Only his face and well-worn boots were visible outside the dark folds of his garment. Neither gave a clue to his origin.

"Well, you need to be careful," Matterhorn advised. "Someone around here doesn't like strangers." He glanced at the wispy smoke in the distance that could have been his funeral pyre.

The man followed Matterhorn's gaze. "That's Karn's place. Did you two have anything to do with that?"

"We were sleeping in the stable," Matterhorn replied. "Someone tried to burn us alive."

"Were there animals inside?"

"No, thank goodness," the Baron said. He did not voice the main question on his mind — What were you doing about an hour ago? — but he did ask, "Have you seen anyone go by?"

"I haven't been here that long." The man swigged his tea from a pewter cup and added, "You're foreigners. I don't recognize your accents. Where are you from?"

"Around," the Baron said, being as vague as his host.

"Fair enough," the man replied. "Do you know who wants you dead?"

Matterhorn wrung water from his ponytail and answered, "We've got a pretty good idea, but catching him will be a major chore in these woods."

"Want some help?"

"That's a kind offer, but no," the Baron said. "Your hospitality has been help enough. This is our fight. We won't put anyone else in danger. By the way, my name's Aaron and this is Matterhorn." He leaned forward and extended his hand.

The man stared at the Baron's open palm for a long time before deciding how to respond. Then he slowly drew his right hand from under his cloak.

It had no flesh on it.

The Baron jerked away as if from a corpse. Matterhorn jumped up and had his Sword leveled at Bonehand's chest in the blink of an eye. But Bonehand didn't blink. He simply said: "Do you always show your appreciation with the point of a blade?"

"We don't appreciate people trying to kill us," Matterhorn said, his eyes boring into Bonehand's.

Bonehand gave a short laugh. "If I wanted you dead, we wouldn't be having this conversation." His words did not have the tinny ring of boast or threat. They came across as a simple fact.

"Are you saying you're not responsible for what's been happening to us?" the Baron demanded.

"Such as?"

"The bone bomb, and the kidnappers, not to mention tonight's fire. You had nothing to do with those?"

Bonehand extended his good left hand and touched the Sword of Truth. "I swear I've not tried to kill you."

This brazen act stunned Matterhorn and the Baron.

Bonehand grinned at their startled faces. "I saw you use this on the dwarfs."

Lowering the blade, Matterhorn said: "If you didn't send them, how did you know about the kidnapping?"

"I make it my business to know what goes on in my forest."

"Do you know why we're here?" the Baron asked.

"To find Ian's Flute."

"Ian thinks you took it," Matterhorn said.

"He's wrong."

"Karn told us you hired the dwarfs," the Baron added.

"He lied."

"It's your word against his."

Bonehand stirred the fire and sent a fountain of sparks skyward. "If you paid more attention to facts than rumors, you'd know who was telling the truth." He watched the flicks of amber rise and blink away.

The Baron and Matterhorn sat down and waited.

At last Bonehand spoke. "There's a common thread in your troubles."

Matterhorn did a flash review of the last few days. They were anything but common. What had he missed? When he asked Bonehand, the man clicked off several points on his bare digits.

Click. "I heard what you said about the bone that fell from the sky, how it was sharpened by a millstone. Who runs the only mill for miles around?"

"Karn," Matterhorn said, trying not to stare at the skeletal visual aid.

Click. "Who did the dwarfs say would pay them for getting rid of you?"

"Karn," the Baron answered.

Click. "Whose building did you almost die in tonight?"

"Karn, again," Matterhorn said. He snapped a twig into tiny pieces and tossed them into the short flames. "The leprechaun's got a sneaky face," Matterhorn admitted. "But we've never even met until today. What could he possibly have against us?"

Click. Bonehand thumbed his little finger against the others. "You're after what he's got."

arn's got the Flute!" Aaron cried. He was leaning so intently forward by now that his forearms slid off his knees and he lost his balance.

Bonehand drew his hands to his lips and pretended to play the wondrous whistle.

Matterhorn could see Bonehand's logic, but he had trouble with Karn's. "Why would Karn steal from his own family?"

"Money and power," Bonehand said. "His father is Ian's younger brother, which puts him close enough to royalty to smell it, but not close enough to taste it. His cousins are princes, but he's a struggling trader. I'd bet my good hand someone offered him a pretty price for the Flute."

"How come Ian suspects you and not his nephew?" the Baron pressed.

"For the same reason you suspected me," Bonehand said. "I disagree with Ian about the Flute. I keep to myself. I dress funny. I have a deformity"—he held up his hand and rattled the bones—"therefore, I'm evil, right?"

The Baron and Matterhorn looked at each other sheepishly. "I guess we misjudged you because of your reputation," Matterhorn admitted.

"Yeah," the Baron agreed, although he still felt uneasy about this dark stranger.

Bonehand shrugged. "I'm used to it. People think they know what a person's like by looking at his skin. When it's different colored or damaged in some way they assume the worst. They never bother to check." He smirked and added, "I get blamed for everything from lightning fires to lost sheep."

"Our apologies for blaming you," Matterhorn said. He stood and offered Aaron a hand up. "I guess we've got a Karn to catch."

"It's too late for that tonight," Bonehand said. "The lep probably took off the minute he set fire to the stable. You'll have to wait till morning to track him."

"He's right," Aaron said. "Besides, I'm tired. Mind if we bed down here?"

Just then, a rustling noise sounded in the dark. The Sword came out, but was put away when Broc trotted into view. Matterhorn gave his four-footed friend a two-armed hug around the neck and rubbed the broccoli birthmark. "Glad to see you found us, Broc."

Aaron fished a candy bar from his pack and tossed it to Matterhorn, who barely got the wrapper off before Broc inhaled the treat.

"Well, I'll be," Bonehand said, more surprised to see the horse than he had been to see Matterhorn and the Baron. "Do you know who this is?"

"I don't know his real name," Matterhorn replied. "I call him Broccoli, er, I mean, Broc."

"He's not a vegetable!" Bonehand said. "He's a noble scion, a direct descendant of Chiron the Wise, the centaur who tutored Jason and Achilles."

"Broc was wise enough not to trust Karn," the Baron said. "He tried to warn us but we didn't listen."

Bonehand studied the steed from hoof to forelock in the flickering light. The animal was a living work of art, perfect in line and proportion. "We are fortunate to have his company," Bonehand said in a reverent tone. "Not many of his kind are left in the world. Their bodies are entirely equine now; they can no longer speak. Still, their minds are as developed as humans. I've seen this one in the forest before, but never as close. I'm amazed he lets you touch him."

"Touch him," Matterhorn said. "I've ridden him."

"You may be the only person who has," Bonehand said. "No offense, but it has more to do with the Sword you carry than with you."

Broc neighed and shook his head. He stepped closer to Matterhorn and touched the hilt with his nose. The blade lit up in response.

The gesture brought a smile to Bonehand's face. "If this animal trusts you, I guess I can, too. You're welcome to my fire. And my help."

"We'll take the first," the Baron said, "but like I said before, we won't need the help."

"I'm not asking," Bonehand said, "I'm telling. I'll not let the Flute be used to harm innocent animals. I warned Ian this would happen. It has to be stopped."

"We can't involve you in—"

"I know these woods," Bonehand interrupted, "and you don't. I also know how to use this." He drew back his cloak to reveal a short sword of exquisite workmanship. The handle was wrapped in faded blue leather and capped with a bronze pommel. Bonehand drew out the blade. The edges of the gray shaft were sharpened to a silver gleam.

Matterhorn let out a low whistle. "Where'd you get that?"

"I found it in the cave where I first hid as a child."

"It looks Roman," Matterhorn said. "Their merchants and scouts were in these parts centuries ago. Can I see it?"

Bonehand let the sword drop back into its sheath. "Look at it in the morning."

Aaron realized there was nothing he and Matterhorn could do. The duo had just become a trio. Counting Broc, they were actually a quartet. Glancing at the horse in profile gave Aaron an idea. His best thoughts often came like that, as bolts of inspiration. Taking off his belt, he held it in front of him and approached Broc. "If you are who this man says, you can understand me, right?"

Broc nodded.

"You know what we're here for, then," the Baron continued. "We think Karn has Ian's Flute. He'll have to play it sooner or later to prove to a potential buyer that it's the real thing. When that happens, will you have to obey its call?"

Another nod.

The Baron's hunch was right. "There's a tracking device in my belt. If I put it around your neck we can follow you and protect you. Is that okay?"

Broc snorted and lowered his head. The belt just fit around his powerful neck. "This will send out a signal for up to three days," Aaron said, activating the beacon. "Something's bound to happen before then." He went to his pack and switched off the beeping noise coming from the homing device. He checked to make sure the green light was blinking in the center of the compact screen.

"Don't worry," Matterhorn said, coming up and rubbing Broc behind the ears. "We won't let anything happen to you."

"Enough for tonight," the Baron said.

Since his bedroll had been lost in the fire, he covered himself with a wool poncho and was soon snoring quietly.

Matterhorn had too much on his mind to sleep. "Can I ask you a question?" he said to Bonehand. "I've seen you tend the fire and tidy up. How is it you can use your bone hand so well?"

Flexing his naked fingers, Bonehand said, "The muscles that work the fingers are in the forearm. Tendons connect them to the bones. My skin was broiled in the fire, but most of the tendons survived. Gradually I've trained myself to use my hand again. It's not pretty, but it works."

Bonehand noticed Matterhorn's gaze sliding up to the goo leaking from around his shirt cuff. "I make this salve from herbs and honey," he explained. "It prevents infection and keeps the tendons lubricated."

"I admire your grit," Matterhorn said. "But tell me, do you regret trying to save those animals?"

"Not a bit," Bonehand said instantly. "I'd do it again if I had to. I can't stand to see animals suffer."

Matterhorn wanted to ask about the soldiers who had started the fire, but Bonehand turned away and pulled the hood over his head.

Follow the Leader

Matterhorn, Broc, the Baron and Bonehand hid in the trees watching a group of farmers poke around the burned building next to the mill. Ghostly dust devils swirled in the morning breeze flush with fresh charcoal. One of the men came out of the smoldering ruin with a silvery sheet in his hand. "Someone must've been in the stable last night."

Matterhorn mouthed the words, "Your blanket."

"The fire was set on purpose," said a second farmer holding up the butt-end of a blackened torch.

"Anyone find any bones in the ashes?" another asked.

Several shook their heads or grunted, "No."

"Karn's gone!" a lad yelled across the clearing from the porch of the trading post. "The hearth's cold and his bed ain't been slept in!"

"Foul play," said the first speaker knowingly.

"Bonehand's work," muttered a middle-aged man leaning on his pitchfork. "The sooner we get rid of 'im the safer we'll all be."

Bonehand gave Matterhorn and the Baron an "I told you so" look.

The farmers drew themselves into a tight knot of concern. "Those who can spare a man or two, send 'em back here in an hour," came a crisp command from the center. "And make sure they're well armed. We'll scour the woods till we catch the blackguard this time."

When the way was clear, Matterhorn and the others made their own quick search for clues. "There was a skiff by the millpond yesterday," he said after circling the area. "It's gone."

"Which means Karn's headed for the coast," Bonehand said. "It's thirty miles and he'll make better time on the water than we can on land. Once he reaches the shore, we won't know if he's gone north or south."

"The best we can do is follow and wait for him to use the Flute," the Baron said. He shaded his eyes and glanced skyward. "It's 9:15 now; we've got a long day ahead of us. Let's go."

Walking beside their new guide, Matterhorn got a chance to study the mystery man in the light of day. At five foot six, he was a head shorter than his new companions. His black hair was drawn back from his forehead and ears, giving his face a severe look. He had high cheekbones and straight, but dingy, teeth. An intricate pewter broach fastened the sleek cloak at the neck. Underneath he wore a dark linen shirt and buckskin breeches tucked into high boots. His stride was easy and confident.

In contrast to Bonehand's subdued outfit, the countryside blossomed with bluebells, blackthorns, butterburs and primroses. Every green-crested hill seemed to have a frisky brook playing down one side or the other. Farther away, thickset stonewalls separated the velour pastures of well-kept farms. Pheasants occasionally fluttered from field to field in bursts of feathery excitement.

Under different circumstances, Matterhorn would have loved to talk to the people who owned those farms. His grandfather, a man he respected for his faith and wisdom, had come from Irish stock. But Matterhorn knew he would be seen as an accomplice of the man in black, who was no doubt suspected of every unsolved crime in the district.

Aaron's horse had never returned and Matterhorn chose not to ride Broc, so they progressed at foot-speed. To pass the time Matterhorn tried to learn more about Bonehand. "What's your real name, if you don't mind me asking?"

"Bonehand will do," came the terse reply.

"You don't sound Irish"

"That's because I'm English."

Remembering what Ian had said about Bonehand's parents, Matterhorn tried a different approach. "I'm sorry about your folks being killed. Do you have any other family?"

"None worth talking about."

"So you live alone?"

"I have a forest full of friends."

"Does that include the leprechauns?"

"Some."

"How long have you known Ian?"

"Years."

"Do you ever visit the nearby towns?"

Bonehand glowered as if the question was too dumb to deserve an answer. "Do you ever stop talking?"

Matterhorn snapped his jaw shut. Just as well; Bonehand might begin asking questions of his own. Matterhorn wouldn't lie and Bonehand wouldn't believe he was a kid from the future given an adult body and sent by the Queen of First Realm to find one of the Ten Talis. Matterhorn hardly believed it himself.

They moved over the next several hills in silence. An easterly breeze kicked up and brought with it a faraway snapping sound. From the top of the next rise they spotted a farmer at the plow. He was using a bull-whip on the slow-footed draft horse in harness. The huge creature shuddered under the rain of blows. His legs strained against the burden of the dull blade. Blood ran down his sweaty sides from the gashes on his back.

The sight was enough to throw Bonehand into a towering rage. He ran to the end of the field and vaulted the rock hedge. The farmer lashed his horse again before turning to face the caped intruder. He was a head taller than Bonehand and broader in the shoulders. He seemed put out by this interruption, but not afraid.

"Should we do something?" Matterhorn asked the Baron.

"Like what?" Aaron replied. They stopped at the wall and watched.

"How would you fancy the lash on your own back?" Bonehand barked.

"Keep yer nose outta my business or I'll peel it off," the man retorted, shaking his whip.

Bonehand ignored the threat and kept coming.

The farmer's face got hard. He drew back his hand and snapped the seven-foot cord forward faster than the eye could follow.

Bonehand raised his right arm and let the leather snake coil itself around his forearm. Then he grabbed it with his bony fingers and yanked the weapon free. He caught the hilt in his left hand and a moment later was chasing the surprised farmer toward the barn. He landed several lashes, and might have seriously injured the man if the race hadn't been abruptly ended by the barn door.

Bonehand slid a board through the brackets and locked the farmer inside. He flung the whip down the well. Returning to the field he cut the horse loose and led him toward the gate near Matterhorn. The Baron didn't look back, and so didn't see the farmer appear in the loft's door with a longbow in his hands. His chest heaved with exertion as he fitted arrow to string and took careful aim.

When the Baron saw the farmer, he reached into his pocket and drew out a compact signal mirror. He unfolded it and directed a flash of sunlight into the man's face just as he fired. He flinched and sent the arrow high of its target and into the wall just below the Baron's waist.

"Hurry up!" Matterhorn screamed at Bonehand.

Aaron blinded the farmer each time he raised his bow. Finally, it dawned on him to back away from the opening and shoot, but by then Bonehand and the horse were safely among the trees.

Not wanting any more trouble with the locals, the Baron suggested they follow the river deeper into the woods, which suited Bonehand fine. He soon had them in timber so dense that Broc and the plow horse could barely squeeze through.

Matterhorn and the Baron trudged along behind the animals, watching where they stepped. "Quick thinking with the mirror," Matterhorn complimented his friend. "You saved Bonehand's life and he didn't even say thanks."

"He doesn't strike me as the kind who says thank you," Aaron replied.

"What do we really know about him?" Matterhorn said quietly. "Maybe he lied about Karn. Maybe he'll keep the Flute once we find it and kill us like he did those soldiers."

"He could have killed us last night," the Baron observed. "Let's not give him a reason to reconsider the idea."

Bounty Men

It was afternoon when they reached a clearing and stopped for lunch. The leafy boughs of the largest tree Matterhorn had ever seen overshadowed the entire glade. Thick limbs splayed from the massive trunk in all directions forming the rafters of the green roof. Gnarled roots dug into the ground like giant fingers.

Bonehand washed the draft horse's cuts and brushed the crusty blood from his coat. Broc paid no attention to the large brute since they had little in common. He chewed at the tender turf while the humans shared jerky and dried fruit. As they rested beneath the great tree, a gray squirrel scampered over the exposed roots and jumped into Bonehand's lap. He had a stick in his mouth that turned out to be the tip of an arrow.

"We've got company," Bonehand said. "And not far away."

This proved an understatement as just then an arrow thwacked into the wood an inch above Matterhorn's head.

A second arrow sliced through the air—and into Broc's right shoulder.

Matterhorn's panic at almost being killed was overwhelmed by his anger at seeing Broc hit. The horse was jolted sideways by the force of the blow and neighed in pain.

Ignoring the danger, Matterhorn started toward Broc, but the Baron grabbed his shirt and yanked him around the trunk. Bonehand dove around the other side a whisker ahead of another thirty-inch bolt of death.

"We've got to help Broc!" Matterhorn shouted as more arrows thunked into the tree. He raised his head and peeked over the root. He couldn't see the horses.

"There he goes," the Baron said, pointing to a break in the trees through which Broc's tail was disappearing at a gallop. He spun on Bonehand and cried: "It's the farmer's mob already!"

Bonehand shook his head. "Bounty men more likely."

"There's a price on your head?" Matterhorn sputtered. "Why didn't you tell us?"

Bonehand slipped off his cloak and rucksack. He handed them to Matterhorn and said: "It doesn't make a difference."

Throwing down the pack, Matterhorn snapped: "It does if someone's trying to kill us to collect!"

"Some soldiers disappeared after the big fire that took my hand," Bonehand said. "That's ancient history. Now, do what I say and you'll live to tell your children about this. Keep these yokels busy till I'm away. Then run straight through there." He pointed to a wooded draw on the far side of the meadow. "You won't be followed: it's me that's worth a hundred pieces of gold." He crouched on the balls of his feet and studied the canopy overhead as he spoke.

"What about Broc?" Matterhorn demanded.

"Judging by his speed, he's not hurt bad," Bonehand replied. "The arrow must have hit a bone. He'll need that shaft removed, though. I'll see to it soon as I can."

Matterhorn wondered at Bonehand's confidence.

"A mile or so from here you'll come to a deep ravine," Bonehand continued. "Below will be the river. Follow it west to low ground."

"And what if—"

But Bonehand was already climbing upward as the squirrel had done when the attack began. His fingers gripped the coarse bark like claws.

"You heard the man," the Baron said. "Draw your Sword."

Matterhorn did so and Aaron draped Bonehand's cloak on the blade. When Matterhorn tilted the garment outward it attracted a hail of arrows.

"Why are you trying to kill us!" the Baron screamed at the attackers. "We've done nothing wrong!"

"Give us the man in black an' ye can go yer way," came a heavy brogue reply.

Matterhorn looked out the top of his eyes to see Bonehand's heels vanish among the leaves. "Let's make a deal!" Matterhorn shouted. "How about splitting the reward?"

"How 'bout we just kill the lot of ye?" came the answer, followed by another pointed volley.

The Baron dug into an inside pocket of his pack and produced a small red ball with a stubby green fuse. He knew what Bonehand would attempt and wanted to give him a fighting chance. He waited a few more moments before lighting the M-80—which had the punch of a quarter-stick of dynamite—and lobbing it toward the voice.

The Baron and Matterhorn covered their ears as the explosion rocked the clearing and filled the air with a caustic smell of gunpowder. Bonehand dropped from a branch thirty feet away and raced into a thicket of ash trees before the bounty men could regain their senses.

When they did, rather than expose themselves to unknown danger, they stayed on the fringe and worked around the meadow to catch Bonehand's trail.

Matterhorn caught glimpses of four men in jerkins, yew bows in their hands and goose-feathered shafts stuffed into their quivers. He prayed Bonehand's head start would be large enough, as a decent bowman could down a running deer at 200 yards.

Running is what he and the Baron did next—in the opposite direction. Bonehand's prediction proved mostly correct. They were not chased. However, one of the men stopped long enough to send an arrow after them, more out of frustration than malice. Had he taken time to aim properly, the missile would have found Matterhorn's back instead of zipping past his ear.

Matterhorn felt the fletching on his cheek and the sensation tripled his speed, which almost cost him his life. After running a few-minute mile, he beat the Baron to the ravine Bonehand had mentioned. It was actually a deep gouge in the earth that plummeted two hundred feet from a sheer cliff to a cauldron of churning rapids.

Matterhorn broke through the thick brush hiding the edge, his feet churning, cartoon-like, in midair.

Cliff-hanger

The foliage that masked the sheer drop is what actually saved Matterhorn's life, for as he fell, he managed to spin and grab a skein of sturdy roots. The weight of his body and pack stretched his arms. His shoulders popped painfully, but his grip held.

The Baron skidded to a halt when Matterhorn disappeared in front of his eyes. "Matterhorn!" he cried. "Matterhorn!"

"Stay back!" Matterhorn warned.

"Where are you?"

"Down here!" Ten feet away a bush rustled. The Baron dropped to his stomach and inched forward. Brambles clawed at his clothes and skin. He reached the edge and looked down.

Matterhorn twisted in space. His face had gone white as his teeth, which were clenched as tightly as his fingers.

Aaron curled his legs around a stout bush and extended himself over the edge. He put one pack strap in the crook of his elbow and lowered the other toward Matterhorn. "Grab on!" he cried.

Matterhorn stared at the loop a few feet away. He told his right hand to let go of the root and grab the strap, but it wouldn't obey.

The Baron crawled a few inches forward and balanced his weight on the knife-edge. "Now!"

Matterhorn said a silent prayer then arched upward in a desperate lunge and caught the strap. He pawed at the dirt wall in front of him with his feet and free hand for traction. When he made it to flat ground, he and the Baron crawled away from the ravine and collapsed back-to-back.

Matterhorn's breath came in raggedy gasps. The Baron started to laugh in sheer relief.

"What's so funny?" Matterhorn croaked.

"You should have seen your face," he replied. "You looked like an albino rabbit."

"I just about died!" Matterhorn shot back. The ordeal had been particularly terrifying because of his fear of heights.

"Close, but no cigar. Remember what I told you about the Sword. You won't die as long as you're wearing it."

Bristling at the Baron's smugness, Matterhorn snapped, "What was it gonna do, turn into a parachute?"

"Perhaps it sharpened your senses so you could save yourself."

"Perhaps I should sharpen your senses." Matterhorn reached for the hilt at his waist. "Yeow, that hurts!" he cried, not knowing whether to grab his shoulder or his chest.

"Take it easy, partner," the Baron soothed. "You can teach me a lesson another day. We'd best get moving in case those archers decide to come after easier prey."

"I should be home reading about adventures, instead of having them," Matterhorn muttered. "In the past few days we've been bombed, kidnapped, set fire to, and shot at." He struggled to his feet.

"Beats being in school," Aaron said, dusting off his pants and adjusting his pack.

They followed the sun westward for hours and gradually made their way down to the river, where they stopped to rest.

Matterhorn had calmed down enough to be thankful for their narrow escape. "I hope Broc's okay," he said as he squatted and drank from his hand.

"And Bonehand," Aaron added, washing the cuts on his face.

Matterhorn picked stickers from his forearm and said: "He's getting what he deserves, but Broc's done nothing wrong." He remembered the look in the horse's eyes after being shot. He could see the arrow quivering in the muscular shoulder just below the Baron's belt.

"That's it!" Matterhorn cried, almost tumbling headfirst into the stream. He straightened up and grabbed Aaron's arm. "We can use your tracking device to find Broc!"

"We could..." the Baron said slowly, "but...there's no time. We're here to find the Flute. Karn may already be at the coast...."

"But Broc could bleed to death!"

"Hopefully Bonehand has found him. The sooner we get the Flute, the sooner we can go back for them."

"What's so important about the Talis?" Matterhorn exploded in frustration. "We've almost been killed several times. Broc may already be dead. Why doesn't the Maker get the Flute Himself? He must know where it is."

"That's not His way," the Baron said. "The Maker doesn't interfere like that. He's written a script, but sometimes people decide to run their own show. When that happens, He doesn't appear and fix everything. Instead He works through those who are true to Him to undo the damage and restore the story."

He put a hand on Matterhorn's shoulder and continued. "The Sword of Truth pulled you into this for a reason. Remember your oath and play your part with courage. What you and I do here will affect the outcome of history."

Matterhorn sighed. "That's too much responsibility."

"I said the Maker doesn't interfere: I didn't say He's not involved. He'll give us the help we need when we need it. He already has and that's why we're still alive."

"And fortunate to be so," said a familiar voice from behind a nearby bush.

"Your Majesty!" the Baron said in surprise. "Where'd you come from?"

"From searchin' fer me flute, where else?" Ian said as he stepped into view.

"Any luck?"

Ian shook his head.

"How did you find us?" Matterhorn asked.

The leprechaun tapped Matterhorn's boot with his shillelagh. "These leave a trail a near-sighted noodge could follow. Where ye be goin' in such a hurry?"

"We're trying to catch Karn."

"Karn?"

"Your nephew's headed to the coast with your Flute," the Baron said.

Ian gave them both a skeptical stare. "Karn has me Flute?"

"We think so," Matterhorn replied. "Or I should say, Bonehand thinks so."

"Bonehand! Have ye seen him?"

"Spent the day with him," the Baron quipped. "Delightful chap."

"Where's the rogue now?"

"Running for his life from bounty hunters," Matterhorn answered.

"Some angry farmers are after him as well," Aaron added. "They think he started the fire at the mill, but he didn't. He didn't hire the dwarfs that kidnapped me either."

"Great Honk!" Ian cried, slapping his forehead with his hand. "Bounty hunters, mad farmers, kidnappin' dwarfs, what have ye been up to the past few days?"

"Up to our armpits in piranhas," Matterhorn said, "but we're pressing on."

"Which we need to be doing," the Baron interjected, "if we're going to find the Flute. You're welcome to come with us," he invited Ian.

The leprechaun chewed his lower lip thoughtfully before declining. "Yer legs be too long. I'll make me own way." But he made no move to leave.

"Is there something else?" the Baron asked.

Ian cleared his throat. "Might I trouble ye for a wee bit more of the chocolate?" The gray hair in his mole quivered with anticipation.

"No trouble," the Baron said, fetching a packet of cocoa from his foodstuffs. "Mix the powder with hot water. Throw the wrapper in the fire when you're done."

The Baron and Matterhorn resumed their journey, walking until darkness made it too dangerous to continue. They pitched camp in a half-moon meadow and ate supper in silence—until a rustling sound from where the firelight frittered into the trees put them on full alert.

Bad Reputation

roc!" Matterhorn cried, jumping up and running to the horse in spite of the Baron's warning to be careful. The noble steed favored his left front leg, which had a mash poultice on his shoulder where the arrow had struck. He tossed his mane in greeting and accepted a neck-rubbing from Matterhorn.

Bonehand walked past without a word and sat down at the fire next to the Baron. He wore his rucksack and cape and acted like nothing had happened. There were, however, three round holes in the woven fabric.

Poking a finger through one of these, the Baron asked, "You went back for this?"

"I sent a badger for it," Bonehand said. He lifted the hem to show a mouth-shaped set of punctures. "It gets cold in the forest at night."

The Baron peered in the direction Broc and Bonehand had come. "Any chance you were followed?"

"None."

"You're sure?" the Baron pressed. He offered Bonehand a cup of cocoa.

Bonehand accepted the warm liquid but didn't bother to repeat his answer.

"I take it this isn't the first time you've been shot at."

Bonehand snorted and took a long drink. "It's the closest I've come to being hit. I was careless."

"Winston Churchill once said: 'There is nothing so exhilarating as being shot at without effect,'" Matterhorn quoted as he joined the conversation.

"Who's Churchill?"

"Never mind," Matterhorn said. "What about the bounty men?"

Bonehand folded his legs Indian-style beneath his cloak. "They won't be troubling us again."

"I don't get it," Matterhorn said, fearing the worst. "You care so much for animals and so little for humans. How can you just kill people without remorse?"

"Who said anything about killing?"

"But the bounty men—"

"—are halfway to Galway Bay on the trail I left them," Bonehand finished.

"Well," Matterhorn said, "what about the soldiers who set the fire that ruined your hand? They're dead, right?"

Bonehand nodded. "They died of stupidity."

"Ian told us you killed them," the Baron said.

"I'd have beaten the potatoes out of those vermin if I'd caught them," Bonehand said, "but I wouldn't have murdered them." He accepted a refill of cocoa before telling the rest of the story. "I tracked 'em through the blaze to a box canyon. They must've been drunk not to read the terrain. The fire swept through like a flood. I buried their charred bones when things cooled down. I wept for their horses, but not for them."

Matterhorn felt relieved not to be sitting knee-to-knee with a mass murderer. Still, he was confused. "If you didn't kill those men, why does everyone think you did?"

"Because I never said otherwise."

"You never tried to clear your name?"

"I've found that the darker my reputation, the fewer people come into these woods. It's better for the animals this way."

"But what about the price on your head?"

Bonehand laughed a genuine belly laugh. "It's all a game. The day a longbow yeoman can pin me is the day he's earned his prize money."

Again they had misjudged the man in black, Matterhorn realized. He pulled his shirt closer against the evening damp and changed the subject. "How much farther to the coast?"

"Twelve miles," Bonehand said without hesitation. "We can be there tomorrow afternoon."

The Baron got up and examined Broc's shoulder. He touched the hardened yellowish patch and said: "I've got an antibiotic for this."

"I've been tending animals for years," Bonehand said. "He's fine."

The Baron decided not to press it. Instead he patted Broc's flank and said, "Can you handle a dozen miles, big boy?"

Broc reared on his hind legs and snorted a jet of steam into the cool air like a dragon.

"Don't patronize him," Bonehand warned as the Baron retreated a few paces.

"Broc may be rarin' to go," Matterhorn said, "but I need some rest."

"We can't all sleep," Aaron pointed out. "Someone has to watch Broc in case the Flute is played. Let's draw for the watch schedule." He snapped a piece of kindling in three and stuffed the twigs into his fist. "Short stick, first watch."

The Baron came up short, with Bonehand drawing second shift.

"Goooood," Matterhorn yawned. "I'm an early riser anyway. You know what they say; the early bird gets the worm."

The Baron grimaced. "If it tastes anything like caterpillar, you're welcome to it."

Matterhorn managed a few hours sleep before being awakened for his pre-dawn watch by a pointy finger in the side.

"Careful," he muttered to Bonehand through chapped lips. "I'm bruised as an overripe banana."

"What's a banana?" Bonehand asked.

"A piece of fruit," Matterhorn said. He sat up sluggishly and accepted a cup of warm tea. "I hope this has some caffeine in it."

"What's caf—"

"Never mind," Matterhorn said grumpily.

After Bonehand was asleep, and before the sun was awake, Matterhorn saw the white horse he had spotted by the lake. Only now he could tell it wasn't a horse. The creature stood in a patch of moonlight across the river. Its perfectly formed body had been shaped for beauty rather than brawn. Its mane and plumed tail glinted with a reddish hue.

An eighteen-inch spike parted the silky hair on the unicorn's forehead.

The spiraling opal horn reminded Matterhorn of something he'd seen recently, but he couldn't quite put his finger on it.

Pirate Cove

Sunrise found the unicorn gone and Matterhorn shivering over the remains of some dying coals. For the past hour, he'd been softly playing his harmonica as a sea mist rolled up the river valley like dry ice fog. The cobwebs in the bushes glittered with dew beads. A nest of robins announced the new morn.

Matterhorn rose and ambled toward the river to wash his face. He scanned the grassy field where Broc stood fast asleep. The horse hadn't twitched a muscle on his watch, but as Matterhorn passed, Broc's head jerked upright, his eyelids snapped open, and after a brief pause he cantered away.

"Hey, Broc," Matterhorn called, but the animal paid no attention.

Reaching the water, Broc veered right and vanished into the fog. Matterhorn couldn't hear anything, but he knew Ian's Flute was being played. He saw no one on either bank and guessed the musician was somewhere downstream.

"Come back!" Matterhorn yelled. This had no effect on Broc, but it roused the Baron and Bonehand. Within fifteen minutes they were packed and tuned in to the Baron's homing device.

"What's that thing?" Bonehand asked. He pointed at the blinking green light under the glass screen.

"It's like a compass," Aaron said, "but instead of pointing north, the green flash points to a piece of metal in my belt."

This was enough of an explanation for Bonehand. He made no effort to keep up with the ways of foreigners.

When the fog burned off later in the morning, the trackers were careful to keep out of sight. They didn't want to give themselves away until they knew who was playing the Flute. It was early afternoon when they topped a breezy knoll and saw the stream pour itself into a spacious bay.

Gigantic fingers of rock reached into the Atlantic on either side. Dingy seagulls and lanky herons fluttered over the ribbon of sand that separated green hills from blue waves. Down the beach, a band of shirtless men were lashing logs together into a large raft. Thinner logs had been roped together to form a makeshift corral that held several unusual animals—including Broc.

Next to Broc stood the unicorn from the night before. The rest of the animals in the enclosure were smaller. A handsome peacock preened his tail. Silent songbirds perched on the top rail as though glued there. Two coppery squirrels the size of Cheshire cats sat in one corner. A few red foxes skittered about, black ears at attention, and white-tipped tails swishing the air. They didn't bother the birds, which normally would have been on the menu for lunch.

Bonehand pulled Matterhorn to the ground next to him. "Keep out of sight," he hissed. He pointed toward the sea and Matterhorn saw a ship lounging at anchor. The twin-masted schooner was rigged with mainsail, foresail and topsails. She also boasted a jib and a flying jib off the bowsprit.

The Baron groaned. "A ship that size will have a lot of hands," he said. "We only have five."

Bonehand gave him a hard look.

"I mean, six," Aaron corrected. He rolled onto his back and fished the signal mirror from his pocket. It was the size of a deck of cards until he unfolded its polished panels. He held this above the top of the hill, so he could see without being seen.

Matterhorn and Bonehand scrunched closer to watch the bayside action. They saw Karn in the middle of the scene, perched on the top rail of the corral with Ian's Flute hanging from a silver chain around his neck. He was arguing with a great white shark of a man who was obviously in charge.

The man was cut square as a ship's beam. His shoulders jutted out at right angles from a pug neck. He wore a white silk shirt, green velvet waistcoat and loose trousers. The ivory-handled dagger on his right hip balanced the cutlass on his left. A tri-cornered hat sat rakishly on his head. Under its brim, bushy sideburns bracketed his brown face.

Gold earrings dangled from each ear. His yellowed teeth had been filed to points, giving him a shark-like appearance when he sneered.

"I wish we could hear what they're saying," Matterhorn said.

"I can tell you that," Bonehand said. "I've seen these ships before. They come from Britain and prowl the coast in search of rare game and careless men. They sell the animals to the royal courts in Europe. The men they auction to merchants who can't get a ship's crew any other way."

"Pirates," Matterhorn concluded.

Below them, Karn was gesturing between the captain and the animals with the Flute.

"He's bickering over price," Bonehand said, resuming his commentary. "If he isn't careful, he'll get the point of a knife for payment."

"That raft is almost done," Matterhorn observed. "We can't let Broc and the animals be taken to the ship."

"Agreed," the Baron said. "But there are a dozen men onshore and who knows how many more on that boat. Our best shot at freeing the animals will be after dark."

"That's no good," Matterhorn countered. "There will be two moons tonight, the one in the sky and its reflection on the water. It will be impossible to sneak up on anybody. Besides, it might be too late by then."

But it was already too late.

"Fie!"

While Karn and the captain continued to argue, a great bird of prey dropped into the picture, landing on a post near them. The huge gyrfalcon was an impressive and powerful creature. Its five-foot wingspan had enabled it to deliver the bone that had almost killed the Baron.

The captain said something in answer to a shrill squawk and the bird took to the air. It flew directly to where the Baron, Matterhorn and Bonehand were hiding in the grass. It folded its wings against its sleek body and screeched to earth like a smart bomb.

This was more than a natural predator guided by instinct. This hunter killed for sport and enjoyed delivering death with its talons. Screeching in fury, it aimed for Aaron's face.

The Baron and Matterhorn saw the danger at the same instant. They reacted to the attack as though their two bodies shared a single brain. As Aaron twisted hard right, Matterhorn drew his Sword and rolled into the vacant space.

A moment later the falcon skewered itself on Matterhorn's upraised blade.

The impact drove the hilt into Matterhorn's breastbone with a jarring crunch and knocked all the air from his lungs. Hot blood spurted over his trembling hands and chest. The extended talons tore his shirt and the open beak scratched his neck.

The Baron jumped up as the sound of shouting men came from below. The air attack was just the beginning of their troubles. "Get ready for more company!" he shouted.

Bonehand needed no encouragement. He straddled the crest of the hill, sword in hand. "There are only six men," he said over his shoulder. "How many do you want me to leave for you?"

Matterhorn crawled out from under the dead weight and stumbled to his feet, visibly shaken. "I, I've never killed anything bigger than a bug before," he stammered.

The Baron put a boot on the bird and pulled out the crimson shaft. He wiped the blade on the grass and handed the Sword to Matterhorn.

"I hate to see any animal killed," Bonehand said, "but that one deserved to die." He glanced down at the approaching pirates, armed to the teeth, and added, "It won't be the only blood spilled today."

The Baron rifled through Matterhorn's discarded pack and found two solar batteries from his security system. He tossed one to Matterhorn, and, a moment later, the toothbrush-sized sensor that went with it. "Set it up over there." He pointed to a spot and hurried to deploy an identical unit on the opposite side of the hill about twenty feet from the top.

Climbing back up, he said breathlessly: "Listen, Bonehand. No time to explain now, but when I say so, point your bony fingers at these guys and shout the scariest word you know at the top of your lungs.

"Get ready, here they come."

The pirates had reached the bottom of the knoll and started up. They snickered when they saw the three young men waiting at the top. These ruffians had brawled their way from the Mediterranean to the North Sea. They wore the scars of countless fights like badges of honor. Adept with knife and cutlass, they didn't expect much of a scuffle. All they wanted was to get rid of these meddlers, put the stinking animals on board ship, sail back to England, and collect their pay.

When the first two pirates reached the invisible line of electrons drawn by the Baron's sensors, he said to Bonehand: "Now!"

Bonehand threw back his cape and raised his right arm. He pointed a long, fleshless finger at the oncoming men and bellowed, "Fie!"

The thunder of Bonehand's deep voice was followed by a loud crackle of sideways lightning. The two men went down like moths flying into a bug-zapper. Their limbs twitched as they lay smoldering on the ground. Smoke leaked out from under their bandanas and the stench of burnt hair wafted up the hill.

106

The remaining pirates froze in mid-stride.

"What in blazes was that?" Bonehand staggered back and stared at his index finger.

"Would you believe sorcery?"

"I don't believe in sorcery."

"How about magic, then?"

"Don't believe in that either."

"If you must know," the Baron said, "it's called electricity. It will be very popular one day. But don't tell anyone you heard about it from me."

Still bewildered, Bonehand asked, "Are those men dead?"

"No. But they won't be any more bother to us." Then the Baron scowled at Bonehand and said, "What kind of scary word is 'fie'? Is that the best you can do?"

Before Bonehand could respond, the Baron nodded toward the rest of their attackers. "Get ready to point again. I bet you can scare these boys back to the beach."

He was right. As soon as Bonehand aimed his finger, the pirates left their smoking buddies and ran away at the speed of fear.

The captain had been watching from the corral when the two men had gone down in a crackling blue flash. A few moments later, he saw the rest of the band beat a hasty retreat. He was too far away to tell what had happened, but he knew how to counter it. Cupping his hands to his mouth, he bellowed to his ship, "Unfriendlies on the hill! Open fire!"

The command carried easily across open water, and the first mate put his spyglass to his eye. He quickly spotted the three locals on the grassy knoll. Since the eight shore-side cannons were kept primed and loaded, the first volley was on its way within a minute.

"Incoming!" the Baron yelled. The warning was unnecessary as Matterhorn and Bonehand were already scrambling into the woods behind the hill. The lead balls punched great holes in the earth and threw up geysers of dirt, but since they didn't contain explosives, they posed little threat to the men now hidden in the trees.

The captain soon realized this and yelled to his crew: "Cease fire! All hands to shore! Make it quick!"

The deck burst into activity as the first mate barked orders. This was his maiden voyage with this crew, but they had quickly learned the captain was not a man to cross. He had tossed two men overboard for nothing more than spilling a keg of rum. He had run the navigator through with his cutlass for a slight error that cost them time in reaching Ireland.

Several sailors scrambled down a cargo net into dinghies that bounced against the wooden hull. They filled the boats to overflowing and strong arms were soon pulling the oars with practiced precision.

The eager crew should have reached the captain in a few minutes—but they never got near the beach.

Water Nymph

As the pirates hurried to obey the shore call, they rowed into unexpected difficulty. Despite the calm day, the water around them bunched into waves and resisted their efforts. Like a riptide, the reverse current pushed them away from land. Three-foot waves became six-foot breakers, then doubled again to twelve-foot monsters! The ocean rose so rapidly that even the most veteran seadogs among them had never seen anything like it. Terror melted their bones and bleached their faces.

The rogue waves not only toyed with the pirates, they easily lifted the schooner and tossed it toward the horizon. The swells had grown so huge that the ship's anchor was useless.

Nothing but panicky screams made it to land. The captain fumed and cursed at his lost ship. He couldn't care less about the men, but this supernatural interference might pose a real problem.

Karn was also upset, but for a different reason. Coming down the beach toward him were the three men in the world he never wanted to see again. He jerked the captain's sleeve and frantically pointed at the oncoming figures. "Don't let them get near me," Karn pleaded. "I'll give you anything you want."

The captain backhanded Karn off the rail. "I'll take anything I want, you sniveling shrimp," he growled.

True, he needed the leprechaun to carry the Flute back to England. But that would be difficult now that his ship was gone. He would have to use the raft until he could steal something better.

First things first. These intruders had to be killed. The captain marshaled his remaining crew. Leaving two men by the animals, he drew his cutlass and led the charge.

Matterhorn, the Baron and Bonehand marched toward the pirates. The trio had decided to go on the offensive, ignoring the fact that they were outnumbered. They were as startled as the pirates by what had just happened out on the bay. But at least Matterhorn and the Baron knew what had caused it. Or, more precisely, whom.

"The water nymph must have followed us," Matterhorn exclaimed as he stared after the receding boats. "She can do incredible things with water!"

Bonehand scowled. "We still have plenty to worry about here on land. These knaves aren't as squeamish about spilling blood as you, Matterhorn. They'll cut us into fish bait." He looked at the Baron and asked: "You got any more tricks in your bag?"

"I'm glad you asked." The Baron produced an eight-inch aluminum tube, unfolded two hinged arms, unscrewed the bottom and removed a heavy rubber band. His nimble fingers moved over the tube, transforming it into a magnum slingshot. Without breaking stride, he scooped up a few golf-ball-sized rocks and opened fire.

The first stone flew over the pirates' heads. They taunted the Baron for his lousy aim.

The heckling stopped when the next rock laid the second mate out like a clubbed seal. He got off a few more rounds before running out of ammo on the sandy beach. He folded the weapon away and pulled a mahogany handle from a pencil-thin sleeve on his other leg.

Bonehand marveled. "Now what?"

"This is what I prefer for close-in fighting," Aaron replied. He pressed a button on the stick and released an eight-foot lash with a polished metal tip. "I call it a switchwhip. Made it myself."

"That's the best you can do for weapons?" Matterhorn cried. "Slingshots and bull-whips!" He was hoping for laser guns and hand grenades!

The Baron patted his pockets and said: "I've got a few throwing stars somewhere. Don't worry, I can hold my own. How about you? Afraid?"

"Terrified!"

"Just hold tight to that Sword," the Baron said, "and you'll be okay."

The blade pulsed and Matterhorn felt the handle throb in sync. The power is in the Maker's Sword, he reminded himself. He was just the delivery boy. No, make that man. He was taller than any of the oncoming sailors and certainly better armed. Perhaps he could hold his own in a fight. Hadn't he and the Sword just saved the Baron's life? He looked down at his sticky hands and the stained silver crosspiece, evidence of their baptism in blood.

The captain who had sent the gyrfalcon would show no mercy to Broc or the other animals in the corral. The thought of what would happen to them, if this rescue attempt failed, doubled Matterhorn's determination. Karn's treachery and the captain's cruelty could not go unpunished.

The faster his mind churned, the faster his feet moved and soon Matterhorn was several paces ahead of the Baron and Bonehand, zeroing in on the captain like a heat-seeking bomb.

The pirate watched the youth's charge and realized the young fool knew nothing about staying alive in a fight. He had committed himself too soon, and narrowed his focus too early. The captain hand-signaled two men into ambush position. Under his breath he snarled: "Let's grant this idiot his death wish."

Matterhorn was so focused on the captain that he never saw the men with the net until they blindsided him. The unexpected blow knocked the Sword from his hand and trapped him like a tuna, arms pinned helplessly by his sides. The air was crushed out of his lungs by the two goons on his back. Their sweaty bulk smashed him into the sand and squeezed bile up into his throat. His muscles quivered beneath the terrible weight. His heart jack-hammered against his bruised ribs.

All the bravery left his body along with his breath. Thoughts of Broc and the Flute disappeared, replaced by images of the family he would never see again. They were hundreds of years in the future and thousands of miles away in a place, where he himself had been only a few days ago. A safe place.

A place he should never have left!

Beach Brawl

Bonehand and the Baron had no chance to help Matterhorn before they came under attack themselves. Four men circled Bonehand, blades carving the air. He parried their flashing steel with his short sword. "You fight like women!" he taunted. "Be thankful I'm not using my good hand!" He raised his skeletal right hand and rattled the bones.

Two sailors drew back in horror, but a third saw his chance and darted in under the uplifted arm. Expecting the attack, Bonehand deftly swirled his cape around the man's sword and jerked it from his grasp. Then he followed up with a side kick to the groin. He feigned to the left with his sword, then leapt to the right and flung the cape over a pirate's head. Yanking his victim forward, he brought his knee up into the man's stomach and the pommel of his sword down on the man's head.

As he spun to face his remaining assailants, Bonehand did not see a fifth man move in from behind. A seasoned brawler, he stayed out of harm's way. He picked up a rock and waited.

The men in front of Bonehand charged. Occupied with this onslaught, Bonehand did not see the rock. Because of that, he did not see anything else for a long time.

Meanwhile, the Baron had troubles of his own. Several pirates tried to get close enough to use their cutlasses on him, but his snarling whip kept them at bay. One man received a deep cut on his arm for his boldness. The Baron counted silently—one, two, three—until the smitten sailor slid to the sand, conscious yet unmoving.

The tip of the lash was coated with a mild form of the poison, curare. The Baron had learned that little paralyzing trick from Nate.

The whip wasn't Aaron's only weapon. A flick of his wrist zipped a throwing star into the forearm of a burly man, who dropped his cutlass and cursed in pain. He twisted away just in time to keep a second star from giving him a close shave.

With calm precision the Baron stunned a second pirate, then a third, with his lash. But more kept coming as those who had knocked out Bonehand came over. Everyone at the beach brawl now clustered around Aaron, except the captain and the two men on top of Matterhorn.

In desperation he whirled the whip overhead like a helicopter blade to create a no-man's-land around him. But that could only last until his arm gave out.

Nearby, Matterhorn's world shifted into slow motion and a single thought bounced around in his head: I'm gonna die! I'm gonna die! I'm gonna DIE!

"No," interrupted a calm voice. "That is not why you are here."

The voice in his head startled Matterhorn more than what was happening to his body.

"You have a job to do," the voice continued. "The only way you can fail is if you quit. I have given you all the power you need."

Who had given him what power? The only thing he had with any power was the Sword, and now even that was gone.

"The Sword is just one of my tools," the voice said. "I can work without it, and so can you. Use what you have. It is enough."

I don't belong here, Matterhorn silently protested. This is all a big mistake. I'm not a knight; I'm just a kid!

"You are what I have called you to be."

Matterhorn lay at a crossroads. He could give in to his circumstances or rise up to his calling. He had been given an adult body; did he have the courage to use it? He had just been told he wasn't meant to die here: did he believe it? He didn't have to be a victim: he could be a victor!

Victor!

That's it!

Matterhorn had learned some great wrestling moves from his older brother Victor, and now he had the body mass to use them to full effect! But would his new muscles remember what his twelve-year-old muscles knew? Only one way to find out.

When one of the attackers shifted to the side to get at his knife, Matterhorn erupted. Despite the net, he raised his head and upper body and did an adrenalin-powered post-and-roll. He got up on his right elbow while curling his leg around the other pirate's left knee. Then he twisted his bulk the opposite direction and flipped the startled man over like a turtle.

He followed this with an illegal forearm chop across the throat. The blow would keep the man from thinking about anything but breathing for a while.

The other brute had his knife out by now. He lunged forward and stabbed at Matterhorn's stomach. But Matterhorn's knee was already coming up to deflect the murderous blow. Still, the blade cut through his pants and sliced his thigh. Through the pain he forced his leg farther upward, then brought his heel down hard into the man's kidney. This straightened the pirate upright in agony. Matterhorn did a power sit-up and head-butted the brute, putting his lights out.

Untangling himself, Matterhorn scurried across the sand like a crab and scooped up the Sword. His ribs ached from a second bruising. His leg throbbed from the stab wound. He ignored the pain as he checked the battle scene.

Bonehand lay unmoving amidst several downed pirates.

The Baron was fighting for his life in the center of a tightening ring of flashing steel.

The captain waited nearby, letting his men do the dirty work.

When Matterhorn locked eyes with him, the captain jeered. "You handle yourself pretty well. Let's see how you handle this!"

Mortal Combat

The captain came forward, cutlass first. Matterhorn raised his Sword to deflect the expected blow. His attacker froze, gaze fixed on the blade, which now glowed like a beam of sunlight. The brilliance cast a shadow of fear on the captain's face and he weighed his chances in this new light. More than anyone else on the beach, he understood the incredible power of that Sword. But did the young man know what he held?

Matterhorn took advantage of the pause to slow his breathing and his heart rate. The anger in his chest cooled from hot flames to embers. A peace settled over him as he recalled the Baron's words from their first meeting: "You're safer with this Sword in your hands than if you were inside a tank." And hadn't he just been told that the only way he could fail was if he quit?

He shook the sweat from his forehead and read the indecision on the captain's face. This raised his confidence. He felt like a fighter pilot at the controls of an awesome weapon. Only a fool would challenge the Maker's Sword in combat.

The captain was no fool. The blade's light and Matterhorn's body language told him he had no chance. The shadow of fear gave way to the thing itself. He drew back from a fight he could not win and dare not start. Yes, the others would be furious with his failure to get the Flute. But if he stayed alive, he could try again later.

The captain took another step backward. Then another.

With amazing speed the Sword pulled Matterhorn toward the retreating pirate, and in a crash of blades the battle began!

Matterhorn had all he could do to hold onto the Sword. The captain had all he could do to block the blows. He knew he had to get the Sword out of Matterhorn's hands, if he wanted to survive. And the best way to do that was to go low.

117

When Matterhorn swung his next roundhouse, the captain met it with his cutlass. But rather than resist the blow, he let it knock him backwards and down. Like a judo master using an opponent's strength to gain the advantage, he rolled and brought his legs forward to sweep Matterhorn's feet from under him.

Matterhorn landed hard and the air whooshed from his lungs in one great UUGGHH! His head smacked a piece of driftwood and everything went out of focus. The Sword lay in his limp hand. He didn't have the strength to grip it, much less lift it.

The captain jumped up and should have run. But seeing Matterhorn down and dazed, a murderous urge came over him. He lunged in for the quick kill.

Not quick enough.

A jolt of power shot from the hilt of the Sword, up Matterhorn's arm and into his chest. His body jerked as though being shocked back to life from a heart attack. His arm came up and the Sword of Truth sliced the captain's cutlass in half as if it were a stick.

It was Matterhorn's turn to use his legs to down his attacker. The captain landed on his back and Matterhorn leapt to his feet. Quickly their roles were reversed and Matterhorn held his Sword point an inch above the pirate's chest.

The man's unblinking eyes were pure evil. His voice dripped with contempt as he snarled: "You wouldn't kill an unarmed man. You don't have it in you."

Matterhorn knew the pirate was right, yet a moment later he stared horrified as the Sword—under its own power—plunged into the captain's chest to the hilt.

Instead of blood pouring from the wound, a foul-smelling mist spewed upward. The body dissolved into a thick black stench and hissed off the blade in sooty steam leaving a pile of empty clothes in the sand.

What had he done?

What had the Sword done?

Maybe the Baron could tell him.

The Baron!

The thought jerked Matterhorn out of his stupor and spun him around. "Aaron! Are you okay?"

118

"I could use some help here!" came a loud yell.

Matterhorn started toward where his friend stood entrapped by attackers. The two guards from the corral had grown impatient and run up the beach to join the skirmish. That put the number of men surrounding Aaron at six.

Adrenaline still pumped through his veins, but Matterhorn was having trouble putting weight on his wounded leg. It would take him a minute to get to his friend.

"You seem to be doing fine!" he shouted as he limped forward. "I'd hate to interrupt!"

"Interrupt! Interrupt!" the Baron cried. "My arm's about to fall off."

Matterhorn feared he wouldn't make it to his partner in time. Suddenly, the flash of an idea lit up his brain. He stopped and yelled to the Baron: "Hang on, buddy! I salute your bravery!" He gave a mock salute, then pivoted his hand down to shield his eyes.

Would the Baron understand?

Aaron saw the hand motion and picked up the signal. He thought he knew what Matterhorn wanted him to do. In an act of supreme trust, he dropped his whip and covered his eyes with both hands.

If he had guessed wrong, he was dead.

End Game

atterhorn put his fingers to his lips and whistled as loudly as he could. The pirates turned at the unexpected sound—and were blinded by a dazzling flash from the Sword. Matterhorn felt the heat surge on the forearm that shielded his face. When he opened his eyes, everyone but the Baron was blind as a barnacle.

"That's some brilliant Swordplay," the Baron said with great relief. "I'm glad we're on the same side."

"That makes two of us," Matterhorn panted. He hobbled forward, using the Sword for a cane.

"Keep an eye on these goons while I get my pack," Aaron said. "I have some rope we can put to good use."

Back at the corral, Karn had cowered behind a post and waited for a chance to escape. When the guards left to join the fight, he took off in the opposite direction as fast as his stubby legs would go. He covered a half-mile of open sand before turning up the nearest stream. He waded in the middle of the water to hide his trail.

Karn splashed upriver like a salmon going to spawn. It frightened him to be in the water since he didn't know how to swim. But he was even more terrified of being caught. Whoever won the fight would come after the Flute—and his head!

His new plan was simple: get to his hidden boat and wait for darkness. Then sneak back to the bay and out to sea. The current would carry him down-coast to a fishing village he knew. He would hide there until he could catch a ship—any ship—away from the captain's wrath and the strangers' revenge.

Grasping the pouch of gold that had been the down payment for the Flute, Karn pushed onward. It was only half of what the captain had promised, but it would buy Karn a fresh start. He would never have to mend shoes or tend shop again. And he still had the Flute. He could sell it again wherever he went. Just a few more hours of luck, and he would be on his way to the life he deserved.

When Karn reached the hills, the stream widened and flowed more swiftly. He stayed in the shallows, but he slipped and fell several times on the slimy rocks. At last, he saw his skiff where he'd tied it to an overhanging branch. Just a few more yards.

But when the leprechaun turned toward shore, the current grabbed his legs and sent him cartwheeling into deeper water. He was dunked, flipped, spun, tumbled, whirled and would have drowned if not for the woman who suddenly appeared and carried his almost lifeless body to a sandbar in midstream.

The turbulent water should keep Karn from escaping when he came to his senses. The woman took the Flute from around his neck and dissolved into a wave to carry it back to the bay.

The animals in the corral awoke from their dream-state at that precise moment. As long as Karn had the Flute, and played it regularly, they remained under his spell. But once the Flute and the player were separated, the enchantment dissolved. The songbirds flew to safety while the squirrels and foxes tried to avoid being trampled by the larger animals.

Broc kicked down the makeshift gate and headed toward Matterhorn. The unicorn followed, trailing a tail of foxes. The horse and rider shared a joyous reunion, standing cheek-to-cheek for a long time; each thankful the other was all right. They had grown so close over these past danger-filled days that words were unnecessary.

Nearby, the Baron tended to Bonehand, using smelling salts to revive him.

"I wasn't much help," Bonehand rasped. "I feel like I've been kicked by a mule." Several of the animals gathered around, licking his face and hands. He smiled and winced at the same time. It was worth the splitting headache to know they were safe.

"You did fine," the Baron said, handing Bonehand two aspirin. "Don't ask what these are, just swallow them."

After taking the pills, Bonehand began picking sand from the honey that coated his wrist. "This is why I don't like the beach," he mumbled.

Aaron walked over and removed his belt from Broc's neck. "Glad you're okay." He turned to Matterhorn and said: "You, not so okay. Let's get a look at your leg."

Matterhorn sat down and rested the Sword across his lap. His hands were shaking. "Have you ever killed anyone before?" he asked the Baron.

"No," Aaron replied as he knelt to inspect Matterhorn's wound. "And I don't intend to. That's why I carry a whip and not a sword." He cut the torn pant leg off above the knee. "You haven't killed anybody either," he assured Matterhorn. "That thing wasn't human."

Matterhorn winced at the Baron's probing. "He seemed human enough—until the Sword pierced him."

"The cut isn't too deep," the Baron said as he cleaned sand from the gash with an alcohol swab.

Matterhorn gripped the Sword hilt with both hands to keep from screaming.

"Put that Sword down and pinch the flaps of skin together," the Baron ordered. "No, like this." From a white tube, he squeezed a bead of clear paste on the laceration.

"What's that?" Matterhorn wanted to know.

"Super glue. It works better than stitches, and it won't leave a scar."

"Do you read this stuff in books or make it up as you go along?" Matterhorn said, amazed at the range of Aaron's knowledge and skill.

The Baron grinned. "I can't answer that or you might sue me for malpractice."

"Well, I appreciate it," Matterhorn said. He borrowed the Baron's knife and sliced off his other pant leg to match.

"And I appreciate you," Aaron said as he put away his first-aid kit. "Thanks for saving my life."

"You're welcome," Matterhorn replied.

"And mine, too," said a voice that sounded like Queen Bea.

But when Matterhorn looked up, all he saw was the unicorn.

Lost and Found

"Is...is that you, Your Highness?" the Baron sputtered. He stood and approached the unicorn.

"Do you like my disguise? Unicorns are one of my favorite animals."

The creature's lips never moved, but Matterhorn heard the words in his mind. Now he remembered what the horn reminded him of: the opals in Queen Bea's throne and crown.

Just then, a luminous glittering began at the tip of the unicorn's horn, transforming it into a sparkling fuse. The horn melted and flattened into a gold-and-opal coronet. The long mane spun into tresses of brown hair. Four feet became two. Open-toed sandals replaced hooves. The face shortened, and the body lengthened, as the regal animal morphed into a royal lady.

Queen Bea stood on the beach dressed in a charcoal gray traveling outfit. On her left wrist she wore a lion-headed charm bracelet from which dangled several beautifully carved miniature animals: an ivory eagle, a coral dolphin, a jade dragon, a gold tiger and a granite mouse. She transferred a tiny opal unicorn from her palm to the bracelet.

The Baron was more upset than happy at the sudden revelation. "You took a terrible risk coming here," he scolded in an older-brother tone. "You could have been injured or killed."

"I am not helpless," Bea shot back. "And I am not in the habit of asking for permission to do what I see fit."

Before the Baron could continue the argument, the two men who had been zapped on the hill staggered into view. They offered no resistance and were quickly tied up with the rest of the pirates at the corral. The men weren't so mean now that their captain was gone.

The interruption gave the Queen time to get over her pique. When the Baron and Matterhorn rejoined her, she said: "I came to

Ireland and assumed this form so I would hear the Flute, if it was played. I thought I would be able to resist its spell, resume my natural form, and recover the Talis." Her gaze dropped to the sand and she added: "I was wrong. The wonderful music completely overwhelmed me. My whole being surrendered to pure joy. I would gladly have followed Karn anywhere, done anything he asked."

"Speaking of the Flute," the Baron said, pointing to a large red fox trotting toward them with the silver tube in his mouth. This animal hadn't gone with the others after being freed from the corral, but had picked up Karn's trail instead. He tracked the leprechaun to the stream. He didn't have to go any farther because he saw the Flute gliding on top of the water. He paddled in and scooped up the instrument, still attached to its necklace, and brought it to the Queen.

"The Maker be praised!" Bea cried, as she knelt to grasp the necklace and put it around her neck. "You have done well," she said, touching the fox with the tip of the Flute. A shimmering spread over the sleek body, darkening the rusty fur to black—all but the tips of the hair, which lightened to silver. "Receive this new coat as a token of my gratitude."

"I thought Travelers weren't supposed to interfere with the natural order of things?" the Baron said as Bea stood.

"Will you find fault with everything I do? There is no harm in rewarding this clever fellow with a bright new outfit."

The fox pranced over to show off his new colors to Bonehand, who had been watching the proceedings with a growing sense of wonder. The unicorn queen's beauty and power left him breathless.

Bea followed the fox and offered Bonehand a hand up. She waved off his normal left hand and accepted his skeletal right without flinching. "I have heard of your love for animals and of your bravery," she said as he rose. "I have seen both today. The fox has his recompense; how may I reward you?"

After a long silence, Bonehand said, "You came for the Flute. If you take it with you when you go, that is enough."

Bea nodded and smiled. "I must explain this to King Ian in person. Will you help me find him?"

126

"Happily," Bonehand said. "Just as soon as I make sure the animals are all right."

"No hurry," Bea replied. "I have other matters to attend myself." With that she herded the Baron and Matterhorn up the beach for a private conversation.

Matterhorn felt great as he walked between the Baron and the Queen. Broc and the other animals were safe. The Flute had been recovered. Maybe he could go home now. But first he had a few questions. "Pardon me, Your Majesty," he said. "The pirate captain I fought; who was he? What was he?"

"He was a wraith from First Realm," the Queen said. "And I owe you an apology. If I had known you would encounter a dark spirit on your first trip, I would never have sent you. His presence here is deeply troubling."

"How did a wraith get to Ireland?" the Baron asked.

"The heretics somehow discovered the Flute's whereabouts and sent him for it. He used the guise of a pirate captain to get a crew and a ship to bring him from the portal in England. Fortunately he did not have the Traveler's Cube or he could have come and gone before we had a chance to stop him."

"Heretics?" Matterhorn said in a one-word question.

The Queen fixed her large brown eyes on Matterhorn. "Even in the Realm there are those who reject the Maker's way," she said. "They ignore the sacred doctrine of noninterference and want to control the destinies of others. These heretics desire the Talis for evil purposes. Their agent, the wraith, learned of Karn and his resentment toward Ian. He put the knowledge to good use, promising Karn a great sum for the Flute."

"The greedy little leprechaun," Aaron muttered.

"All was going according to plan until you two arrived," Bea continued. "Karn tried everything to get rid of you. He made the bone bomb. He hired the kidnappers. He even torched the mill at his trading post."

"How do you know all this?" Matterhorn asked.

"I have been keeping an eye on you," the Queen replied. "For a couple of secret agents, you sure attracted a lot of attention."

"It's not our fault," Aaron protested.

"Now what?" Matterhorn wanted to know.

"Karn must pay for his crimes," Bea said. "Bonehand and I will find the scoundrel and take him with us to see Ian. The king can decide how to deal with his nephew. And as a Queen," she added in a regal tone, "I know how to deal with you."

Knight Time

he trio had reached a secluded inlet and the Queen turned to her rescuers. "Kneel before me," she commanded. Matterhorn and the Baron exchanged puzzled looks and then did as ordered.

She stepped up to Aaron first and said: "You have served well on many assignments and shown surprising skill with the Traveler's Cube. The Praetorians were right about you. For this, as well as your cleverness and courage, I grant you in the Maker's name the honor of keeping the Cube. You may come and go as you please. No other Traveler has ever been given such freedom. Use it wisely."

Ever since his first trip with the Cube, Aaron had devoted himself to learning its intricacies. Now he could take it to the next level. "Thank you, Your Majesty," he said.

"As for you," Bea said, shifting her attention to Matterhorn. "When we first met, I sensed you had great potential. The Sword would not have called you otherwise. Still, one never knows if a person will become all he or she can be, or stay who they are. You have grown from an untested youth into a knight. Give me the Sword."

Matterhorn drew the hilt, extended the blade, and handed the Talis to the Queen.

Dubbing him on both shoulders, she pronounced: "For bravery in serving me and the Maker, I grant you in His name the rank of Queen's Knight. Henceforth you will be known as Matterhorn the Brave."

"I don't deserve the honor," Matterhorn protested. "I've been more scared than brave these last few days."

"It is not true bravery unless you are truly afraid," Bea said.

Aaron the Baron nudged Matterhorn. "That's one for your little book."

As he stood, Matterhorn thought of all that had happened since he'd been pulled into the Propylon and sent to Ireland. He saw a swirl of faces: Aaron, Ian, Bonehand, Broc, Karn, the captain. He recalled the faceless voice that had said, "I have called you a knight." And now he was one!

He had been chosen.

He had been called.

He had obeyed.

There was only one thing he hadn't done.

"Your Majesty?"

"Yes?"

"May I hold the Flute?"

Bea smiled as she laid the ten-inch silver shaft in his palms. It was more like a miniature recorder than a modern flute, Matterhorn noticed. It had no valves, just six finger holes and a thumb-hole. It felt cool to the touch and heavier than he expected. He sensed both the lilt of a morning sunrise and the bass of an afternoon thunderstorm in its short span. A deep joy bubbled in his heart as he ran his fingers over the words inscribed in flowing script: *Play with joy in creation's symphony.*

"This is the Talis of the Maker's Joy," Bea explained as Aaron the Baron took a turn with the sacred instrument. "The Chief Musician of the Realm plays it on special occasions to celebrate the joy of creation. Now she will be able to do so once more."

As the Queen put the Flute back around her neck, there came a loud splash from behind her. She turned toward the sea and said, "There is someone else I need to reward." Presently the spray above the rocks formed into the shapely lady from Karn's mill: Sara, the Naiad, who with the unicorn had protected the travelers

"We met a few nights ago," Aaron said. "She got us out of a real hot spot."

"That was a neat trick getting rid of the schooner and her crew today," Matterhorn added.

"Thank you," Sara replied with a twinkle in her voice that matched the sparkle in her eyes. Her delicate features were unchanged, but today she wore an ocean blue gossamer frock accented by a purple amethyst necklace and earrings. Her nail polish had deepened to purple.

"Your help has been invaluable," Bea said. "What can I do to show my appreciation?"

"Ireland is lovely," Sara said, "yet there's so much more to see and experience of the Maker's creation. Let me travel in your service. You have seen what I can do." Lowering her voice, she added, "These men are strong and resourceful; still, they could use a lady's help from time to time."

Bea smiled. "So they could."

"Now wait a minute!" the Baron spoke up. "We don't travel all the time. And when we do, it's dangerous."

"All the more reason I should come along," Sara said coyly.

"I think it's a bad idea," Aaron grumbled.

"And I think it is a good one," the Queen announced. "Request granted. Baron, what sort of containers do you have in those pockets of yours?"

"He's got a vial of smelling salts," Matterhorn offered, for which he earned a scowl.

"That will do. Empty it."

The Baron did so and scrubbed out the ammonia smell with sand and salt water. The plastic tube with its rubber stopper was about as long as his little finger. "This is awfully tiny," he said. "I don't know what good this will do."

"It is sufficient for me," Sara said.

"What?" You're going to live in this?"

"It will hold my essence," Sara explained. "Whenever you open the vial, I can make a body and clothes to suit me out of any nearby water."

"Won't you be lonely in the meantime?" Matterhorn asked.

The nymph shook her head. "I don't experience time except when I'm in a body. My next thought will be when I take shape again. I can't wait to see where that will be!"

"Before you go, Sara," Bea said, "would you mind returning the pirate ship? We have some beached sailors who need a ride home."

"I only pushed it a few miles away," Sara said. "The evening tide will bring it back. And now, by your leave." She bowed and then dissolved into a fine mist that condensed into the vial. Her gems plunked into the sand at the Baron's feet.

Aaron capped the tube, feeling uneasy about the arrangement; yet secretly glad he would see Sara again.

Fond Farewell

hus began the good-byes. When Bea and the Travelers rejoined Bonehand and the others, Matterhorn's spirits sank. Everyone he'd met in Ireland would be long dead when he returned to his own time. He would never get to ride Broc again. He would never know if Bonehand and Ian patched up their differences. Still, the prospect of going home helped to offset the sadness.

The Baron, who wrestled with the same mixed emotions, was first to speak. "We have to be going now," he told Bonehand. "We couldn't have found the Flute without you. Thanks for your help."

"You saved my life," Bonehand said. "Let's call it even." He held out his hand and both the Baron and Matterhorn shook it without reservation. The grip was firm even though the fingers felt like a bundle of sticks. "You are welcome in my woods any time."

"Probably won't happen," the Baron replied. "We live a long way from here."

Broc pushed his way amongst the humans. Matterhorn pulled a squished Snickers from his pocket. He had been saving it for the post-rescue party. He rubbed Broc's birthmark while the horse ate the treat.

"I know you're a free creature and you go where you want," Matterhorn whispered. "Still, you might check on Bonehand once in a while. He's got a lot of territory to watch over; he could sure use your help."

Matterhorn hardly needed to mention this. Bonehand's respect for the horse's intelligence and the care he had taken for Broc's wound had started a friendship that would last a lifetime.

Aaron tapped Matterhorn on the shoulder. "We should be on our way. With your permission," he said to the Queen.

"Granted. Walk with the Maker."

"Always."

"That's it?" Matterhorn said, staring at Bea. "We just stroll into the sunset?"

Bea smiled. "Only if you can walk on water like Sara."

"It's a figure of speech. But seriously, we just leave?"

"I will see to the final details. You are free to go. Do not look so worried my brave knight," Bea added. "Remember what I told you when we first met—serve well, serve long. You will be summoned again."

The Baron and Matterhorn left the crowd at the corral and started along the beach. They took time to find all the Baron's throwing stars. They would leave no evidence of their presence behind except their prints in the shifting sands of memory.

On the climb up the knoll to retrieve their packs, the Baron asked: "How did you manage that great escape from the goons with the net?"

"Have you ever heard the Maker's voice?"

With a knowing smile Aaron said, "What you can become..."

"You already are," Matterhorn completed the sentence. He stopped on the spot and wrote the phrase on the first page of his quote book.

Once atop the hill, Aaron collected his electric eyes while Matterhorn stared at the bloody gyrfalcon, its beak open and its talons empty in death. That had been a close call. He thought of the Sword that had saved his life. Already he missed the weight of it on his hip, the feel of the soft leather in his palm, the brilliant hardness of the blade.

"Change your clothes," the Baron said, handing Matterhorn his pack. "Put everything in here. Then I'll take you home."

"It's pretty cool that the Queen let you keep the Traveler's Cube," Matterhorn said while switching shirts.

"It's a great honor," the Baron said. "And so is being called by the Sword of Truth. It makes you a Traveler."

Matterhorn knelt to tie his shoes. "What exactly do Travelers do?"

"First Realm opens portals on other worlds and monitors the civilizations there," the Baron explained. "If they mature to where all the cultures are living in harmony, the Realm makes contact and invites them into the Alliance."

"You mean like a United Nations of the universe?"

"Sort of," the Baron replied. "When Praetorians from the Realm set up the portals, they select and train locals to become Travelers. They are recruited as kids and retired when their bodies can no longer handle the strain of time jumping—usually in their twenties. Travelers gather information and make progress reports."

"How many portals are there on Earth?" Matterhorn asked.

"About two dozen that I know of, probably more. Some are in well-known places like the Great Pyramid in Egypt and near Stonehenge."

"The rock formation in England?"

"Yeah," the Baron said. "That's how both the Queen and the wraith got here."

Aaron ran his fingers through his short-cropped hair and put on his red baseball cap. "Everything changed not long ago because of the trouble in First Realm," he went on. "I'm sure that has something to do with me getting to keep the Cube." He put the Talis in his pack.

"Don't you need that to take me home?" Matterhorn asked.

"I don't know your time-space coordinates," Aaron said as he pulled out the hilt of the Sword of Truth. The Queen had given it to him for just this purpose. "You're returning the way you came." The diamond blade extended and he stuck it in the ground. Then he rested his left hand on Matterhorn's shoulder in the Traveler's salute.

Matterhorn returned the gesture of respect and said, "I'm going to miss you, Aaron. As Ashleigh Brilliant once wrote, 'We've been through so much together, and most of it was your fault.'"

The Baron responded with a quote of his own. "Methinks the gentleman doth protest too much." He stepped back a few paces and said, "Put your hands on the hilt."

Matterhorn widened his stance and did so.

"Serve well, my friend ..."

"... serve long," Matterhorn finished.

The ground beneath him dissolved and as he stretched into nothingness, he heard the Baron say, "Try to land on your feet this time."

Lucky Charm

The ringing in his ears persisted. Matt tried to lift his head, but a swirl of dizziness kept him facedown. When the noise died away, he gradually realized it had been a bell. Opening his eyes, he found himself back in the library at David R. Sanford Middle School. The clock above Miss Tull's desk read 3:01.

Impossible!

He'd been traveling for days, yet the clock had ticked off only a few minutes.

Matt sat up and rubbed the bump on his forehead. He must have dozed off and smacked his head on the desk. There was something large in his lap. An open book. He flipped it over and read the title printed on the spine.

The Sword and the Flute.

The book was much lighter than when he had pulled it off Mr. Rickets. The pages were filled with words, whereas before they had been blank. The hole in the middle was gone.

As he skimmed the story, Matt realized he had just lived it. He read of the Propylon and Queen Bea. Of Aaron the Baron and the Sword of Truth. He flipped ahead to Ireland. Ian, the king of the leprechauns was described just as Matt remembered him. So were Broc and Bonehand.

Matt slammed the book shut and closed his eyes.

He could feel the Baron's hand on his shoulder in a Traveler's salute.

He could sense the Sword of Truth pulsing in his palm.

He could recall the texture of Broc's birthmark.

He could remember Bonehand's skeletal grip.

He could taste burnt caterpillar.

He could hear the Maker's voice. "What you can become you already are."

Another voice was speaking to him now.

"Are you all right, Matt?" Miss Tull asked. "What happened?" She touched the bruise on his forehead.

"I'm okay," Matt said. "I must have fallen asleep and bumped my head." He got up a little shakily and walked over to Mr. Rickets to return the book. As he slid it in place, the gold lettering on the spine faded. The disappearing act made his vision swim. He stumbled backwards and rubbed his eyes.

"I'd better take you to see the nurse," Miss Tull said, coming toward him.

"I'm fine, really." Matt hurried away before she could grab his forearm and steer him to Mrs. Serveen. Mrs. Serveen had been the school nurse since the days of Florence Nightingale. She had the bedside manner of a drill sergeant. No kid ever went to her of his own free will.

Matt's first stop when he left the library was the boy's bathroom. After he examined the bruise on his forehead, he checked his right leg. There was no sign of a knife wound. And when he peeked down his shirt, he found no bruises on his chest. His ribs felt fine.

His ponytail was gone, too, he noticed sadly. His twelve-year-old body looked small and feeble. Had he really been an adult only a few minutes ago?

The halls were almost deserted by the time Matt reached his locker, this being Friday afternoon. He walked out to where his sister usually met him, but she was gone. Probably got tired of waiting and went home alone. That was okay. Matt needed time to think.

Trudging past the park, he waved off his friends who were kicking a soccer ball around. "See you tomorrow!" one of them yelled. "We're gonna be champs!"

So he hadn't missed the district championships. He hadn't been gone for days. His overactive imagination had simply created a far-out story. Clocks don't lie, he scolded himself. Neither do mirrors. Still, something scratched at the back of his mind that wouldn't let him dismiss his adventure as a daydream.

The scratching turned out to be on his left wrist. Matt noticed it as he swung his arms in stride. When he finally realized what it was, a slow smile spread across his freckled face and a deep joy settled in his heart.

He had been to First Realm and back.

He had fought in Ireland alongside the Baron and been knighted by the Queen.

The Sword and the Flute were not figments of his imagination. They were Talis from another world.

He was a Traveler now.

All the proof he needed was right there on his belt. And the rest of the way home he couldn't stop rubbing his new lucky charm.

A scritch pad.

Epilogue

he Monday after Matthew Horn had returned from Ireland, he arrived at school by 6:30 a.m. When the custodian unlocked the doors, Matt mumbled something about an unfinished assignment and begged to be let into the library. Once there, he headed straight for Mr. Rickets. With shaking hands, Matt pulled out The Sword and the Flute. He sat on the floor and speed-read it once more.

How these words got into the once-blank book wasn't the only question on Matt's mind. He wanted to know if there were other stories among Mr. Ricket's treasures that had "holes" in them. Carefully at first, then more frantically, he checked every book. All of them seemed normal.

When Miss Tull showed up an hour later, Matt strolled over to her desk and asked his favorite librarian: "Is there anything special about the books on Mr. Rickets?"

"All books are special," she replied with a smile that tilted the glasses on her long nose.

"Have you read these?" Matt asked, trying to sound casual.

"Most."

"How about *The Sword and the Flu?*"

Over the top of her spectacles her gray eyes locked onto him: "You must be mistaken. There is no such title."

Matt showed her the book.

She frowned and said: "Hmm, I will have to enter it into the catalog. What is it about?"

Matt stepped back from this question, and mumbled something about getting to class. No sense having Miss Tull concerned over his sanity. He hadn't even told his parents about what had happened.

The next few days he poked around Mr. Rickets, whenever Miss Tull wasn't looking. He was dying to find a way back to the Propylon.

He needed to know if Queen Bea had made it home with Ian's Flute. Were there other Talis on Earth that needed finding? Would the Sword summon him to help find them?

Evidently not.

Life went on as it had before his adventure. Eventually, Matt gave up searching for portals. However, he did decide to prepare himself in case he was called upon again. Since he was now a knight, he would learn how to handle a sword. He read books on fencing and checked into martial arts built around swordplay such as aikido and kenjutsu. He even discovered the Society for Creative Anachronism, a group that recreated medieval jousts and tournaments. Finally he settled on Kendo, the Way of the Sword.

No one in his family understood Matt's sudden interest in swords. His mom and dad worried about injuries. But they both knew that once Matt got an idea into his head, he was more stubborn than crabgrass. And so they signed the permission slip and bought the uniform, the body armor and several shinai—bamboo practice swords.

For the next few months, Matt went to the dojo every day after school. He skipped indoor soccer and focused on kendo. He worked hard on his eye-hand coordination, practicing attacks and defenses as though his life depended on it.

One day it might.

The seasons worked their way around to spring. On a fresh Friday afternoon, Matt came home from school, changed clothes, grabbed his pack and headed for The Loft. The Loft was an eight-foot-square tree house nestled in the heart of an ancient apple tree. Matt had helped Vic and his dad build it many years ago. It perched six feet off the ground, which was plenty high for Matt. Thick branches and lush leaves shielded it from prying eyes while still letting in lots of sun.

This marvel of backyard engineering had been built without pounding a single nail into the venerable tree. It had running water—a plastic jug that tipped into a bucket sink at the pull of a rope—and even a garden-level basement made by hanging tarps from floor to ground.

Matt scrambled up the ladder and plopped into a scrunchy green beanbag. He had checked out *The Sword and the Flute* to re-read his adventures with Aaron the Baron. Halfway through the book, he heard a faint hissing, like air being sucked through a tiny straw. The noise was coming from a period on the page in front of him.

The spot of ink was growing.

Matt's eyes grew bigger along with it.

A portal?

At long last!

For months Matt had dreamed of this moment. Now he panicked. Butterflies banged into each other in his stomach. Beads of sweat called an emergency meeting on his forehead. His feet wanted to head straight for his bedroom.

He had almost not returned from his first tumble into a portal. Pirates had tried to kill him and a dark spirit had almost succeeded. If he knew what was good for him, he would run to the house.

Why would he risk taking another plunge into the unknown?

The answer came to him with caffeine clarity.

Because the Sword of Truth was calling.

Because he was the Queen's Knight.

Because he had sworn to serve the Maker.

Because he would not ignore his destiny.

The spot on the page had grown to the size of a CD. Matt could detect the swirling and could feel the pull. His muscles tensed in anticipation. He patted his pockets to make sure he had his quote book and harmonica. Satisfied, he pressed his palms together, tucked his head and leaned forward.

First came the tingling in his fingertips, then the painless stretching.

Matt had been unwittingly sucked through his first portal and deposited in a heap of arms and legs. This time he would make a better entrance. He would somersault his body as he passed through the portal and come out the other end like a superhero.

Fat chance.

The End

TALIS HUNTERS

Mike Hamel

Contents

Royal Reunion

Matterhorn the Brave came rolling from the cave like candy out of a gumball machine. When the skittering mass of elbows and kneecaps came to rest, a red head popped up from the tangle of limbs. Hazel green eyes blinked open and took in the surroundings. Stately Sitka spruce and bushy western hemlock crowded the landscape. Through their spiked green heads, Matterhorn saw the horizon being tickled pink by the setting sun.

Where was he?

When was he?

Why was he here?

An evening breeze rustled the trees and raised goose bumps on his skin. He stood and rubbed his arms for warmth. They were well muscled since the trip through the portal had accelerated him to adulthood. He had fallen in one end as a preteen and out the other as a young man with an athlete's body.

Matterhorn grinned. This physical change was one of the best things he remembered about time-space travel. He checked his hair. Sure enough, the fire-red ponytail was back. His legs were twice their normal size, though his feet looked about the same. Not surprising since he had big feet for his age.

A good thing his clothes also grew, he thought, as he dusted sticky pine needles from his pants, or he would be very uncomfortable right about now. He stretched his new muscles and did a 360. He was in the middle of nowhere and unprepared for the fast-approaching night. He didn't even have a coat, much less a tent or any way to make a fire. Aaron the Baron had been with him on his first adventure, and the Baron came equipped for every situation. From inflatable backpacks to collapsible weapons, he had more gadgets than a secret agent. Without his resourceful partner, Matterhorn felt lost.

But not for long.

First he heard the voices of two women, and then their forms emerged from the forest with arms full of firewood. He recognized the taller woman as Queen Bea of First Realm. Even without her throne and crown there was no mistaking her royal bearing. Her arrival made Matterhorn feel 1,000 percent better.

When the Queen caught sight of Matterhorn, her face crinkled into a smile. "Ah, here is my knight now. How good of you to come." She turned to her companion and said, "Princess Jewel, this is Matterhorn the Brave. Matterhorn, this is Princess Jewel."

"Yell-O," Matterhorn said.

"Hi," Jewel replied in a rich alto voice.

He had seen her once before on a computer in the Baron's workshop. She was prettier in person, with wide-awake brown eyes and cinnamon skin smoother than jeweler's felt. An onyx wolf earring dangled from her right ear. A dark flow of coffee hair ran down her back in a heavy braid. She wore buckskin pants and a leather vest over a hunter green shirt. Standing five foot five in her moccasins, she looked almost petite. Matterhorn recalled Aaron's respect for her and assumed she must be tougher than she appeared.

Jewel was sizing him up at the same time. Six foot four, she guessed, and about 210 pounds. Rangy limbs, indoor complexion, nice ponytail.

The Queen cleared her throat to regain Matterhorn's attention. "We have much to discuss and you are not the only knight to arrive. Make yourself useful by finding some water. Jewel has a water skin you can fill."

Matterhorn followed the women to the beginnings of a campsite and got the skin. "There's a stream about a quarter mile beyond that bank of deer ferns," Jewel said, pointing with her chin. "Don't get lost."

She meant it. Moving downhill from the cave, Matterhorn was swallowed in a confusing riot of green. Tall trees overshadowed him as he pushed through the dozen different kinds of ferns that wrestled for space on the forest floor. Sleek squirrels eyed him warily while the more suspicious gray jays squawked in alarm. The air pulsed with evening sounds and evergreen smells.

150

Drawn by the gurgling, Matterhorn located the stream. His arrival startled a gang of black-tailed deer, but not the fat rainbow trout lounging in the pool. The crystal water stung his hands as he filled the skin. He remembered how the Baron taught him to squat, not kneel, at a riverbank to make him less vulnerable to attack.

Was there danger of attack here? From wild animals? Natives? Matterhorn glanced around uneasily. He liked being outdoors, but the wildness of this place unnerved him. Whistling for his courage, he started back to camp. The cheerful noise died on his lips a few moments later.

It wasn't the size of the animal that froze his face and feet, but the white racing stripes running down the creature's fur.

Staring up at him was the biggest polecat Matterhorn had ever seen. His nose wrinkled as he recalled the rank smell of the neighbor's dog after her encounter with a skunk. He had no wish to be sprayed by this mobile stink-dispenser.

As the skunk sauntered past him, Matterhorn counted four small skunks waddling in her wake. He drew on his kendo training to focus himself into perfect stillness. Momma passed close enough to brush his leg with her tail. Skunklet number three stopped and shoved its nose up Matterhorn's pant leg.

Were baby skunks armed and dangerous? He did not want to find out.

When the family moved on, so did Matterhorn. He retraced his footprints to camp and found Jewel busy peeling some strange-looking roots.

"You're sweating," she said, taking the water skin. "Did you have any trouble?"

"Just met a few of the neighbors."

Indian Heaven

Jewel filled a cooking pot and placed it on the fire. She added the camas roots, along with some greens and spices. When the mix began to simmer she sprinkled in a yellow powder to thicken it.

Cornstarch, Matterhorn figured. The aroma reminded him of his mom's vegetable stew. He got comfortable and waited for supper.

"Have you been well since our last meeting?" Queen Bea asked from the other side of the fire. The light danced in her brown eyes and gave her cheeks a healthy glow. She had on loose jeans and a long-sleeve russet blouse, accented by a teardrop sapphire at her throat and a golden charm bracelet on her wrist. Her thick hair was wound into a bun at the nape of her neck. There was a small object in her right ear Matterhorn couldn't make out. A knapsack rested against her leg.

"Yes, thank you," Matterhorn said. "I was beginning to think I'd never see you again. How long has it been, anyway?"

Bea smiled. "For you, months, but for me, days."

The time difference didn't come as a complete shock to Matterhorn. Uncle Al had often told him time was relative. It depended on factors like the speed and direction you happened to be going. Evidently Earth and First Realm, while being mirror worlds, were not in sync.

"What have you been doing with yourself?" the Queen asked.

"Studying kendo," Matterhorn said, pressing his palms together and bowing. "It is the Way of the Sword."

"Then I suppose you will be wanting this. It is the reason you are here." She reached down and pulled a red leather hilt from her pack. The three watched a diamond blade grow from the handle. A liquid sunbeam appeared in its center. This was the Sword of Truth, one of the Ten Talis, fashioned by the Maker to represent His integrity and truthfulness.

Matterhorn reached over and took the weapon. He noted the inscription on the silver crosspiece, etched there by the Maker: Truth is a Blade sharp as Light. The scritch pad was still attached to the hilt. It matched the square pad on his own belt. Scritch was the Baron's Velcro-like invention, only stronger.

Matterhorn willed the blade to vanish and stuck the hilt to the pad. In a strange way he felt whole again, as though an amputated limb had been miraculously restored.

"Did the Baron explain to you about portals and what they are used for?" Bea asked.

"Yes," Matterhorn said. "He told me your people opened portals on planets they wanted to observe. On Earth they're in mystical places like Stonehenge and the pyramids."

"The cave you came through is also a portal. I used it to bring Jewel here this afternoon. You, of course, were summoned by the Sword."

"Summoned where?"

"Tomorrow morning, if you look above those trees, you will see how Mount St. Helens appeared before she blew her top. Over there," Bea pointed in the opposite direction, "you will see Mount Adams. Between these two giants is the very unstable piece of real estate we are sitting on. In your day it is called the Indian Heaven Volcanic Field."

That had an ominous sound to it.

"Princess Jewel is a Chinook Indian," Bea continued. "Centuries from now her people will live on this land. Her knowledge of the area will be helpful to you and the Baron."

"So will my cooking," Jewel said, handing them each a bowl of steaming stew.

"Anything is better than the Baron's cooking," Matterhorn mumbled as he took the bowl.

Jewel shot the Queen a knowing glance. "The Baron has many skills," she said. "Cooking is not among them. Where is he anyway?"

"I do not know," Bea said. "He should have arrived by now."

Conversation stopped while they ate. Matterhorn used the silence to do a quick mental review of what he had learned when his family had camped in the Pacific Northwest last summer. The guide who took them fishing on the Columbia River had told tall tales of the Chinook, Kwakiutl, Nootka and Tillamook tribes. The Native Americans had lived undisturbed on the banks of the big river until the white man "civilized" them on reservations.

The Queen finished her stew and resumed her explanation. "The volcanoes in this place make it prone to earthquakes. A major one is due in the next few days, hence the urgency of your task. The quake may collapse the entrance to an underground city. One of the Ten Talis is there. You must retrieve the Talis before it is too late."

"A few days!" Matterhorn sputtered. "Couldn't we have come any earlier?"

"We do well to be here at all," Bea said. "And do not forget whom you are addressing."

"I'm sor—"

The Queen cut him off with a gesture. "I owe you an explanation since you will be risking your life."

These words fell like cold rain on Matterhorn's excitement, reminding him that he had been brought here as a soldier, not a tourist.

Bea became strangely silent. A single tear formed on the inside corner of her right eye, but refused to fall. Princess Jewel moved closer and rested her hand on the Queen's arm. She seemed to be sharing, and thus easing, Her Majesty's pain.

When the Queen could speak, she said, "Our worlds are almost identical in so many ways; size, climate, geography. Yet our histories have unfolded differently. We have made different moral choices. Yours have caused you untold miseries. We have been spared such catastrophes— until recently. There is growing dissent in First Realm and bloodshed in the Palace of Peace. The King—my father—was murdered."

"I'm sorry," Matterhorn said. "When did this happen?"

"Not long before the Sword called you the first time."

"Did you catch the murderers?" Jewel asked.

"We caught the assassin, but not the traitors. Everyone pays me lip service as Queen, but there are heretics in high places. Otherwise my father would still be alive."

"Are these the heretics who sent the wraith after Ian's Flute?" Matterhorn asked. He remembered the pirate captain melting into black smoke upon being run through by the Sword of Truth.

"I suspect so," Bea replied.

"What do they want?"

"To take over your world," she said bluntly.

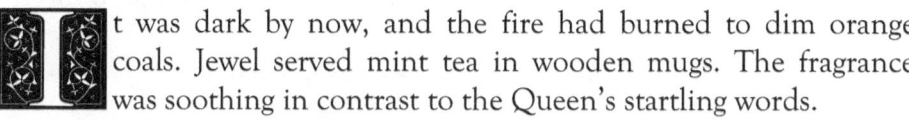

It was dark by now, and the fire had burned to dim orange coals. Jewel served mint tea in wooden mugs. The fragrance was soothing in contrast to the Queen's startling words.

"Because your world is so like ours," she explained, "it has attracted great attention. There is growing concern you will destroy yourselves and turn this paradise into a nuclear wasteland. You have come within minutes of doing this several times already."

Bea shifted on her log seat and sipped her tea. "It is against everything we believe to interfere with other races before they have matured," she continued, "but some heretics are calling for direct intervention. Others have gone farther. They are secretly working to write themselves into your future by changing your past. My father strongly opposed them and was killed as a result."

"What can we do to help you?" Jewel asked.

"The role of the Travelers has changed because of something my father did before his death," the Queen replied. "He realized the heretics would need some of the Ten Talis to carry out their plan, so he had the Captain of the Praetorians hide several of them on Earth. The Captain never returned from this mission. The heretics must have followed and murdered him as well, although that would have been a difficult task indeed."

Matterhorn was temporarily distracted when a large rabbit hopped from the bushes and plopped between Jewel's feet. Without taking her eyes off the Queen, Jewel began scratching the furry newcomer's head. Only then did Matterhorn notice the lizard lying by the fish tattoo on her ankle. The Princess seemed to be an animal magnet.

He tuned his mental radio back to Queen Bea and heard, "The Captain left some clues that we have since uncovered. We know he hid the Talis among creatures that are separate from your mainstream history."

"Such as the leprechauns," Matterhorn spoke up. "He hid the Talis in our fairy tales."

"What better place to hide fantastic treasures than in fantasies," Jewel put in.

The Queen smiled at their perceptiveness.

"And you think there's a Talis hidden in an underground city near here?" Matterhorn asked.

"My people have many legends about a secret city," Jewel said. "They say that Sesqec once lived there."

"That is true," the Queen said. "They have what I seek."

"What are you talking about?" Matterhorn wanted to know. "Who has the Talis?"

Jewel stood to stretch her legs. The Man-in-the-Moon beamed over her right shoulder. Her face was in the shadows but there was no missing the gleam in her eye as she said, "Sesqec is the Native American word for Sasquatch. Your people call them Bigfoot."

First leprechauns, Matterhorn thought, now Sasquatch. "So Sasquatch are real," he said to the Queen, who was also standing now.

"Many of the Native American stories about the Sasquatch are true," Bea said. "The legends will help you find the city. When you do, look for this." She bent and retrieved an article from her knapsack. Matterhorn threw more wood on the fire so they could see better.

"This is a replica of the Band of Justice," the Queen said, handing Jewel a circular band of material about an inch wide. Webbed to its smooth white surface with delicate gold filigree was a triangular-faceted ruby. Inscribed around the woven cloth in ruby chips the size of rice grains were these words: "I know in depth your deepest thoughts."

"The real Band of Justice is made from Morning Cloth," the Queen said. "The Maker cut and set the gem Himself. This Talis represents His all-knowing mind. It allows the wearer to know the thoughts of anyone he or she touches." Bea paused for effect. "Invading someone's inner privacy is never to be done lightly. The Band is used by the King or Queen only when the truth cannot be learned any other way. I need the true Band of Justice to find my father's killers."

158

Jewel half raised her hand as if she were in school. "If you know where the Talis are hidden, why not go to the exact locations and get them?"

Reaching down for her pack, Queen Bea sighed. "I wish it were that easy. The Captain was careful not to reveal too much in his clues in case the heretics found them. We know to whom he committed some of the Talis, but not the exact times. Also, we must be discrete in searching; there are spies among us. I do not want to repeat my earlier mistake when I went to look for Ian's Flute."

"What mistake?" Matterhorn asked.

"I was gone too long," she said. "Time moves more slowly for those we leave behind when we travel. Still, it does move. Trayko is covering for me, but I must return before I am missed. I do not want to draw attention to your whereabouts."

Matterhorn remembered the tall Praetorian whom the Baron had introduced to him.

Jewel handed the Band back to Bea.

"Keep it," Bea said. "It might come in handy. Be careful, Princess." With that, she motioned for Matterhorn to follow and started uphill toward the cave.

"One more question, please," he said as he caught up. "Does my being here mean I'm an official Traveler?" The Baron had called him one, but Matterhorn wanted to hear the words from the Queen.

She regarded him thoughtfully. "You are something different. A Traveler, certainly, but unique."

"I know it's not my age," Matterhorn replied. "I was told kids are recruited as Travelers. Why is that? Why not use scientists or psychologists to keep an eye on humanity's progress?"

"Because young minds are not yet hardened into categories like 'possible' and 'impossible.' Children are much better at believing than adults. Faith comes naturally to you. Do you know what faith is? It is being certain of what you cannot see. Without faith it is impossible to know the Maker or hear His voice."

They had reached the cave. Queen Bea stopped and stared up into Matterhorn's eyes. "Conduct yourself with courage my brave knight. Find the Talis. Protect the Princess with your life. The Baron will have the supplies you need. Nate the Great may come also, who knows. He travels by his own rules." Standing on her tiptoes, she placed her right hand on his shoulder and squeezed. "Serve well."

"Serve long," Matterhorn replied, returning the salute.

Then the Queen spun on her heels and walked into the cave.

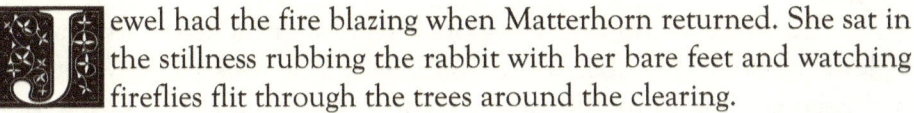

ewel had the fire blazing when Matterhorn returned. She sat in the stillness rubbing the rabbit with her bare feet and watching fireflies flit through the trees around the clearing.

Matterhorn resumed his place across from her. He played with the hair behind his left ear and wondered what to do next.

The night crowded closer, its Cyclops-eye watching them from a dark face pimpled with stars. Jewel looked up and said, "I do love being outdoors. It's so, so majestic!"

"You're not frightened being in a strange place?"

"Of what?"

"Well, there might be wild animals around," Matterhorn said.

"Like that grizzly bear?" She glanced to his left.

He spun and searched the gloom for animal eyes. Seeing nothing, he turned on Jewel, expecting a "made you look" remark.

She was serious, yet calm.

"What bear?" he asked.

"The one sitting thirty yards away."

"How do you know?"

"I can smell her for one thing. Also, I have this sixth sense about animals. It's like I can feel their feelings. My dad says I'm empathic. Whenever I travel, my senses get sharper. You know how our bodies mature. Well, my animal awareness also becomes more acute."

"Will the bear bother us?" Matterhorn asked nervously.

Jewel laughed. "No, she's just curious about the fire. It's new to her. Is it okay if I invite her over?"

"You can do that?"

"Sure." As Jewel closed her eyes, the rabbit at her feet opened his and a second later bounced into the underbrush. In a few moments Matterhorn could hear the grizzly approaching. A big, black nose on the end of a long, brown snout poked into the firelight. The bear sniffed at the wisps of smoke floating overhead then strutted past Matterhorn and harrumphed down where the bunny had been.

The brute weighed six hundred pounds and measured four feet at the shoulders. Five-inch claws made each paw a formidable weapon. Matterhorn put his hand on the hilt of his Sword. He relaxed somewhat when the blade didn't extend. Evidently they weren't in danger.

Becoming as still as the log on which he sat, Matterhorn gawked as Jewel stood and scratched the bear's neck. She took the stewpot that had been cooling in the dirt and gave it to their guest. The bear's long pink tongue scrubbed it shiny clean.

"I so love animals," Jewel said, burying her fingers deep in the grizzly's coarse fur. "My people have always had a deep respect for all living things; I inherited it from them. My great-grandfather was a famous chief. My dad says that makes me a princess. That's how I got my nickname."

When she finished with the stewpot, the bear pawed at the fire. She quickly dropped the orange coal she had scooped up to examine. After that she gave Matterhorn a good sniffing, which made him sweat despite the night chill. Finally she bestowed a goodnight lick on Jewel and wandered off, leaving behind a steaming memento of her visit.

Matterhorn scooted the scat out of the way with a branch.

Jewel laughed at his fussiness. "Come on," she said. "I'll show you which ferns make the most comfortable sleeping mats."

While they were collecting their feathery bedding, a skittering of rocks sounded from the direction of the cave. Matterhorn's face brightened. "Maybe it's the Baron."

"No, it's the bear," Jewel said. "The Baron doesn't make much noise."

"Have you traveled with him before?"

"A few times. He's one of the best Travelers ever. Did you know that? No one's more trusted by the Praetorians."

Matterhorn wasn't surprised by the Baron's reputation, having seen him in action.

"Those fronds to your left are good," Jewel said. Her own arms were full by now and she headed back to camp where they made beds on opposite sides of the fire circle.

"One time the Baron went after a fellow Traveler who had been in a mountain climbing accident," Jewel said from across the dying embers. "He found the guy in a blizzard and brought him down, even though the man had a broken leg. This was before he had the Cube, and the rescue took two weeks. They survived on what the Baron had in his pack."

"He's got some amazing gear," Matterhorn agreed. "Most of it he made himself." Matterhorn picked at his teeth with a twig and glanced sideways at his new partner. "The Baron thinks highly of you as a Traveler as well. He was disappointed when you weren't available to help him find Ian's Flute and he got stuck with me."

"From what the Queen told me, you did quite well."

"Beginner's luck," Matterhorn said.

"I don't think so," Jewel replied, "or you would be called Matterhorn the Lucky, not Matterhorn the Brave."

Assuming she was an adolescent like himself and Aaron when not traveling, Matterhorn asked, "How old are you?"

"Thirteen."

"What grade are you in?"

"That depends on the subject. I'm home-schooled because of where I live." She thought for a moment and added, "I suppose I'm mostly in the seventh grade."

"I don't know much about your tribe," Matterhorn admitted.

"Most people don't. The Chinook lived peacefully in the Great Northwest for centuries. After Lewis and Clark arrived with their germs and diseases, we went from being one of the most powerful West Coast tribes to near extinction."

Although bringing diseases had not been a deliberate act, Matterhorn did know enough history to feel ashamed of other things done by his ancestors to the Native Americans.

"Some Chinooks ended up on reservations in Washington and Oregon," Jewel went on. "The rest scattered. My family lives in a national park. My dad's a U.S. forest ranger."

"How did you become a Traveler?" Matterhorn asked.

"My grandmother is a healer," Jewel said. "I found out on my tenth birthday that she was also a Traveler in her youth. She told me about her adventures and asked if I wanted to travel. I learned later that this happens a lot. Those with personal experience can often spot others who would make good Travelers."

Jewel leaned up on one elbow. "Several weeks after I said yes, grandmother brought me to the portal you came through this afternoon. It's just a few hours' walk from my house. I met a Praetorian who took me to the Propylon to begin my training."

"Did you meet Queen Bea?"

"Later," Jewel replied, touching the onyx earring Bea had given her. "Only she wasn't a Queen—"

Just then, a tremor rolled through the ground and shook loose a volley of pinecones that peppered the campsite like brown hail.

It was an unsettling omen of things to come.

Morning Briefing

Matterhorn awoke stiff and cold, but not as chilled as he should have been. During the night he had been covered to conserve his body heat. The shiny space blanket he found on top of him seemed familiar.

"It's 7:15 already; about time you woke up." Warming his hands by a crispy fire sat a bronzed and buzz-cut young man. A red corduroy baseball cap kept the morning sun out of his eyes, which were the color of faded denim. Under his insulated vest he had on a gray T-shirt that stretched across his muscular chest. The pockets of his cargo pants bulged with who-knew-what. Two oversized backpacks lined with silver tape leaned together a few feet away.

Matterhorn sat up and draped his arms across his knees. "Hey Aaron, great to see you. How've you been?"

"Fine, Matterhorn. And you?"

"No complaints." Noticing that the Baron wore no watch, Matterhorn asked, "How do you know what time it is?"

"Internal clock," the Baron said, tapping his temple. "I always know what time it is."

"When did you get here?"

"An hour ago."

Gazing around the campsite, Matterhorn said, "Where's Jewel?"

"I haven't seen her. She's probably getting breakfast."

"While you two chat the morning away," Jewel said.

The Baron stood as Jewel came through the trees carrying her stewpot brimming with strawberries almost the size of apples.

"Hello, Princess," he said, scooping her into a great hug and swinging her round and round. Strawberries flew everywhere.

Jewel laughed. "Put me down, you brute."

"You must be thinking of someone else," he said, lowering her.

"I'm thinking it's about time you got here," Jewel said.

"I wouldn't have missed this adventure for anything. Especially if you're doing the cooking."

"The Maker made today's breakfast," she said, handing the half-empty pot to the Baron. "Pick up what you spilled and I'll make some tea."

Matterhorn would have preferred hot chocolate but the tea was hot and flavorful. The strawberries tasted sweeter than anything he could remember. He chewed slowly, savoring each bite, and listened as the Baron and Jewel got caught up.

"How's your mom doing?" the Baron asked.

Matterhorn now recalled that Jewel hadn't gone to Ireland with them because her mom was dying of cancer. He felt ashamed at having forgotten such an important detail.

Jewel took a large breath and let it out slowly. "Mom didn't do well with the last round of chemo, so she's stopped going to the clinic. Her older sister—my Aunt Anna—died of cancer two years ago, which scares Dad and me. We're praying for a miracle."

The Baron patted her hand. "I don't know what I'd do if I lost my mom. It must be hard for you to leave her, even for a short time."

"She's at Grandma's for a few weeks," Jewel replied. "Grandma wants to try some herbal treatments. Besides, when I found out this trip was to where my ancestors lived, I couldn't resist." She told Aaron what Bea had said last night about the trouble in First Realm, the missing Talis, the Band of Justice and the Sasquatch.

The Baron listened quietly, nodding from time to time. "The Queen briefed me about the heretics and the Talis," he said when Jewel finished. "She also said there were clues in the Chinook legends about the Sasquatch."

Jewel topped off their mugs of green tea and said, "I've been thinking about that. The stories tell of a hidden city in a valley somewhere between two fire mountains, which have to be Mount St. Helens and Mount Adams."

Matterhorn scanned the two peaks visible above the treetops. "Both of them are volcanoes," he said.

"And those are just the big ones," the Baron added. "This whole territory is like an underground nuclear test site."

"The Queen said a major earthquake could seal off the city any day now," Jewel went on. "We should get going. Yesterday I spotted the canyon of a large river. It's as good a place as any to start."

"The oracle has spoken," the Baron quipped, wiping strawberry juice from his chin and slurping the last of his tea. He pointed at the packs and said to Matterhorn, "These are much newer than the ones we used in Ireland. I brought you a change of clothes and a pair of lightweight hiking boots. Size thirteen, right?"

"Yeah. How far into the past have we gone?" Matterhorn asked as he dug into the pack.

"To around 10,000 B.C.," the Baron said.

Matterhorn moved a coil of lightweight rope and a flat roll of duct tape to find the boots. Noticing a blue bundle beneath them he asked, "What's this?"

"A small parachute," the Baron answered.

"A parachute! What am I supposed to do with that?"

"The terrain around here is pretty rugged. We might have to drop into a canyon or check out a crater or two." He poked Matterhorn in the side. "Besides, BASE jumping is exciting."

"Extreme sports aren't my style," Matterhorn protested. "The only thing I'm going to use this for is a pillow."

"Stop talking, start walking," Jewel said. She shouldered her own pack, which Matterhorn hadn't noticed before. He scolded himself for not being more observant. Sherlock Holmes would scoff at his inattention to details.

But not even the world's greatest detective would have spotted the keen red eyes watching from the cave as the trio broke camp and headed west. Even Jewel, with her ability to sense the presence of other creatures, was unaware they had company.

Three Faces West

With a belly full of sweetness and a heart ready for adventure, Matterhorn followed Jewel and the Baron into the multicolored forest. Blue and purple huckleberries grew among the drooping pink clusters of flowering currants. Blades of yellow sunlight sliced through the leafy canopy overhead and splattered on the ground.

"Do you realize we're in a temperate rainforest?" Jewel asked over her shoulder. "Even in our day this place gets almost fourteen feet of rain a year. That's why it's so lush. I should know; I live here." She led the way through the matted undergrowth of cloverleaf oxalis and blunt sword ferns, jumping over fallen trees with deer-like grace.

They hiked through stands of Ponderosa pines and red cedars thicker than bear fur. The Baron and Matterhorn were thankful when Jewel settled on an animal trail that made the going a bit easier. In half an hour they came to a large tear in the earth's skin. The canyon was deeper than it was wide. At its bottom a frisky river could be heard playing among massive boulders.

Shying away from the edge, Matterhorn asked shakily, "Now where?" He had a sinking feeling behind his belly button.

"Down," Jewel said. "This trail goes to the bottom. It's steep, but if animals can use it so can we."

Patting the bottom of his pack, the Baron said, "Or, we can use the parachutes."

Matterhorn didn't like either option. As the Queen's knight he was supposed to be courageous. Hadn't he tackled a gang of pirates? Hadn't he wrestled a wraith? So why couldn't he hike down the side of this canyon?

Acrophobia.

Matterhorn the Brave was afraid of heights. He scratched the hair behind his left ear while his face flushed. How embarrassing not to be able to follow their female guide. "Sorry to make this difficult," he mumbled. "I have this thing about heights."

"That's okay," Jewel said, understanding at once. "We can walk the ridge for a while. Maybe there's a safer way down. No sense taking unnecessary risks."

"The view up here is better anyway," the Baron said, deciding not to tease Matterhorn about his phobia. After all, Matterhorn hadn't made fun of his fear of snakes when they encountered one on their last adventure.

The rest of the morning they tickled the lip of the canyon. A few more downward possibilities came along, but none that Matterhorn could bring himself to take. Along the way they pooled their knowledge about the Sasquatch.

They would have kept their voices down had they known who was listening.

"In my research for this trip," the Baron told his companions, "I read that Sasquatch is an Indian term meaning 'hairy man.' The adults can be nine feet tall and weigh half a ton. They're solitary creatures who have never been seen in groups."

"If they're so solitary," Matterhorn asked, "why are we looking for a whole city of them?"

The Baron shrugged. "Their habits must have changed over the centuries."

"Native Americans regard them with great respect," Jewel said. "We have many tales about our great elder brothers. Some believe they possess both animal and human consciousness. Others say they can sense when people are hunting them. That's why no Sasquatch has ever been killed or captured. It also helps that they're stronger than grizzlies and faster than horses."

"Will they know we mean them no harm?" Matterhorn wondered.

"If they don't figure that out," Jewel said, "we'll never get close enough to find the Band of Justice."

"Finding the Talis won't be easy," the Baron said. "Did the Queen mention Nate?"

170

"She said he might show up, but she wasn't sure," Matterhorn replied.

"We could use his help. That bushman could track a polar bear in a blizzard."

They walked and talked for several more hours. At one point Jewel climbed alone to the top of a ridge where a buck and two does were nibbling bushes. When she came back she announced, "There's a river not far ahead that cuts a gentler path to the canyon floor. We can follow it down."

"The deer told you that!" Matterhorn said in amazement.

"No," Jewel said. "I could see it from the high ground."

The lazy tributary took its own sweet time yielding to gravity. It preferred to double back on itself rather than risk steep drops. Following the winding water and using the dense vegetation as handholds, the Travelers made it to the bottom by sundown. The river noise made it difficult to carry on a conversation, which didn't matter since everyone was talked out. Exhausted from their trek, they didn't bother with a fire.

The Baron dug out three MREs—meals ready to eat. He cut the large plastic casing in which they were issued and dumped out the contents: chicken-and-rice main course, crackers, cheese spread with jalapenos, fudge brownie, Skittles, cherry-flavored beverage powder and a baggie of spices. He showed Matterhorn and Jewel how to slide the meal pouch into the green sleeve with a chemical heating wafer. The result wasn't gourmet, but it was hot and filling.

They spent the night on moss-covered ground that smelled of humus and awoke before the sun could haul its round bottom over the canyon rim. Jewel scrounged for fruit and nuts while the Baron started a fire.

"We should head downriver," Jewel said, as she brewed her morning tea, "not upriver like we discussed last night."

"Why the change?" Matterhorn asked.

"The canyon narrows upstream. Downstream looks more promising."

She must have been up for hours to have scouted both directions, Matterhorn realized. He felt guilty for sleeping in.

Jewel and the Baron let Matterhorn take the point this morning. Even he could follow a stream. This particular one was on its way to make a deposit of melted snow in the Pacific. The atmosphere above was crisp and clean, thanks to a vigorous routine of daily showers. The rocky walls were serrated on top and studded with trees that grew wherever a few inches of dirt had collected over the ages.

Hawks circled on updrafts. Deer and elk signs littered the canyon floor as it widened. A set of fresh tracks in the soft earth caught Matterhorn's attention. He knelt and studied the prints. "Keep your eye peeled for a large wolf," he said. "These paw prints are huge."

Jewel smiled but said nothing.

At one o'clock they reached a fork in the river. Jewel suggested the left prong—and regretted it two hours later. The banks on both sides of the chasm had narrowed and then disappeared in the spray of churning rapids.

They would have to shoot Class V white water or turn back.

e could make a raft and keep going!" the Baron yelled as they rested on a granite slab not far from the mouth of the cataract. "I've got some rope, and there's enough fallen birch around."

Matterhorn snapped a branch off a downed tree. "How are we supposed to trim these trees into logs?"

"With a wire saw!" the Baron said. "There's one in your pack!" From his own gear he pulled out a small loop of flexible black-oxide-coated wire. The twenty-four-inch strand had ring handles on either end. "These babies will zip through wood, metal, bone—you name it!" As he spoke, he deftly trimmed one side of the log on the ground between them.

"A raft might work if the rapids don't go on too long!" Jewel said, cupping her hands to her mouth. "That chop will shred it otherwise!"

"I'm good with knots!" the Baron cried, rolling the log over with his foot and starting on the other side. "The SS **Princess** will hold together and get us through, Captain!" He gave Jewel a military salute.

Jewel tossed one of the severed branches into the stream and watched it vanish into the swirling vortex. "Have you ever played Rock, Paper, Scissors?" she asked. "Well, in Rock, Rapids, Raft, the Raft loses!"

"Speaking of losing!" the Baron countered, "we'll lose too much time if we have to backtrack!"

"Better than losing our lives!"

"Do you think the Maker would let that happen?"

"Do you think He will protect us from our own stupidity?"

Matterhorn interrupted the squabbling, "Jewel has a point!" he yelled at the Baron. "We have no idea what's ahead!"

Jewel shielded her eyes with a hand and studied the terrain. Finding what she wanted, she scampered uphill to a towering Sitka

173

spruce. She kicked off her moccasins and climbed out of sight like a long-haired squirrel. Ten minutes later she was down with news that the narrows got much worse beyond these first rocks.

"Forget a raft!" she insisted. "I wouldn't go in there on a submarine!" She scooped up her pack and started upstream.

By the time they backtracked to the fork, darkness was already pouring over the sides of the gorge like spilled ink. They would have to wait till tomorrow to explore the other branch of the stream. With nothing to show for the day's effort but sore feet, Matterhorn, Jewel and the Baron settled for another night in the canyon. They camped in a broad meadow far enough from the water to be able to converse without yelling.

Jewel found a secluded pool where they took turns washing up. It was the coldest, and shortest, bath Matterhorn had ever taken. They fished for supper and feasted on brookies. After dinner, Matterhorn asked to see the copy of the Band of Justice. "If this is a fake, the original must really be something."

"I think the ruby is real," Jewel said. "I've never seen a gem that big. It must be worth a mint."

Matterhorn was more interested in the inscription. He compared it with the writing on the crosspiece of his Sword. Both matched the script he had seen on Ian's Flute. Assuming each Talis had been inscribed by its creator, he asked the Baron, "What's written on the Traveler's Cube?"

Aaron tossed the Talis to Matterhorn. "See if you can find it."

Returning the Band to Jewel, he held the Cube close to the fire. The alien object reminded him of a warped Rubik's cube. The twisted ball was a mosaic of flat gemstones seamlessly welded together. The surface shifted under his touch as if the ball were full of thick jelly. He had a severe case of eyestrain by the time he found the thin blue line threading among the gems.

The barely legible writing read: *I am Beginning, End, and all Between.* "The inscriptions are in English," Matterhorn noted.

"They're in whatever language the reader knows," the Baron replied.

"What aspect of the Maker does the Cube represent?" Matterhorn asked.

174

"His omnipresence. The fact that He's everywhere all at once. There's no place we can go where He isn't."

"Who had the Cube before Queen Bea gave it to you?"

"The Praetorians," the Baron replied. "They used it to open new portals."

Fingering the fantastic device, Matterhorn got a flash of inspiration. "Why not use this to go back in time and ask the Captain of the Praetorians where he hid the Talis? Better still, have him give them to you!"

Matterhorn was disappointed that the Baron didn't share his excitement. "You could even go back and warn the king of First Realm of the assassination plot!" Matterhorn added. "Bea wouldn't have to lose her father!"

The Baron shook his head. "If only it were that easy. I suggested the same ideas after my first trip with the Cube. That's when I learned that Realm time is absolute."

"There's no such thing," Matterhorn said. "Einstein showed that time is relative."

"Einstein never visited First Realm," the Baron replied. "There's no going back there, no revisiting or changing the past."

Jewel wanted to see the Cube next. "How many trips have you taken with this?"

"Quite a few," the Baron said, "but only when I can't use a fixed portal. The Cube consumes a lot of energy and takes time to recharge."

Looking at the shiny strips on their packs, Matterhorn asked, "Is it solar powered?"

"No. The power source is in its core. Probably some form of quantum energy transfer. I've been ordered not to take it apart to find out."

"Why do guys want to dismantle everything?" Jewel said.

"Curiosity."

"Isn't that what killed the cat?"

"Only cats that aren't careful."

"I'm all for curiosity," Jewel said in self-defense. "None of us would be Travelers if we weren't curious. But there's also such a thing as common sense. And taking apart one of the Ten Talis isn't sensible."

The Baron laughed. "The Talis are indestructible. The worst I could do is get it out of alignment."

"Is it worth the risk?"

"I'm trying to learn how it works. That knowledge may come in handy someday."

"Or get you stranded somewhere."

Moose Meadow

All the next morning they kept moving west until the canyon walls finally petered out. The terrain opened up and by early afternoon the Travelers found themselves on a gently sloping plateau. Warm grass engulfed their legs and Matterhorn felt like he was wading in a shallow green swamp.

A flock of birds feeding on some scraggly bushes caught Jewel's attention. She went to investigate and returned with a shirttail full of sour berries for lunch.

"Are you sure these are safe?" the Baron asked through puckered lips.

"Most black or blue berries are edible," Jewel said. "Red berries are riskier. White berries are almost always poisonous."

"What do you eat when berries aren't in season?" Matterhorn wanted to know.

"If you are desperate, you can eat the birds. All species are edible."

"Especially chicken and turkey," the Baron said. "With a side of mashed potatoes and gravy. Mmm."

A bull moose bellowed at them from a stand of trees. The hump on his back loomed up between the sides of his five-foot rack. His shoulders bulged outward from a thick neck that supported a long, ugly head.

Whistling in awe, Matterhorn said, "Now I know what 'big as a moose' means. He's enormous."

"They're the largest members of the deer family in North America," Jewel said. "A bull like that can weigh up to 1,200 pounds. He's warning us to stay out of his meadow. See how his ears are laid back and his hump is arched."

"A wide berth it is," the Baron said, getting up to leave. "I got chased by a moose once in Alaska. They're much faster than they look."

177

"They can charge at thirty miles an hour," Jewel said.

"You've had experience with them?" the Baron asked.

"Some. They're not the brightest beasts in the forest, but they're good-natured, as long as you don't come between a cow and her calf."

"Which is exactly what we did."

"Who's 'we'?" Matterhorn asked. "And what were you doing in Alaska?"

"My uncle Shaun took me there for my twelfth birthday," the Baron replied. "Sort of a 'rites of passage' deal. We spent two weeks in Denali National Park." The Baron's face brightened with the memory. "He's a fireman now but he used to be a PJ."

"Your uncle used to be a pair of pajamas?" Matterhorn teased.

"He was an Air Force Para-Jumper," the Baron said, unimpressed by Matterhorn's attempt at humor. "They're the most highly trained search and rescue forces in the world. Anyway, we had a great time. He taught me all sorts of survival skills."

"Which one did you use to escape the moose?" Jewel asked.

The Baron put both hands on the base of his spine and stretched his back. "Tell me what you would have done."

"I wouldn't have walked between a cow and her young," Jewel said.

"A white man's mistake," Aaron admitted.

"If attacked," Jewel said, "I would drop to the ground, curl into a ball and pretend to be a rock. Moose are color-blind; if you don't move they can't see you."

"I did the exact opposite," the Baron said. "I was so scared I bolted. My uncle kept his head, though. He grabbed a rotting branch off the ground and smacked it into a tree. It sounded like a gun shot and distracted the moose long enough for me to climb a tree."

It started to drizzle, so the hikers put on their ponchos. Soon real raindrops were splattering them and glazing the grass. They moved closer to the river, which didn't need this added encouragement as it picked up speed on the slight incline.

Matterhorn wiped rain and sweat from his steamy face. A half mile away he could see where the highland ended as abruptly as a table.

He could faintly hear the water barreling over the edge. "So much for following the river," he said to Jewel.

"We'll have to find another—" An ominous thunderclap cut her off as the weather took a rude turn. The rain plops hardened to pellets fired from a shotgun gray sky. The stinging barrage of hail left Matterhorn unsure of what to do. He didn't like getting blasted, but he had been taught to avoid trees during a storm.

Not far ahead a compromise presented itself in a stand of pines on the riverbank. Jewel pointed out a stunted tree on its fringe, more of a bush than a tree. Being shorter than its neighbors, it was a less likely target for lightning. Its splayed branches would provide at least some protection and she led the others toward it.

Just as they reached the pines, the earth joined the sky in objecting to these trespassers being here before their time. It gave a sudden, massive shudder and everything shifted sideways. The trees cracked heads. The river sloshed out of its bed. The humans went sprawling.

The Baron grabbed for a branch.

Matterhorn grabbed for the Baron.

Jewel grabbed for Matterhorn—and missed!

She slid down the bank and into the rushing stream as helpless as a flipped turtle.

Raging River

hen the earth stopped shaking, Matterhorn struggled to his feet and went after Jewel. The Baron had already rolled out of his pack and was sprinting downriver. He managed to shed his poncho and kick off his boots while gaining on the Princess.

Matterhorn had no idea the Baron could run so fast.

Neither did the Baron. But a friend's life was at stake. He caught up with Jewel and dove into the torrent. Ice water rushed up his nose and froze his sinuses. Wet clothes tangled around his limbs, which soon became stiff with cold. The noise of the waterfall ahead filled him with dread, but he blocked out the sound and concentrated on reaching Jewel.

By the time he got to her, she had stopped moving. He flipped her over and kept her head above water. But with his arms full, he had only his legs to propel them back to shore.

It wouldn't be enough.

He had used every ounce of energy to get this far and strained every muscle to the limit. If only Jewel could help, but she was unconscious. The turbulence pounded them. Icy fingers clawed at their skin.

While his body strained against the inevitable, the Baron's mind went strangely calm. *So this is what it feels like to die,* he thought as he sped with his nearly lifeless burden toward the end of the plateau. He would never see his mother again. Throw a baseball. Watch a movie. Joke around with Matterhorn. A quiet sadness closed over him; he prepared to meet his Maker.

Back on shore, Matterhorn charged through the buckshot rain, straining to catch up. He realized he would lose the race to the cliff. The current, swollen by snowmelt, was too swift, the edge too close. His friends were going to die and he couldn't prevent it. Fear squeezed his chest and congealed his blood to jelly.

No longer careful of his footing, he slipped on the rocks. Scrambling to his feet, he stumbled on. How could the Baron and Jewel die like this? What about their calling as Travelers? Where was the Maker when they needed Him most?

Matterhorn screamed into the dark sky, "Help us!"

Amidst the surrounding chaos, he heard a voice that had spoken to him when his own life had been in peril. It spoke the word that could save the Baron and Jewel, and Matterhorn began yelling that word with all his might!

"SARA!"

He cupped his hands around his mouth and screamed over and over as he ran.

"SARA! SARA! SARA!"

Above the din of the stream, the Baron heard Matterhorn's shouts. What was he yelling?

Sir?

Air?

Sara!

SARA!

Why hadn't he thought of her before! The Baron let go of Jewel with one hand and fished the vial from his thigh pocket. He yanked the stopper out with chattering teeth. A fine mist rose and became the most gorgeous woman he had ever seen. And what made Sara especially beautiful at this moment was her ability to do wondrous things with water.

The revived water nymph took in the situation. Although she had been in the vial for a long time, to her only a second had passed since she'd been speaking with Queen Bea on the Irish coast. Her Majesty had commanded the Baron to take Sara with him. It was a good thing for the human that he had obeyed.

Sara diverted the rushing water to one side of the Baron and Jewel while she pushed their bodies toward land. She also made the water around them bubble with oxygen to keep them afloat. By the time the half-drowned couple drew near enough to shore that Matterhorn could haul them to safety, they were less than fifty yards from the edge of the plateau.

The Baron was exhausted, but waved off any help. Jewel needed CPR, which Matterhorn applied, thankful for what he'd learned at swimming lessons.

After coughing up a chest-full of water, Jewel sputtered weakly, "What a ride." She rolled her head to the side and saw the Baron lying nearby, his clothes soaked and his skin pale. "Thanks," she mouthed.

The Baron smiled feebly and gave her a thumbs-up.

Glancing above her to where Sara hovered, Jewel blinked several times. Each time her vision refocused, Sara was still there. Befuddled, Jewel said, "I must have hit my head; I'm seeing things."

"I'm not a thing," the water nymph said. "My name is Sara. I'm from Ireland."

"How did you get here?"

"I came in this," Sara replied, holding up the vial the Baron had dropped in the river. Her bright blue eyes twinkled in her doll-like face. A gray shift draped her petite figure, leaving her arms and legs bare.

"I'll explain it to you later," Matterhorn said, patting Jewel's arm. To Sara he said, "Good to see you again. You're a lifesaver."

"That's my line," the Baron rasped. "Sara, I take back what I said about your traveling with us being a bad idea."

Sara giggled like a mountain spring. "Let's see about getting everyone dry." She dissolved upward and a few moments later the rain stopped. Ten minutes later she reappeared. "What a delightful country!" she announced. "The forest is so much thicker than in Ireland. And it's so humid!" She flung her arms wide and twirled like a ballerina.

Matterhorn moved Jewel and the Baron away from the river before going to retrieve their packs. He set up camp in a glade, but had difficulty finding dry kindling and branches to make a fire. Then he hit on the idea of asking Sara to dry the wood, which she did before sailing off to explore this new wonderland. Soon the Travelers were sharing a toasty blaze. The sun shooed away the spent clouds. Birds opened their beaks without fear of drowning, and the forest once more trilled with music.

The Baron got dry but couldn't get warm. His teeth were chattering so hard he couldn't speak.

"You need some medicine and hot food," Jewel said. She wobbled to her feet and told Matterhorn, "Tend the fire; I'm going shopping."

Special Delivery

Matterhorn did what he could to make the Baron comfortable. He put a pot of water on the fire and collected ferns to dry out for bedding.

The Baron thought about the last time he had been this sick. It was a few summers ago, which meant he was at his grandparents. His time at the ranch was the best part of every year. True, a few medical emergencies had occurred there, but the good memories far outweighed the bad.

His grandpa was the closest thing to a father in his life. His real dad had walked out when Aaron was three. Before taking early retirement and buying the 3,000-acre spread, grandpa had been an engineer. He converted one of the barns into a world-class workshop and loved to tinker with everything from computers to hay balers. It was in this magical place that Aaron discovered his love of machines and his flair for invention.

The Baron didn't have the energy to share his memories with Matterhorn. Instead he curled up and tried to sleep. He woke up when Jewel returned. She fixed a supper of tossed greens and wood sorrel soup, flavored with venison jerky from her pack. Plump blackberries did a fine impersonation of dessert. But all that the Baron managed to get down were a few sips of broth.

Jewel feared he might have pneumonia.

His shivering got worse after sundown. Even under the space blanket he couldn't keep warm. Matterhorn extended the blade of his Sword and placed it under the blanket. Recalling what he had done in Ireland, he willed the blade to heat up. He didn't understand the link between his mind and the Talis, but the longer he carried it, the more confident he felt using it.

After the Baron was settled, Matterhorn dried out his quote book and harmonica. Then he lay down and played lullabies. The music calmed his nerves, which were still raw from the day's events. If his friends had gone over the falls, what would have happened to him? He didn't know how to work the portal to get home. He wasn't even sure he could find it again.

Mother Earth hiccupped a few more times that night, but the sleepers were too exhausted to notice. The tremors were a sure sign of more trouble ahead. The Big One was coming.

Shortly after dawn, Jewel woke Matterhorn from a troubled sleep. Worry creased her pretty face. "The Baron is getting worse," she said. "This morning I thought of something that might help. If I can find some mountain mint, I can brew a fever-breaking tea."

"I'm going with you this time," Matterhorn insisted. "Four eyes are better than two."

Jewel didn't argue. She made the Baron as comfortable as possible and whispered in his ear, "We won't be gone long. We'll bring back something to make you better."

Matterhorn didn't have Jewel's skill with animals and he dreaded going into the wilderness unarmed. Yet if he took his Sword he would be depriving the Baron of its warmth.

Seeing Matterhorn's concern, the Baron said, "Take my switchwhip."

"Thanks." Matterhorn pulled the smooth stick from its narrow pocket on the Baron's leg. The press of a button on the weapon would release an eight-foot leather lash with a poisoned tip.

Jewel described what they were looking for as they left camp.

"Where did you learn about plants?" Matterhorn asked.

"My grandmother has been teaching me the medicinal benefits of plants and herbs. For hundreds of years my people have been filling our prescriptions at nature's pharmacy. Many modern drugs are based on natural remedies." To illustrate, she pointed out the scarlet fruit of devil's club and the single nodding flower of Indian pipe and described their curative powers.

Matterhorn would have been more interested in the lecture if he wasn't so focused on finding a single stalk of mountain mint, which they never did.

Jewel peeled a chunk of bark off a willow tree and said, "At least this is better than nothing."

"What's in that?"

"Salicylic acid." When Matterhorn's face remained blank, she added, "Aspirin."

Back at camp the Baron was getting worse. He had dosed himself with penicillin from his first-aid kit, but it hadn't helped. The chill burrowed deeper into his bones. He hated feeling this weak and vulnerable and his thoughts turned homeward. With a twist of his Cube he could be there. He could rest in his own bed and let his mom fill him with homemade chicken noodle soup when she got home from work.

Aaron loved the excitement of being a Traveler and of having contact with First Realm. He got an adult body and the ability to journey through time and see the world. The job used to involve observing and reporting, but since the death of the King and the undeclared war for the Talis, it had become much more dangerous. The great privilege now carried greater peril.

As in any conflict, there would be casualties. Continued service to the Maker would include hardship, perhaps even death. Hadn't he and Matterhorn come within a whisker of being killed over Ian's Flute?

His mood grew more somber, yet in the end he decided to stick it out with Matterhorn and Jewel. They wouldn't quit or slink home and neither would he. He dozed fitfully, only to be awakened by bouts of uncontrollable coughing.

Around noon, Matterhorn and Jewel returned and found the Baron asleep. Everything appeared as they had left, except for the stalks of mountain mint spread out to dry on rocks near the freshly stoked fire.

Matterhorn awoke Aaron and asked about the plants. The Baron had no idea how they had gotten there. Ignoring the mystery for the moment, Jewel put some water on to boil. Then she set about stripping the downy, lance-pointed leaves from their square stalks. She sang over the leaves as she shredded them, mingling her sweet voice with the fresh fragrance. She also thought to add some lemon balm from her supply of herbs. The Baron forced down almost a cup of the steaming liquid before falling back to sleep.

In the meantime, Matterhorn searched the campsite for clues to the identity of their unknown benefactor. Footprints, broken branches, bent ferns, disturbed moss, anything.

Nothing.

Jewel wandered off and eventually came back shaking her head. "None of the nearby wildlife seem out of sorts," she said. "We're the only strangers that have raised their curiosity."

Over a late lunch they traded theories. "Someone knew the exact plant we needed and where to find it," Matterhorn pointed out. "But there aren't any humans around yet. So that only leaves—"

Leap of Faith

"So the Bigfoot know we're here," Matterhorn said to Jewel as he fidgeted with the pile of kindling at his feet. "Does that mean they know what we're after?"

"Maybe," she replied. She was busy grinding the willow bark to red powder. "Some tribes like the Hopi and the Lakota believe Sasquatch have psychic powers. They think they have medicine that makes them invisible when they want to be. The Chinook believe Sasquatch are just physical beings like humans and animals."

As the day wore on, the mint tea laced with aspirin worked its herbal magic. The Baron's eyes became more blue than gray and his fever broke. He was awake and alert for supper, and Matterhorn brought him up to speed while they ate.

"It's obvious the Sasquatch know where we are," Aaron agreed. "But they don't want us to know where they are. There's nothing to do but keep searching for the city." To Jewel he said, "What else can you tell us about the place from the legends?"

"The entrance is supposed to be shrouded in a rainbow and guarded by the god of thunder."

"That's rather mysterious."

Jewel shrugged. "It's the best I can do. Now drink your tea and be quiet. Save your strength for tomorrow; you'll need it. We have to get moving before the next earthquake hits."

"What kind of bedside manner is that?" the Baron said. He emptied his mug and lay back down.

The next thing he knew it was bright blue morning. Sunshine filled the uncluttered sky and bleached the day moon's already pale face. Moss on white birch and weeping willows made them look like old women draped in wet shawls.

189

The Baron's melancholy and chill had gone and he felt 80 percent better. Time to get on with the task of finding the Talis. He sat up and scratched his stubble.

"You're starting to look like your old self," Matterhorn said from across the fire. "I guess some things can't be helped." Lofting the switchwhip to the Baron, he added, "Time to trade back." He missed his Sword.

After a breakfast of fruit and nuts, the trio walked the short distance to the edge of the plateau. The forest grew thin as a receding hairline as Jewel led them onto a massive forehead of bare granite. Eight hundred feet below, she and the Baron saw the oval pool into which the waterfall splattered.

Matterhorn had no interest in the view. He was frantically thinking of how to get off this high ground.

"It's awesome!" Jewel yelled at the Baron over the thunderous noise.

The Baron didn't answer. He was staring down at the colorful halo the sun painted on the spray above the large pool. He had never seen a round rainbow before. He signaled Jewel and they rejoined Matterhorn a safe distance from the cliff.

"A rainbow and thunder," the Baron said. "I think we've found the front door to Sasquatch City. And I have just the thing to get us down off the roof." He pulled two silk bundles from his gear and handed one to Jewel. "I knew these would come in handy."

"You're crazy!" Matterhorn cried, taking a few steps backward.

"Are we high enough?" Jewel asked casually as she studied the super lightweight harness.

"High enough!" Matterhorn was beside himself. "You're crazy, too! How can you hang your life by a few threads of silk? My pajamas weigh more than these parachutes!"

"I'm trusting in more than the equipment," Jewel said. "The Maker will get us down."

"Gravity will get us down!" Matterhorn cried. "It's the landing that concerns me!"

"Don't worry," the Baron tried to assure him. "You'll be fine."

His breezy confidence irked Matterhorn. "How do you know? Have you ever done this before?"

"Yes."

That caught Matterhorn by surprise. "Your mom lets you jump off cliffs?" he said in disbelief.

"She doesn't know I jump off cliffs, or scuba dive, or snow camp. She doesn't know I've had survival training or search-and-rescue experience."

"How could she not know?"

The Baron cast an impatient look at Matterhorn as if the answer were obvious. "Because I do them when traveling, which is a secret occupation. I can't exactly get her to sign a permission slip."

Matterhorn took out his own parachute and fingered the harness straps. "Where'd you get this fancy gear?" he asked.

"Are you curious or just stalling?"

"Both," Matterhorn admitted.

"Tell you what," Aaron said in a sympathetic tone, "I'll explain it to you tonight. Right now we need to get down from here." A slight tremor just then emphasized his point. Who knew how much longer they had before the promised earthquake would make their mission impossible?

Matterhorn spread his feet to keep balance. The Baron was right. They had to do something. Any way off this plateau would be torturous. Might as well get it over with. "If we gotta jump, we gotta jump," he concluded. "Show me how this rig works."

"Shift your pack to the front and put your harness on like so," the Baron began his show-and-tell explanation. "Make sure the straps are tight. This is your pilot chute. Hold it in your hand and release it as soon as you clear the cliff. It will pull out your main chute, which will blossom into two hundred square feet of silk. These are your brake lines; make sure they stay outside the keeper rings on the risers . . .."

The instructions lasted a few more minutes and ended with a warning. "The most important thing is to jump far enough from the ledge so you don't hit anything on the way down. You'll be dropping at seventeen feet per second, so you'll have about a fifty-second ride." Showing them once more how to steer by pulling the guidelines, the

Baron concluded by saying, "Aim for the water. It will feel better than landing on top of a tree."

"Fifty seconds is way too long," Matterhorn lamented. "Would it go faster if I put rocks in my pocket?"

The Baron's laugh resounded above the falls. "Your pack provides plenty of extra weight. Release your harness when you hit the water so you don't get tangled in the lines. If you need to, you can inflate your pack lining to keep from sinking." He pointed to the tab on the pack's yellow backing.

"Are you two done yapping?" Jewel said. "This eagle's ready to soar!"

The phrase reminded Matterhorn that mother eagles pushed their young out when the time came to leave the nest. No practice runs. No safety nets. No do-overs. Eaglets had to fly or die. He had the same options, only he felt more like a chicken than an eagle.

Jewel retreated several yards. When the Baron gave her a thumbs-up, she zoomed toward the cliff with a yell that would have made Geronimo proud, even though he was an Apache and she was a Chinook.

"You're next," the Baron said. "Remember that you carry the Sword of Truth. It will protect you."

Matterhorn decided that was enough truth on which to take a leap of faith. He checked his harness while walking to where Jewel had begun her takeoff. Clutching his pilot chute in one white-knuckled hand, he gave the okay signal with the other.

Without another thought Matterhorn began pumping his strong legs toward open sky. No matter how fast they churned they couldn't keep up with his speeding heart. As he shot past the Baron and long-jumped into space he heard, "Serve well!"

To which he shouted with fervent hope, "Serve loooooooooong!"

Water Landing

Matterhorn wanted to close his eyes during his descent, but they were frozen open in fear and wonder. As he sailed over the edge, the wet updraft slapped him in the face and ripped the pilot chute from his grasp. A few seconds later, the main chute jerked him upright with a force that threatened to dislocate his shoulders.

What the Baron saw from the ledge—and what he never mentioned afterward—was how close Matterhorn had come to whacking his head on an outcrop before the parachute opened. The silk actually brushed the rock, but slid off without catching or tearing.

Hanging suspended in space, Matterhorn took his first breath since the jump—a deep, ragged gasp. The spray from the falls drenched him. It felt like he was swimming to earth instead of falling. Between his feet he saw Jewel's yellow-and-red canopy coasting toward the pool. Circles of green surrounded the blue bulls-eye, which grew larger as he watched. He remembered his guidelines and pulled the left one, then the right, struggling to keep sight of Jewel.

He heard the Baron's exuberant laughter from somewhere overhead. The guy was having way too much fun. Matterhorn had to admit the feeling of floating was exhilarating. The drag on his canopy offset the relentless tug of gravity just enough to create a sense of serenity. He even imagined doing this again—in another thousand years or so.

The leap off the cliff hadn't killed him. The opening of the chute hadn't torn his arms off. That left him free to worry about the splashdown. He focused on Jewel and tried to copy her movements. At the last second she jerked hard on the right side of her canopy and swerved to a stand-up landing on a slim ribbon of ground by the pool.

"Sweet move!" Matterhorn yelled down. He was still trying to figure out how to duplicate it when he hit the water. The impact stunned him from feet to brain. His pack pulled him under and he got snarled in the guide-lines as the turbulence twisted him round and round. Precious seconds struggled by, each one taking a piece of his life. He couldn't wiggle free of his harness and his petrified fingers couldn't find the tab on his pack. He gritted his teeth and prepared to suck air through them as if they were gills.

I can't die, he reminded himself. Not while I have the Sword of Truth on me. But did he still have it, or had it been torn off in this maelstrom? If the Sword was lost, could he still count on being saved? His survival might depend as much on the Baron's scritch pad as on the Maker's Sword.

Neither, it turned out, failed him. The hilt was still on his hip. He yanked it loose, extended the blade halfway and slashed at the tangled lines. The spot of yellow on the edge of his vision turned out to be the tab on the pack liner. He managed to pull it with the last of his fleeting strength. The yellow bladder inflated and hauled him to the surface.

After several gulps of air, Matterhorn expected the grayness in his vision to clear. It didn't. He was floating in a murky world whose only light seeped through a wall of water to his left.

He had landed in broad daylight in front of the falls, but had risen in the gloom behind them. When his eyes adjusted, he could make out a stone anteroom about ten feet high, forty feet long, and twenty feet across. Roots grew down from the ceiling like albino serpents. The walls were slimed with mucus-green moss and lichen. Dog-paddling to the edge, Matterhorn crawled out onto the chamber's stone floor. He heated his Sword and huddled over it in an attempt to get warm.

On the opposite side of the waterfall the Baron had landed next to Jewel. Together they looked for the silk lily pad of Matterhorn's parachute.

"There!" Jewel yelled as the blue fabric bubbled up from beneath the falls.

Still feeling the effects of the pneumonia, the Baron responded sluggishly. Jewel swam out and grabbed the chute and Aaron helped drag it to shore. It was remarkably light.

Too light.

"Something's wrong!" the Baron cried, pulling the parachute hand over hand until he held the severed lines. He scoured the frothing pool for signs of the yellow airbag or Matterhorn's red hair. Seeing nothing, he began to slip off his pack to go in after his friend when Jewel stopped him. She grabbed his shoulders and pushed him toward the bank.

"You're too weak!" she shouted over the din of crashing water. "If the undertow has Matterhorn, you'll never be able to pry him loose! Where's Sara?"

The water nymph had been exploring her new surroundings since being freed from the vial the day before. She had checked on the humans occasionally and had been close by when they jumped from the cliff. On a whim she had decided to follow them down. She needed no artificial help, but simply dove into the stream and tumbled over the edge like a kid on a water slide. Then she floated back to the top in the mist and cascaded down again.

She was so busy playing that she never heard the frantic calls for help.

Open Sesame

The Baron was the first to notice the slivers of unnatural light leaking around both sides of the waterfall. It dawned on him that the brilliance could only be coming from one source—the Sword of Truth. He clutched Jewel's arm and shouted, "Matterhorn's behind the falls!"

"I see it!" Jewel cried. "How do we get back there?"

"We'll find a way!" The Baron didn't take time to repack his chute, but shucked out of it and let it float away. Jewel did likewise. This broke one of the rules of traveling—you pack it in, you pack it out—but they had no choice. The fabric would rot long before humans reached this area anyway. Still, he might have some explaining to do if the Queen found out. He began picking his way around the pool's rocky lip.

Jewel took off her moccasins and followed. Years of running barefoot through the woods had hardened her feet. This way she could use her toes to grip the slimy stones. "I saw no signs of a hidden city on the way down!" she hollered as they approached the falls. "Did you?"

"No! But Matterhorn may have stumbled onto what we're looking for!" Pointing ahead he yelled, "What a great place to hide a secret entrance!" A narrow rock ledge cut between a wall of granite and a wall of water. The Baron and Jewel squeezed through the slit and into the Sword-lit cavity.

"I thought you said to land in the water!" Matterhorn yelled at his friends. He sat Indian-style at the far end of the room, the glow of his blade drenching the chamber. "Am I the only one who knows how to follow instructions?"

"I also told you to be careful!" the Baron shouted back. "What about that part?"

"Jumping wasn't my idea in the first place!"

"Stop arguing you two!" Jewel scolded with a smile. She reached Matterhorn first and asked, "Is anything broken?"

"I don't think so!"

Before Aaron could join them, Sara materialized next to him. "You three can't seem to stay out of the water!" she said in her lilting voice. She had finished frolicking and decided to check on the solid-bodies. Since her unplanned appearance at the river, she had changed her dull gray shift into a silvery sundress. As was her custom, she accented her outfit with local gems. Her jewelry for today—pinky ring, bracelet, pendant, earrings, and ankle bracelet—featured brilliant orange red garnets.

The reunited adventurers sat in a circle and discussed their situation. "The entrance to the city has to be in here somewhere!" the Baron shouted over the water's roar. "Mind if I use this?" He reached for the Sword.

Matterhorn handed over the Talis and watched the Baron approach the back wall. He began scrambling through the wet greenery until the bright light and sudden commotion dislodged a family of bats. The leathery creatures swooped away in a huff, startling the human intruders. The Baron slipped and stuck out his hand to keep from smashing his face into the rocks.

His hand disappeared into the foliage, followed by his arm, and then his whole body.

The curtain of secrecy had been parted.

Aaron's smiling face popped out a moment later draped in a wig of soggy green dreadlocks. "Spelunking, anyone!" he beamed.

They cleared the camouflage from the cave opening, which turned out to be a ten-foot semicircle that reminded Matterhorn of a giant cartoon mouse hole. The interior was blacker than day-old coffee.

"Let's get inside!" the Baron yelled.

Jewel balked at the suggestion. "Now it's my turn to be scared! Do we have to go in there! It looks like a narrow grave! I can't stand closed-in places!"

"You can do it, Jewel!" the Baron encouraged. "The hidden city might be at the other end of this tunnel."

So in she went, heart beating in her throat and hands shaking in her pockets.

When they were far enough underground to dampen the water noise, the Baron called a halt. He took three baseball caps from his pack-of-plenty, switching one for his red corduroy cap and giving the others to Matterhorn and Jewel. Silver foil lined the inside of each cap. A thin piece of unbreakable glass about two inches in diameter perched above the bills.

The disc on the Baron's cap began to glow as he explained the headgear. "Most of our body heat radiates out of our heads. That's why hats help keep us warm. But these babies aren't designed for warmth. The lining captures one form of energy—heat—and converts it to another form—light."

Matterhorn looked at the Baron's light, which wasn't getting any brighter. "You're a pretty cool head," he quipped. "Are you sure your hat isn't reading brain wave activity?"

"Very funny. I know the lumens aren't much; that's why we also have these." The Baron flipped a thin plastic visor down from underneath the bill of his cap. Matterhorn reached up and flipped his own visor. Everything became brighter in a greenish sort of way.

"I added night vision visors to magnify ambient light," the Baron said.

"That helps a lot," Jewel said, relieved the passage was larger than it had felt in the stifling darkness. Still, she hated being underground.

"And here's something to make it easier for us to keep tabs on one another." The Baron handed out glowing yellow patches. "Put these reflectors on the heels of your shoes. There's a patch of the same material on the back of our caps. Seeing the water nymph behind Jewel he said, "Sorry, Sara, I only brought three caps."

"I can see fine. Besides, I don't produce any body heat."

"Will you be all right down here?" the Baron asked.

"It may be hard to stay with you if the air gets drier," she said.

"Maybe you should return to the vial. Then we'll be sure not to lose you."

"All right," Sara agreed, "if you promise to let me out as soon as you can. I don't want to miss anything."

199

"I promise."

Sara's jewelry clattered to the floor when she atomized into the vial.

Jewel adjusted her cap and tried to stop shivering. Matterhorn sympathized with her, having been a recent victim of his own phobia. Squeezing her shoulder he said, "Since you got to be first off the cliff, I'll go first in the cave."

With that, he led the trio forward and down. The blade of his Sword gave enough light to make the visors unnecessary. An eerie stillness replaced the clamor of the falls as they moved under the plateau they had jumped from a half-hour ago.

They had no way of knowing this would be a one-way trip.

Spelunker's Paradise

Aaron the Baron was the only one with much spelunking experience. Running his hand along the tunnel's ebony sides he said, "Feel these walls. We're in a lava tube. Flowing lava can develop a shell of cooled magma. The molten rock keeps moving underneath and leaves behind a hollow tube."

"I've been in a lava tube before," Matterhorn said with a shiver. "The Ape Cave near Mount St. Helens. It's the second longest tube in the world." What he felt too embarrassed to add was that he had wandered away from his family and gotten hopelessly lost in the lower cave. It wasn't the first time his curiosity had led him into danger, but it was the scariest. When his flashlight died of exhaustion, the darkness was so thick and terrible that he had to close his eyes for a more manageable shade of black. He might still be down there if not for a kind elderly couple with a lantern who showed him the way out.

"Knowing how this cave was formed won't tell us where it goes," the Baron said. "We'll have to discover that for ourselves."

"Elementary my dear Watson," Matterhorn said in a poor British accent. "All we have to do is keep going straight." He pointed with his Sword, thankful its light wasn't dependent on batteries. But going straight was only possible for five more minutes. Then the passage split in two.

"Now which way?" Jewel wondered out loud.

Matterhorn held up his index finger and replied, "As Yogi Berra once said, 'When you come to a fork in the road, take it.'"

The Baron rolled his eyes. "Sherlock Holmes, Yogi Berra. Who's next, Yoda?" He turned to Jewel and asked, "Anything in the legends about this?"

She shook her head.

He took a small LED light from his pocket and shone its laser-like beam down one branch of the tunnel, then the other. In both cases the light seemed to go on forever. "Any ideas?"

"I picked the wrong way on the river," Jewel said. "You choose."

"Since you picked wrong," the Baron said, "I'll pick right." He produced a piece of chalk and drew a large arrow on the wall pointing back to the entrance. "This will help us find our way out. Remember the first rule of spelunking."

"Which is?" Matterhorn asked.

"Never go into a cave," Jewel said with an uneasy laugh.

"Exit takes more effort than entry," the Baron corrected. "Good spelunkers always plan with their return in mind."

"I've a mind to return to the surface right now," Jewel said. "You can come get me when you find the Sasquatch."

"We need to stay together," the Baron said. "Don't worry, we won't let anything happen to you." He glanced at Matterhorn who nodded his assurance before leading the way into what he hoped was the longest leg of this stone wishbone.

After a few hundred yards, Matterhorn questioned their choice as a foul breeze wafted by. He grimaced and pinched his nose shut with his fingers. "What's that smell?"

"I don't know," Jewel said, sniffing the rancid air. "I've smelled it since we started this way. And it's getting stronger. Don't tell me you're just noticing it?"

"Of course not," Matterhorn fibbed to protect his ego. A sizzling jolt reminded him why the Talis he carried was called the Sword of Truth. He yelped and dropped it like a hot poker. He tucked his smarting hand into his armpit and did the pain dance.

The Baron's laughter filled the tunnel.

Jewel clicked her tongue at the Baron and asked Matterhorn if he was okay.

"I'm just a slow learner," Matterhorn mumbled as he rubbed his sore palm. The Sword remained lit so he had no trouble finding it. He gingerly picked it up with his left hand and started forward again.

"I didn't notice the smell before," he said to Jewel, "but I'm picking it up now. If it becomes any more obnoxious I say we go back and take the other tunnel. This might be the way to the latrine."

The Baron and Matterhorn adjusted to the catacomb-like atmosphere around them while Jewel grew more agitated. At least the passage was roomy as far as caves go. Jagged lava stalactites stabbed down into the passage, but none far enough to furrow their bobbing brows. Stubby stalagmites jabbed from the floor in odd places, making the cave an obstacle course.

The one bright spot for Jewel was the strange iridescence now surrounding her. It was as if the passage had been sprayed with liquid moonlight. "Matterhorn, could you turn off your Sword?" she asked.

Matterhorn obliged. When their eyes adjusted to the dim light of their headlamps, the walls came alive with multicolored glitter.

"It's so pretty," Jewel whispered. She reached toward the luminescence. "What is it?"

The Baron grabbed her arm. "This beautiful stuff goes by an ugly name. It's called cave slime. It's a form of light reflecting bacteria. If you touch it, you'll kill it."

"I don't want to do that," she said, retracting her hand.

"I've been to some remote places," the Baron said, "and I'm always amazed at how the Maker decorates His creation. Even the parts no one sees."

The Travelers admired the view and enjoyed a snack of energy bars and water before pressing on. Matterhorn noticed that the shinier the walls got, the more slanted the floor became. No more forks or side passages came along to confuse them. They kept up a good pace for the next twenty minutes. Still, a growing unease crept over them as they burrowed downward like blind earthworms. This unease bloomed into full panic when the cave began jumping up, down, and sideways.

Another quake! This one was more powerful than anything they'd experienced topside. Being aboveground during an earthquake had been frightening. Being underground was absolutely terrifying!

The violent motion rolled the trekkers into a human cue ball that ricocheted down the tunnel, bouncing off stalagmites in a dangerous game of bumper pool. The jumble of arms and legs finally smacked into a solid wall and shattered into three dazed and bruised pieces.

Matterhorn felt the rocks, but not the pain, as he tumbled in the dark. He felt every twist and turn in surreal motion, an elbow jabbing into his left eye, his foot catching in someone's pack straps, the surround-sound of falling stones.

He lost the Sword almost immediately.

Then he lost consciousness.

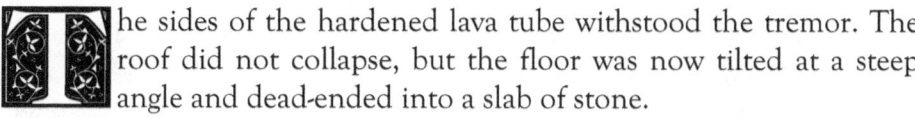

Tunnel of Doom

he sides of the hardened lava tube withstood the tremor. The roof did not collapse, but the floor was now tilted at a steep angle and dead-ended into a slab of stone.

"Whew!" the Baron grunted. He struggled to sit up. "Everyone okay?"

Jewel moaned. "You mean other than feeling like I fell down a flight of stairs?"

"On top of me most of the way," wheezed Matterhorn from between a rock and a hard place. He was still in shock from the fall; that's why he didn't notice the pain until he tried to push himself off the floor. The agony that screamed up his arm was different from the sting of the Sword. Even before he saw the awkward angle of his wrist he knew his arm was broken.

Matterhorn had a high pain threshold. He'd taken his share of hits in kendo. The bamboo shinai raised nasty welts, even through the protective body armor. Once, he broke his index finger in a soccer match while stopping a penalty kick. He refused to let the coach pull him and played the rest of the game without allowing a single goal.

He'd cracked a rib bodysurfing in the ocean.

He'd even been stabbed in the leg by a would-be killer.

But this pain was fiercer than all those injuries. Matterhorn rode the wave of nausea to the black edge of consciousness and hovered there.

Realizing something was wrong, Jewel crawled to Matterhorn's side. Her adept fingers soon found the problem in the dim glow of her headlight. "His arm is broken," she told the Baron as she helped Matterhorn sit up.

The Baron began scrounging in his pack for his first-aid kit. He had lost his cap in the tumble and had to feel his way to the square plastic box. Inside he found the pain pills left over from when he'd fractured his collarbone. Stumbling over to the two haloed figures, he said to Matterhorn, "Take these." To Jewel he said under his breath, "We'll have to set the bones. At least it's not his sword arm."

"What do we do now?" she whispered back with a calmness she didn't feel. "I don't want to die down here."

"We've made it this far. The Maker will see us through."

The Big Shaker had broken more than Matterhorn's arm. It had also split the floor of the cavern behind the falls. Water gushed into the cave and down its slanted throat much faster than the Travelers had covered the distance. The first wave soon splashed into the stranded spelunkers.

"The quake must have sprung a leak in the pool!" the Baron shouted when the frigid water hit.

Jewel stared at the stone wall that blocked their path. "Can we make it back the way we came?"

Aaron helped Matterhorn to his feet and answered, "No way. The water's coming too fast."

"I don't suppose you brought any scuba gear," Matterhorn said.

The Baron's eyes brightened. "I've got something better." He reached in his pocket for Sara's vial.

"I can't be gone for a second without you getting into trouble," the water nymph said when she grasped the situation. She was glad to be able to save the day—again—by quickly creating an ice barrier to stop the flow.

This deliverance would last only as long as their air supply, Matterhorn realized. He slumped against the wall and slid to the floor. The water lapped at his chest. The pain in his arm throbbed with every heartbeat and he tried to slow the one to ease the other.

Jewel couldn't stop shaking. She rubbed her arms and asked Sara, "Is there any way you can get us out of here?"

"That will take some doing if the cave is flooded," she replied. "Do you want me to go check?"

"No!" the three humans shouted. They knew if the ice broke while Sara was gone they would be goners. Sweeping the area with her headlamp, Jewel soon found the Baron's cap hooked on a stalagmite. A

206

short distance away she located Matterhorn's Sword, hilt-deep in a pile of debris. She brought it to him and he increased its light with a thought.

The Travelers silently surveyed their stone tomb.

Matterhorn fought for clarity through the pain and the pills. He couldn't just sit here waiting for death. He leaned his head against the stone and stared upward. It dawned on him that this wall was different from the others, more ragged and edgy. He ran his fingers over the rough surface. There was no cave slime on it.

With difficulty he stood, turned and raised his Sword higher. The wall was only eight feet high and stopped well short of the roof. But that wasn't the amazing part. A broad brown face beamed down on him with a Cheshire cat grin.

"G'day mates. Need a lift?"

Break Point

The Baron snapped his head upward at the sound of the Australian accent. He realized at once what had happened. The quake had caused this section of the passage to break and drop below the rest of the tunnel. The ledge above them was actually the cave floor; and there on its lip squatted Nate the Great.

"How did you get here?" the Baron burst out.

"Let's get you out of there," Nate said, extending a hand. "Then we'll talk. Wounded and sheilas first."

The Baron and Jewel managed to get Matterhorn partway up the wall. Nate grabbed Matterhorn's good arm and helped him the rest of the way. Next came the Princess, the packs, and the Baron, who hugged Nate like a long lost brother. The two men, however, could not have been more different.

Aaron's face was angular, stubble-chinned, and white. Nate's was round, brown, and fringed with wiry black hair. His sideburns and beard were the same length as the steel-wool hair on his head. Between his eyebrows and moustache was a flat nose with flared nostrils. His dark eyes seemed large, as did his ears, but only by Western standards.

Born in the bush of central Australia, Nate was large for an Aboriginal, standing just under six feet and weighing just over 180 pounds. He had a short neck, wide shoulders, long arms, deep chest, and thin legs compared to his upper body. His physique was apparent because he wore khaki shorts and a tank top. There was a kangaroo-skin bum bag resting in the small of his back and a dingo-hide belt around his waist from which dangled various pouches. A short boomerang carved from mulga wood nestled against his left hip. He had on a most unusual pair of sandals. They were pure gold with emerald-studded soles. The green gems sparkled against the black floor.

"Bonzer trick with the ice," Nate said to Sara as she floated up beside them. He obviously knew who and what she was.

"Thanks," she replied.

"This crew's kept you busy," Nate chuckled.

The Baron frowned. "How do you know that?"

"Been following you since the portal, mate. Easy as tracking a herd of turtles."

"Who are you?" Matterhorn asked. "How did you get down here?"

"There's an alcove ahead," Nate said. "Let's yak there."

In a few minutes the five were sitting around a lighted can of paraffin at a wide spot in the tunnel. Once settled, the Baron introduced Nate the Great and Matterhorn to one another. Jewel already knew the bushman. "What were you saying about following us from the portal?" the Baron asked.

"You and the dunny rats on your tail," Nate said.

"Dunny rats?" Matterhorn asked.

"Vermin. Two of them have been stepping on your shadows since you got here. I've been stepping on theirs." Nate inspected Matterhorn's arm as he spoke.

"I have a very good sense for people and animals," Jewel said. "I didn't detect them."

"The creatures look like Bigfoot but aren't."

"Careful!" Matterhorn cried.

"How do you know they aren't Sasquatch?" the Baron wanted to know.

"Disguises are good," Nate said, tickling Matterhorn's palm and tugging each finger. "Found a piece of fur where one scratched against a tree. It's genuine, but they're not."

"Have you seen Bigfoot before?" Jewel asked.

Nate nodded and rested his other hand just below Matterhorn's elbow.

"What's not right about these two?" she pressed.

"They don't stink," Nate said. Then, without warning he tightened his grip and yanked on Matterhorn's hand.

Matterhorn screamed in pain at this unexpected assault.

"Steady, mate," Nate soothed, not loosening his hold. "That break needed to be set. Best get it over with."

"You could've warned me!"

The bushman gave Matterhorn a toothy grin. "You would've tensed up like a tick on a dingo."

Jewel bent forward to study the arm. "He's right," she told Matterhorn. "The bones are back together. Now you can heal."

The Baron inflated the air splint from the first-aid kit and eased it onto Matterhorn's forearm. "This will keep the break immobile," he said.

Jewel found a yellow bandana in her pack and made a sling.

The stab of agony was gone, replaced by a pulsing, yet bearable, ache. What Nate had done might have been for the best, but Matterhorn determined to keep a close eye on this frizzy-haired wild man.

Returning to the conversation that had been so rudely interrupted, the Baron asked, "What did you mean when you said the Sasquatch don't stink?"

"Everything has its own scent," Nate explained as patiently as a tour guide instructing eager tourists. "I could've tracked your smell with my eyes closed."

The Baron sniffed his armpit. "We've been in the water so much we haven't had a chance to get ripe."

"Any creature with body heat gives off an aroma," Nate said. "Humans smell different from dogs, which smell different from wolves. Bigfoot have their own scent."

Jewel knew what Nate meant. Her sense of smell was more acute than Matterhorn's or the Baron's. "Is that what we've smelled in the cave?"

Nate nodded. "Wait till you get close to a Bigfoot. Bigstink's more like it. A mix between BO and methane. One Bigfoot puts out more gas than a herd of cattle."

"And the creatures following us don't smell right?" the Baron said.

"Don't smell at all," Nate replied.

"If they're not Bigfoot, what are they?"

"Wraiths in disguise," Matterhorn said with a flash of insight. "They must have followed the Queen."

Dark Spirits

Wraiths," Jewel said with a start. "That's what Queen Bea was afraid of."

The Baron nodded. "We ran into one on our last trip. Matterhorn killed it."

"The Sword killed it," Matterhorn corrected.

"What are wraiths?" Sara asked.

"This is as good a time as any for a background briefing," the Baron said. Having spent more time in First Realm, he knew more about the wraiths than the others. "There is a Hall of Portals where Queen Bea is from. The Hall is called the Propylon and those who serve there are known as Praetorians. They are the elite Guardians of the portals used for time-space travel."

Sara, who had never been off-world before, nodded. To a creature like her, nothing seemed unbelievable.

"As with all moral beings," the Baron continued, "Praetorians have a choice to obey or disobey their calling. In the long history of First Realm, a few have chosen to use their high position for selfish and evil purposes. When these renegades are discovered, they are stripped of their powers and exiled. They become wraiths of their former selves, but are still very formidable. They hate the Maker and all who serve Him. They have sided with those who killed Queen Bea's father."

Sara wanted to know more, but Jewel whispered, "I'll tell you what happened later."

"Praetorians don't time-travel, except for their captain," the Baron said. "It's too risky. But wraiths seem willing to take the chance in coming to Earth."

"How come the one in Ireland looked human," Matterhorn asked, "while the two Nate has been tracking look like Sasquatch?"

"Apparently they can take any form they want when they travel. That will make them as hard to find as they are to kill."

Matterhorn shivered as he recalled his battle with the wraith. Now two more such creatures were hunting them. If Nate had managed to find the Travelers, so could these dark spirits.

But wait a minute. How had the bushman gotten here?

"Followed you to the edge of the plateau," Nate answered when asked. "Came down last night to have a look about."

"Where's your parachute?" Matterhorn wondered.

"Don't have one."

"Then how'd you manage?"

"Trade secret."

The Baron brought the discussion back to the present. "Any signs of the Sasquatch-wraiths down here yet?"

"No. Checked both arms of the Y you passed. They lead to the same place."

"Where's that?"

"A hollow volcano that puked its guts out eons ago. That's where the Bigfoot live. Wouldn't call it a city, though. More like a couple of villages." Turning to Sara, he said, "You blocked the water in this tunnel, but there's nothing keeping it out of the other branch. The flooding will cause problems for the Bigfoot."

"Are the villages in danger?" Jewel asked in alarm.

"For certain. Unless there's an outlet on the other side of the mountain."

"And if there isn't?"

Nate patted his neck. "The Bigfoot better grow gills in a hurry."

Matterhorn lumbered to his feet and stretched. His joints were stiffening and he wanted to get moving before he seized up altogether. Besides his broken arm, his right ankle was slightly sprained and he could feel a garden of colorful bruises blossoming on his backside. He noticed the Baron rubbing his left knee. Only Jewel seemed none the worse for their tumble. "Since we don't have gills ourselves," he said, "we'd better find the Band of Justice before this mountain becomes an indoor swimming pool."

"You have the light," Aaron said. "You have the lead."

Sara excused herself to go back and strengthen the ice wall she had hastily made.

Matterhorn limped into the unknown with Jewel glued to his side. The Baron fell in step next to Nate. "I haven't had a chance to thank you for bringing the mountain mint to camp yesterday. It really helped."

"You're not welcome."

"Why not?"

"Didn't bring it."

"Then who did?"

Nate said nothing.

The Baron finally figured it out. "You mean it was the bogus Bigfoot? Why would they do that? They want to destroy us, not help us."

"They need you to find the Band of Justice," Nate pointed out. "You need to be alive to do that. They're smart enough to know real Bigfoot won't come within a hundred yards of them because—"

"I know," the Baron interrupted. "They don't stink right."

"They'll keep their distance until you get what you came for, then they'll take it from you."

"Do you know where they are?"

"No."

From the front of the strung-out group Matterhorn tried hard to listen backwards. He caught most of what was being said, including the part about not knowing where the wraiths were. He spoke over his shoulder to the Baron. "How do you think the dark spirits followed the Queen?"

"I have no clue."

The party lapsed into an eerie silence. They trekked deeper into the mountain, picking their way around quake debris. Several minutes later Matterhorn turned to do a head check. Jewel's hat glowed a few yards in front of the Baron's, followed by—darkness.

Nate the Great had disappeared!

Green Giants

Matterhorn stopped and sucked in a breath to shout for Nate, but the Baron put a finger to his lips. "No sense warning the Sasquatch we're coming. Don't worry about Nate. He knows what he's doing."

"Did anybody hear him slip away?" Jewel quizzed. "Where could he have gone?"

Not far, it turned out.

A hundred yards back, Nate had scurried up the wall and wedged himself between two stalactites. Pulling his legs up, he covered his shirt and shorts with dark shin-skin. He pointed his toes down and lowered his forehead to his knees so that his black hair faced forward instead of the whites of his eyes, which reflected light. He blended into the dark and became invisible in the span of four heartbeats.

For him that meant six seconds.

Nate was great at disappearing when he wanted to. He preferred to work from the shadows. That Sword gave off too much light; it hampered his night vision. The others made too much noise. And in this closed space their scents clogged his ability to smell danger.

When the others started forward again, Matterhorn said to the Baron, "That guy must be part ninja."

"The ninjas were assassins," the Baron said. "They used darkness as a cloak for evil. Nate serves the light."

"Now that you mention light," Jewel interjected, "is that what I see ahead?" She drew their attention to a faint oval down the passageway. Matterhorn retracted his blade so they could see better. They slunk through the widening tunnel and soon arrived at the hollow heart of the prehistoric volcano.

An immense cavern opened before them, suffused with soft light from ragged skylights punched into the steepled roof hundreds of feet above. The sunshine nourished a wild variety of plants, shrubs, and stunted trees that covered the floor and crowded partway up the insides of the mountain.

"It's like an indoor forest," Matterhorn gasped.

"It's divine," Jewel said as somewhere in the distance a choir of birds warmed up for the evening service. She noticed pools of rainwater collected in natural stone basins under the skylights. "Sara will love this place."

In the middle of the chamber, beneath open sky, a small lake filled the throat of the once fire-breathing beast. The Baron pointed up and said, "Those holes were steam vents at one time. The giant one in the center was the main blowhole. And look at all the stuff growing in here. Plenty of sunshine and water, cooled lava to insulate the walls. It's like a giant nursery!"

"If this is a giant nursery," Jewel said with a gesture, "then those must be the giant gardeners."

A group of tall creatures stood by a stream that poured from a second tunnel a hundred yards away and gushed toward the lake.

"A bunch of Bigfoot," Matterhorn said. "And we're the first humans to see them." The manlike beasts were similar to the mental picture he had of the Sasquatch—except for one contrary detail. He checked to make sure his night-vision visor was up. "Is it the light in here," he said, "or are those things green?"

"They look green to me," Aaron said.

The thick hair on the Bigfoot reminded Matterhorn of pine needles. It carpeted everything but their palms and faces, which were wide and ape-like. The Bigfoot had sloped brows, flattened noses, and fleshy jowls. Their large eyes glowed red with reflected light, showing them to be nocturnal creatures. Below the neck they were barrel-chested and slump-shouldered. Their arms seemed too long for their bodies, their legs too short. The biggest creature stood over eight feet tall, the shortest was around seven feet. The smaller ones were obviously female. The group was bristling with gestures and grunts. They seemed to be arguing about the water now pouring into their private lake.

"That tunnel must be where the other branch of the cave comes out," Matterhorn said. "We won't be going back through the waterfall entrance. I hope there's another exit."

Bigfoot have big ears and one of the females heard the newcomers talking. She spotted the humans and squealed.

Voices froze in mid-grunt.

Heads turned like turrets.

Red-laser eyes locked on targets.

Not sure what to do, Matterhorn waved a greeting with his good arm. "Yell-O!"

One of the larger males bent down and picked up a rock. He rolled it in his long fingers until his grip was just so, then wound up like a softball pitcher and hurled it at the intruders with blinding speed.

Matterhorn had drawn his Sword and stepped forward when the Bigfoot had picked up the stone. The Queen had charged him to protect Jewel, and that's what he would do.

The fastball was on target.

But so was the Sword.

Quicker than the eye could follow, it deflected the rock with a shock that knocked Matterhorn off his feet. "Yeow!" he bellowed as he landed on his already bruised backside.

The pitcher snarled and picked up a larger stone. Other Bigfoot also reached for rocks. Before they could unleash their deadly volley, the tallest Sasquatch barked a restraining command. A moment later he started toward the humans. The other Bigfoot watched him go but did not drop their rocks.

Blocking out the pain, Matterhorn stood and flowed into tai— correct fighting stance—learned from hours of kendo training: shoulders squared with hips, right foot in front of left, weight slightly forward. His sword grip was firm, yet relaxed. In the normal, two-handed grip, the left hand provided the power while the right gave guidance. Matterhorn had only his right hand now; the Sword would have to provide its own power.

The Baron drew his switchwhip and extended the poison-tipped lash.

"Don't do anything stupid," Jewel warned.

"What!" Matterhorn barked. "Like trying to save our lives!"

"The Sasquatch is more curious than hostile," Jewel said. "Let him make the first move."

"Even if it's ripping my head off?"

"Ssshhh."

The Bigfoot planted himself ten feet away from the Travelers but his scent kept coming. It was the smell from the cave, only stronger. Nate was right. These creatures stank!

Seymour and the Band

The Baron walked up next to Matterhorn and blinked his watering eyes. The smell reminded him of a feedlot he had visited with his grandpa. The stench coated the top of his mouth and the back of his throat. He put away his weapon and pulled a small metal box from his pocket. He took out a plastic plug and stuck it in his right ear. Then he put a round, clear patch on his Adam's apple.

"What's that?" Matterhorn asked out of the side of his mouth.

"A self-programming universal translator. Let's see how long it takes to pick up Sasquatch." Facing the towering creature, the Baron raised both palms to show he was unarmed. "My name is Aaron the Baron. What's yours?"

Silence.

"All I hear is English," Matterhorn said.

"The Bigfoot has to say something before the translator can learn the lingo." He spoke to the Sasquatch again. "We mean you no harm. We come in peace."

Raised eyebrows but no response.

"Say something, big guy."

The Sasquatch scratched his ribs and stared at these stubby, hairless wonders with their dull eyes. His expression brimmed with curiosity. Or was it contempt?

While the men played with their toys, Jewel used her animal telepathy to read the Bigfoot as she'd read the bear a few days ago. Both creatures radiated raw power, yet this one was much more intelligent. Focusing on the expansive face three feet above her own, Jewel saw supreme confidence. He knew he could easily kill these strangers if it came to that. Above his luminous, wide-spaced eyes she caught a glint of red. Studying it, she saw patches of dirty white peeking through the tangled bangs on either side. She stepped closer to Matterhorn and said, "Check out his forehead."

Matterhorn had been staring at what gave the Bigfoot their name. The creature's foot was fifteen inches long and eight inches wide, with five long toes. At Jewel's suggestion, Matterhorn raised his sights to the colorful bump. "Biggest pimple I've ever seen."

"Try ruby," Jewel said, "as in the Band of Justice. He's wearing the Talis. And from the looks of the band, he's had it on for quite a while."

"Do you suppose he knows what it is?" Matterhorn asked.

"One way to find out." And before he could stop her, she walked within arm's length of the Bigfoot.

"Hold it," the Baron said, grabbing Matterhorn's shirt. "Let her try."

Jewel reached out and took hold of a massive, hairy hand. She stroked the palm for almost a minute. Then she placed it on the left side of her head. Holding it there with her left hand she used her right hand to put the creature's other hand on the right side of her head. There was hardly room for all of his fingers. He could have squished her skull like a grape.

The Bigfoot and Jewel stood that way for a long time, his hands on her head, her hands on his. All Matterhorn and the Baron could do was wait.

Near the end of their silent dialogue, the Bigfoot squatted so that his eyes were level with Jewel's. She rubbed his cheeks and touched his forehead above the ruby. At last he stood and returned to the other Sasquatch, who were as anxious to learn what had happened as Matterhorn and the Baron were to question Jewel.

"What did you find out?" the Baron asked.

Jewel didn't answer right away. When she did speak, it was in a respectful tone. "He's amazing, very sensitive and bright. He's chief of the Bigfoot. They call him "One Who Sees Farther" or "Sees More" for short."

"Seymour the Sasquatch," Matterhorn said with a smile. "How were you able to communicate? The Queen didn't say anything about the Band working both ways."

"We understood each other," Jewel said. "Maybe the Band amplified my natural empathy. However it happened, I could see the pictures in his mind." She sat down and rubbed the tension from around her eyes. The Baron flopped beside her and handed over a water bottle.

After a noisy drink, Jewel continued. "He's curious about us, who we are, where we come from, what we're doing here. He's also concerned about our weapons. He has to decide if we pose a threat to his tribe."

"Threat," the Baron said. "Next to them we're children. But then, he's never seen humans before, so he doesn't know what to expect."

"That's not completely true," Jewel said. "His ancestors have had contact with a creature like us."

"How can that be?" Matterhorn said. "This area is supposed to be uninhabited."

"The Sasquatch have an old song about a man who brought them the Thinking Stone. That's what they call the Talis. The chief of the Sasquatch wears it so he can understand the others. Seymour has worn it for many seasons. I think it's increased his IQ. The song is beautiful. It tells how the Giver came long ago to the Salmon Waters. He made friends with the tribe and put the Band on the head of the strongest Sasquatch. The Giver made them understand that it was a sacred treasure, something to cherish and protect."

"Did he tell the Sasquatch it also had special powers?" the Baron asked.

"They're very smart," Jewel said, "much smarter than apes or gorillas. They soon learned how to use the Band to communicate. It's one of the reasons they've built such a strong tribal structure."

"Then they're not likely to part with it," Matterhorn observed.

Jewel nodded. "Probably not. However, the song says the Giver would return someday for the Band. That may be why Seymour stopped the others from killing us; because we look like the Giver."

"The Giver must have been the Praetorian captain," the Baron said. "But he's dead now. Do you suppose we can convince Seymour that the Giver sent us for the treasure?"

"I wouldn't try," Jewel said with a stern glare, "because it isn't true. We can say the original owners sent us to retrieve the Band. I'm not sure Seymour will accept that, though. And right now he has more pressing business." She looked at the water pouring from the other cave. "Seymour knows the earthquake caused this flooding. He was puzzled why we came out of this tunnel instead of more water. I told him about Sara and the ice wall she built. He wants her to make a wall in the other tunnel. I said we would ask her to do it when she returns. This would go a long way in winning his trust."

Thinking aloud, the Baron said, "In the meantime we should check for another outlet from this place."

"I asked Seymour about that," Jewel said. "There's a tunnel at the far end of the cavern. He hopes it can handle the water flooding in from this side. Sasquatch don't like water. That's one reason they live underground. It rains too much outside."

"That may be why they stink," Matterhorn said.

"Has Seymour sent someone to make sure the other tunnel wasn't damaged by the quake?" the Baron asked.

"It's not that easy," Jewel sighed. "That side belongs to the Browns."

"The Browns? Who are they?"

Wave Pool

Princess Jewel leaned against the wall near the cave they had come through a short time ago. It had been a long and grueling day. Her side hurt and her psyche was taut with the stress of being underground. The mental contact with Seymour had also been draining. He was an intimidating presence, almost human in intelligence, yet beastly wild.

Matterhorn touched her shoulder in concern. "How are you holding up?"

"Just tired, that's all."

"Who are the Browns?" the Baron asked again.

"It seems there are two tribes of Sasquatch living in here," Jewel replied, "and they are enemies. Seymour tried to explain it to me. The Greens—Seymour's clan—came to America long ago across an ice bridge."

"Must have been the Bering Strait between Alaska and Siberia," the Baron put in. "It froze during the various ice ages and connected the continents."

"Anyway," Jewel said, "the Sasquatch moved south until they came to the Salmon Waters. My guess is the Columbia River. They love fish, and so they stopped there. Over time they adapted to the pine forests and their thick hair evolved from brown to grayish green."

"You said Bigfoot don't like water," Matterhorn interrupted. "So how do they fish?"

"They love the taste of salmon more than they hate getting wet. When Seymour thought about fishing, I got an image of a Sasquatch standing in the shallows and swatting salmon out of the stream. The others catch the fish like footballs. It's a game to them. When they have enough, the wet Sasquatch rolls in dirt and pine needles to get dry. It's pretty funny."

"I'm sure it is," the Baron said. "But get back to the Browns."

"In the not too distant past, another bunch of Bigfoot crossed the ice and came down the coast. Sasquatch view time differently, so I can't tell how long ago that was. Anyway, the newcomers haven't been here long enough for their coats to change. They're still brown. The Greens resent the Browns since they compete for food and living space. And when the Browns found their own way into this underground paradise, the Greens attacked them. The fighting was fierce, but the tribes were evenly matched. Neither could drive out the other. Today they live in a tense stalemate—the Greens on one side, the Browns on the other."

Closing her eyes, Jewel faltered. "I've seen the battles in Seymour's mind. They hurl rocks at each other and use clubs or bare hands. They are incredibly strong. Seymour doesn't like the fighting, yet he has to protect his tribe. The chief before him was killed by the Browns. Seymour knows the fighting has to stop someday, but he has a lot of bitterness over the—"

Just then Nate came barreling out of the cave behind them. "Make like lightning and bolt!" he yelled over his shoulder. "NOW!"

Matterhorn, the Baron, and Jewel stumbled into Nate's wake as he sped past. His tone left no room for arguing. They followed him at a dead run toward the lake.

The Sasquatch near the other tunnel stared in wonder at the sudden flight.

When Nate reached the water he stopped to help Matterhorn, who could not swim with a broken arm. The Baron inflated the airbag on Matterhorn's pack and then his own. Nate pulled Matterhorn toward the center of the lake while the Baron and Jewel put an arm each through his pack straps and paddled behind.

The quake began as a slow rumble deep in the earth. It shook the cavern floor and then climbed the walls to rattle the roof. Chunks of rock fell and burst like bombs. The shrapnel wounded several Sasquatch as they scurried about in terror. There was no place to hide.

Meanwhile the humans bobbed like rubber toys in a bathtub. The lake was deep and narrow, which made the waves sharp and choppy. The frigid water numbed Matterhorn's broken arm, along with the rest of his body. Without the airbag he would have drowned. So would the

Baron and Jewel, who clung to the pack between them. "Didn't we almost drown together already?" the Baron joked through chattering teeth.

Nate coped by rolling into the fetal position. He filled his lungs with great gulps of air that kept him afloat like a beach ball. He had led the others here because it was the safest place to ride out the quake since it put them beneath the open crater.

The seismic shocks lasted over a minute, which seemed like forever to the humans and Bigfoot trapped inside the mountain. When the violence subsided and the lake settled down, the exhausted foursome floundered toward the shore.

Jewel sat on the stony floor, arms wrapped around her legs to control her shivering. "How did you know the q-quake was c-c-coming?" she asked Nate.

"Felt it," he said, pointing to his feet. "Seismic waves travel through rock like waves through the ocean."

"This must be the quake Queen Bea warned us about," Matterhorn said. He readjusted his soggy sling. The feeling was returning to his arm—the feeling of pain!

"This would register as a whopper on the Richter scale," the Baron said, "but it hasn't been invented yet."

Matterhorn had trouble hearing the Baron. He tilted his head sideways and tried to pound the water out of his ears. It took him several seconds to realize that the roaring wasn't in his head. It filled the chamber and bounced from wall to wall, crashing into its own echo. Looking back he saw water spouting from both tunnels now. It billowed outward then flattened into great satiny sheets. "Sara's ice wall must have shattered!" he yelled.

"Where is she anyway?" Jewel cried.

"No worries about Sara," Nate reassured them. "Water nymphs can take care of themselves. We'd best see to the Bigfoot."

Talis Hunters

More light filtered into the chamber now because several of the roof vents had been enlarged by the quake. From the relative safety of the lakeside the Travelers saw that several Sasquatch had been hurt. Those still on their feet were dragging their companions away from the flooding. Both tunnels were now spewing water like broken fire hydrants. "Nate's right," Jewel said. "We've got to help them."

"1 should've brought a bigger first-aid kit," the Baron muttered as they started toward the quake victims.

"I've got some medicines we can use," Jewel said, patting the pouches on her belt.

As they approached the disorganized Bigfoot, Matterhorn remembered the rock-throwing incident and thought about drawing his Sword. He decided against it, not wanting to give the wrong impression.

The Sasquatch were indeed suspicious, as if the humans had somehow triggered this disaster. A few reached for stones when the unwelcome strangers got close.

"We'd better find Seymour before we get killed," Matterhorn said nervously.

"That him?" Nate nodded toward a path through the shrubbery leading to a series of shallow cavities in the mountainside. Seymour was supporting a female whose foot had been crushed. Nate put his fingers to his mouth and gave a loud, piercing whistle. Every head turned at the sound, including Seymour's.

Jewel waved both hands in the air and cried, "We want to help!"

The chief looked at her blankly.

Thinking quickly, Jewel reached for Matterhorn's broken arm and pretended to set the bones.

Matterhorn winced in pain and said, "I hope he's good at charades."

Seymour understood the mime. He howled a safe-passage order and his tribe went back to collecting their wounded. When the humans caught up to the chief, he shifted his burden to another Bigfoot and conferred with Jewel as they had earlier, hands to head. After they finished, Seymour headed uphill with the humans in tow.

The Sasquatch village was honeycombed along the volcano's inner wall. There were no buildings or freestanding structures, just sleeping niches scraped out above an open area used for tribal gatherings. Now the place looked more like an emergency room. A dozen Sasquatch were laid out in various states of trauma with more on the way. Seymour checked the casualties with Jewel at his side.

After these initial rounds, Jewel reported that two Bigfoot had been killed and that some of the injured might not make it through the night. "I have some herbs and teas to prepare. Can you gather dry wood for a fire and boil some water?"

"Fire's risky," Nate said. "These creatures haven't seen it except for forest fires. Could cause a panic."

"Get the wood anyway," Jewel said without hesitation. "I'll explain it to Seymour."

"Is it safe to go off without his protection?" Aaron asked.

"He told the tribe to leave us alone—for now. But I wouldn't go too far in case you run into some Bigfoot who haven't heard the word."

This was a distinct possibility since there were dozens of Sasquatch bustling about.

A half hour later Jewel watched the boiling pot hanging over a crackling fire. It proved not to be a big deal. The Sasquatch knew about fire but didn't bother with it. Their fur kept them plenty warm and they couldn't imagine burning perfectly good fish.

As the sky darkened, Jewel made the rounds with her teas and medicines. Some would not accept the steaming potions while others were desperate for anything to relieve the pain. Nate and the Baron showed the Sasquatch how to set broken bones. Gradually their assistance was accepted and appreciated. Matterhorn fussed with the fire and fumed at not being able to do more. He felt for the patients, having a painful injury of his own.

When they ran out of things to do, the tired Travelers sat around their fire and ate supper. Below them the flooding continued. The Baron massaged his sore knee and said, "This place will be an aquarium in a few days if this water doesn't have a way out. We've got to make sure the tunnel across the cavern is open. Jewel, can you persuade Seymour to take us into Brown territory tomorrow?"

"I can try," she said.

Matterhorn pointed to the patch on the Baron's throat and asked, "How did your translation gizmo do?"

"Pretty well. I should be able to speak with Seymour myself soon." He took the plug from his ear and held it in the light of his headlamp. "This earpiece analyzes voice patterns while the throat patch converts speech into modulated sound waves. The two units are wirelessly synched. When they've picked up enough vocabulary and syntax, they can translate what's heard into English and what's said into the corresponding language."

Matterhorn whistled softly. "Did you invent that?"

"No. U-Trans are standard issue for Travelers. They're preprogrammed with most languages, and what they don't know they can quickly learn. It's how Queen Bea can speak perfect English," he added. "Hadn't you ever wondered about that?"

Matterhorn hadn't.

The Baron put the device in its metal case and plugged it end to end into a second, identical case. Green lights blinked three times on both units. Then the Baron unplugged the boxes and threw one to Matterhorn. "Welcome to the club. Now your unit has all the data from mine." He repeated the process with the boxes handed to him by Nate and Jewel.

"Why didn't I get one of these?" Matterhorn asked as he put in the earpiece.

"For the same reason you didn't get any specialized training," the Baron said. "You're different from other Travelers. The Praetorians selected us; the Sword of Truth called you. Queen Bea told me it's never happened before."

"Makes you special," Nate said, touching his forehead in salute. The gesture was genuine, not mocking.

This attention embarrassed Matterhorn. "I may be special, but I'm not 'Great.' Where'd you pick up that tag?"

"From being such a large baby," Nate said. "Mum said having me was like birthing a watermelon. Always been big for an Anangu."

"How old are you?" Jewel asked.

"Fourteen." This made him the oldest of the group. He was also the most traveled, both in normal life and as a Traveler. "At the mission school," Nate continued, "the first books I read were about a boy detective named Nate the Great. That made the nickname stickier."

When he finished speaking, the bushman plucked a small hide pouch from his bum bag and put a pinch of what looked like salt mixed with green flecks in his mouth. He worked it around with his tongue and rinsed with water.

"Sand and peppermint," he responded to Matterhorn's puzzled gaze. "Works better than toothpaste." He offered the pouch and said, "Try some."

Enemy Territory

Nate went exploring the next morning while the Baron and Matterhorn took Jewel to find Seymour. The chief was easy to locate and soon he and Jewel had picked up where their last discussion had left off. Standing nearby was the Bigfoot who had thrown the rock yesterday. He was recognizable by the brownish fur on his chin that made for an off-color beard.

Wanting to get some data for his U-Tran, the Baron said, "That's quite a throwing arm you have." His voice sounded garbled to Matterhorn, but the noise seemed to make sense to the Sasquatch.

The creature walked over and stared down at the strangers who had come just before the shaking. Did their arrival anger Mother Earth, or was she upset that the tribe had not properly welcomed them?

Handing a rock to the hairy creature, the Baron said, "Show me how you get that kind of speed."

The Sasquatch palmed the stone, then dropped it at Aaron's feet.

Matterhorn tensed for trouble, but the creature just stooped and selected a larger rock. He wound up and zinged a pitch against the wall near the sleeping niches.

"Strrr-ike!" the Baron cried.

The Sasquatch jumped back and picked up another stone.

"It's okay," the Baron reassured the skittish creature. He slowly picked up a rock with his left hand and mimicked the Sasquatch's underhanded throw. "Like that?"

The Sasquatch threw again with three times the speed of the Baron's toss. They traded throws for a few minutes, then the Baron said, "Now try it overhand." He selected a baseball-size rock and pegged a perfect strike of his own. Back home he was an All-Star Little League pitcher with a couple of no-hitters to his credit.

The Bigfoot responded to the challenge, trying to copy the strange motion. His first attempt barely missed Seymour's head, which earned him a sharp rebuke.

Jewel scowled at the Baron. "Can't you play somewhere else?" She turned back to Seymour, who was waving his arms and shaking his massive head in disagreement.

"Come on, Thrower," the Baron said to his new friend. "We need more room."

Matterhorn walked over to listen to Jewel and Seymour. "Too . . . dangerous," he heard Seymour's gravelly voice croaking in his right ear. This thing works, Matterhorn thought, tapping the earpiece.

"We have to try," came Jewel's velvety response. "The water is rising."

Seymour glanced at the expanding sea and his shoulders sagged. "Well," he said at last. He gestured for several Sasquatch to join them.

Jewel shook her head. "Not a good idea," she said. "We won't get safe passage. The Browns may think you are attacking."

Seymour made a growling noise deep in his chest that the U-Tran couldn't translate.

"We don't want to put you in danger," Jewel said. "Send someone to guide us across. That's all we're asking."

This made Seymour indignant. He rose to his full height and Matterhorn thought the Bigfoot was going to backhand Jewel halfway into next week. But she stood her ground and repeated her request.

"Someone's got to check the other tunnel," Matterhorn said. "Just point me in the right direction."

Seymour scowled at Matterhorn and thundered, "I am the One Who Sees More. I fear no Brown!"

"Certainly not," Jewel replied. "But the last thing you need now is a fight. They may let us pass if they don't feel threatened."

"They . . . not understand," Seymour said. "Your speech . . . poor." He tapped the ruby on his forehead to indicate that it was the only reason he could understand the strangers. "The Browns will kill you."

"The flooding will do that if we don't do something," Matterhorn spoke up. Patting the hilt on his hip he added, "We can take care of ourselves."

Looking down into Matterhorn's eyes the chief saw courage. "I take you," he said finally.

"Good," Jewel said. "Let's go."

Seymour led them downhill and along a curving path at the base of the mountain wall. Several Bigfoot followed at a distance. This made Jewel nervous until Seymour snapped at them to go back.

The yelling attracted the Baron and Thrower, who were not far away. Thrower refused to stay behind and Seymour didn't object.

It took thirty minutes for the party of five to cross beneath the crater and into Brown territory. The central lake was fast becoming an inland sea. Fallen pieces of roof stuck above its expanding surface like coral reefs. Circles of sunlight floated on the tide that flowed from the ruptured tunnels.

Dark shapes began to appear on either side of the group. They were being surrounded by rock-armed Bigfoot. To Matterhorn these Browns looked like the Greens—same muscular builds, same intelligent faces and reflective eyes, which now scanned the trespassers.

The Browns recognized Seymour as the Green chief by the icon on his brow. But what were these strange creatures with him? Only curiosity made them hold their fire.

Matterhorn drew his Sword and its light scared the Sasquatch back several yards.

Seymour halted and snarled an "away" at Matterhorn. Then he addressed the Browns. Sasquatch communication seemed to be mostly gestures tied together with occasional growls. The gist of Seymour's speech was a demand to be taken to his Brown counterpart. His tone and bearing were fearlessly regal. Regardless of color, he was a chief and expected to be obeyed.

For their part, the Browns considered him with contempt. One of them pointed at the humans and demanded to know what they were. Seymour refused to say anything about the "strangers from outside," except to their chief.

The Browns argued among themselves until the leader of the patrol smacked the loudest protester up the side of the head—end of discussion. The intruders would be taken to the village. They could be killed later if necessary, something the leader made clear with a graphic gesture.

"Ouch," Matterhorn said to the Baron. "I hope it doesn't come to that."

The Browns tightened into a hairy cocoon around their prisoners and started walking. Along the way they attracted more company so that by the time they reached their clearing the fur ball had grown to more than thirty Bigfoot. Their smell was so rank that Matterhorn couldn't keep from gagging.

Jewel took a mountain mint leaf from a pouch and shredded it. She put the flakes in her nostrils and offered some to Matterhorn and the Baron, who did likewise.

Mercifully, the end of the cocoon twisted open and the patrol leader nodded toward a group huddled around a young Sasquatch. Gooey red blood oozed from an ugly cut above the youth's right ear and matted the rusty fur on his limp shoulder. The female who cradled the lad in her lap glanced up at the visitors. She panned from Seymour's headband down to his tiny entourage.

Touching the Thinking Stone, Seymour said, "I am One Who Sees More."

"I know you," the female growled in a deep bell voice. "What are these?"

"Strangers from outside . . . came with the waters."

Matterhorn cringed at being linked to the flooding. What if the Bigfoot decided the humans were the cause of the crisis?

Sure enough, the Brown's next question was, "Did they bring this trouble?"

Seymour looked from Jewel to Matterhorn to the Baron and shook his head. "They are like the Giver," he said. "They come to help."

Without waiting for more of an introduction, Jewel slid around Seymour and knelt in front of the female. This uninvited move brought a swift reaction from the Browns.

236

Good Medicine

everal Sasquatch surged toward Jewel, but the seated female restrained them with a raised hand. Jewel ignored the danger, being absorbed in the shared pain of this mother and child. The lad had lost a lot of blood since being felled by a chunk of ceiling. His eyelids drooped. Saliva dribbled from the corner of his mouth. His wound was too broad to scab over properly. A few more hours and he would bleed out.

Jewel began chanting in Chinook, asking the Maker for wisdom about what to do. Her soothing voice was the only sound in the clearing for a long time. She massaged the child's head while she sang. Slowly she brightened with an idea. Reaching into a belt pouch, she produced a palm full of fine white powder. She showed it to the mother before dusting it on the gaping wound. Next she took three long, porous leaves from a different bag, wetted them from her water bottle and applied them as a dressing.

The crystals swelled in the warm fluid to form a gossamer crust and seal the wound. Jewel put shavings of willow bark in her remaining water and gave it to her patient to drink, after which she sang him to sleep. When she finished, she stood and patted the mother's shoulder.

"Will he live?" the Baron asked softly.

"If he hasn't lost too much blood," Jewel said. "At least his skull's not broken."

The Sasquatch rose with her son in her arms. She was seven feet tall and almost as broad as Seymour. She said something that was followed by the sound of falling rocks. The Sasquatch were disarming.

"The chief has extended her hospitality," Jewel confirmed. "We are not to be harmed."

"The chief's a female?" Matterhorn said in surprise.

237

"Don't look so shocked," Jewel said. "Many tribal groups are matriarchal. They submit to the rule of their better halves."

Matterhorn ignored the dig since it had been delivered with a smile. "What happens next?"

"A powwow," Jewel said.

Seymour and Thrower sat down and motioned the humans to join them. The Brown chief carried her son to one of the wall niches, which looked similar to the sleeping grooves in the Green village. When she returned and sat opposite Seymour, Jewel got up and went to her side. This move pleased the chief. She called two males to complete the circle before motioning for Seymour to speak.

Matterhorn didn't need the U-Tran as Seymour acted out his tale. The wobbling back and forth indicated the earthquake. Hands jabbed skyward, then thwacked on the ground, illustrating the deadly reign of stones. Arms swooshing forward meant water spurting from the tunnels.

None of this was new to the Browns, but they listened respectfully to the Green chief because he wore the Thinking Stone. They knew of its legendary power.

Pointing eastward, Seymour asked about the tunnel beyond. Was it open?

The chief looked to the male on her left. He shook his head and pancaked his hands together to show that the cave had collapsed.

Bad news, Matterhorn thought. He had a good mind for math and spatial dimensions and did some quick calculating. With the drain plugged, this chamber would fill quickly. And long before the water reached the top, the air breathers inside would all drown. He leaned over and said to the Baron, "Unless we can stop the water somehow, we've only got a few days."

"Too bad the trees in here are stunted," Aaron replied, "or we could build rafts and float out the top."

"Noah and the Bigfoot," Matterhorn mumbled. "We'll need a better plan than that."

The Sasquatch had no idea how to cope with the flooding and the meeting ended with Seymour saying he would come back tomorrow for more talks.

Jewel and the Brown chief continued a private conversation after the circle broke up.

The Baron tried to talk to the Brown who had given the report on the tunnel, but all the Bigfoot did was repeat his pancake routine.

One curious Brown touched Matterhorn's yellow sling. Another yanked his ponytail. A third hooked a long fingernail into his belt, painfully scratching his waist. Matterhorn twisted away from the unwanted attention, feeling like an animal in a petting zoo.

Thrower came over and slapped the hairy hand away. The Brown snarled and turned on Thrower, but Seymour pushed Thrower toward the path.

Dim shafts of evening light slanted eastward across the water as they headed back to Green land. The expanding sea was lapping at the path by now and they had to watch their footing.

"Did you see the hatred on all those Brown faces when they first saw Seymour and Thrower?" the Baron said to Jewel. "Your healing touch with the chief's son saved their lives and ours."

"See it," Jewel shuddered, "I felt it. Seymour did a brave thing in approaching the Browns. So did Bertha in receiving us. It's the first contact between the tribes that hasn't ended in bloodshed."

"Bertha?" Matterhorn and the Baron said in unison.

"My name for the Brown chief," Jewel responded. "She's known to her tribe as 'Honored Birth Mother' because she's had several healthy offspring. Birth Mother, Bertha."

Matterhorn chuckled. "Seymour Sasquatch and Bertha Bigfoot."

"It's not funny," Jewel said. "This could be the beginning of a peace process."

"It'll be a short process if we don't find a way out this volcano," the Baron said.

Matterhorn had a terrible thought. Maybe the reason there's no solid evidence of Sasquatch in modern times is that they never made it out.

ate was waiting for the others by a fresh campfire.

"Where have you been all day?" the Baron asked, taking off his boots and warming his feet by the fire.

"Around," the bushman replied. He was cutting the ends off thick yellowish pods with an unusual knife. The five-inch blade was black with red streaks and looked like a narrow stone arrowhead. The handle was carved from a wild boar tusk. "How'd the parley go?" he asked.

Jewel filled him in on the meeting with the Browns, including the part about the far-side tunnel being collapsed.

Nate nodded as if he already knew this. He split a husk with his thumb and ejected a string of olive-sized seeds and said, "I'm hungry as an anteater with a broken nose."

"What are those?" Matterhorn asked.

"Supper."

Jewel knew a lot about forest plants but didn't recognize these waxy beans. Perhaps because they grew underground.

"How do you know they're not poisonous?" the Baron quizzed. He didn't like trying new foods.

"Lift your shirt," Nate said.

The Baron looked at Jewel for an opinion.

"Black and blue I know," she said with a shrug, "and red and white. But yellow?"

The Baron reluctantly raised his shirt.

Nate squished a large seed and smeared the paste near Aaron's armpit. "Underarm skin's sensitive," he explained. "Toxins will cause a rash. If the plant doesn't harm the outside, it shouldn't hurt the inside."

"Clever," the Baron said as he pulled his shirt down. "But why not test it on yourself?"

"Easier to see a rash on white skin."

"Is that true?" Jewel asked.

Nate winked and went back to shucking pods.

Matterhorn laughed, thankful he hadn't been selected as the food tester. "While we're waiting for the word on dinner, let's review our situation, starting with the negatives. First, we can't get out the way we came in. Second, the exit tunnel is blocked so the water can't get out either. Third, our favorite water nymph isn't here to help."

"I'm worried about Sara," Jewel said.

"We all are," Matterhorn agreed. "For now we have to plan without her. On with the bad news: Fourth, we can't even take a raft out the top. There isn't enough lumber in here to get all the Bigfoot afloat. There must be a couple hundred Sasquatch between the Greens and Browns."

"Right direction," Nate said, "wrong number."

The Baron frowned. "What's that supposed to mean?"

"Don't have to get everyone out. Just me and you."

"What do you have in mind?" the Baron asked.

"Popping outside tomorrow and shutting off the water," Nate said as calmly as if suggesting a morning jog.

The Baron gazed at the roof arching overhead into darkness. "And just how are we going to manage that?"

"Climb out the nearest vent hole and hike to the falls," Nate replied. "As for stopping the water, I see you still wear your belly pack. Is it stocked like on our last trip?"

Nate was referring to the slim body-pouch the Baron wore under his shirt. Among other things it held a flat strip of C-4 plastic explosives. The detonators rested in the heel of his right boot. These were only part of the Baron's arsenal. His belt had five hidden tools while his pockets and pack bulged with everything from Chinese throwing stars to solar-powered electric eyes.

Their last trip had been to the Mayan empire in Central America. A mudslide had buried the entrance to a portal and a month of sun had baked the earth to concrete. The Baron had resorted to C-4 to blast open the tunnel.

Aaron patted his midsection. "Are you thinking what I'm thinking?"

"Blowing the mouth of the cave shut should tuck the stream back into its own bed," Nate said.

Matterhorn craned his neck backward. The nearest star-pocked vent hole loomed hundreds of feet overhead.

"How much rope you got?" the bushman wanted to know.

"Two rolls of 100-foot, 5mm Kevlar rope," the Baron said. He pulled a neon yellow coil from his pack and a second from Matterhorn's gear. They weighed one pound each. "I've also got a few metal spikes."

"You carry more stuff than an army surplus store," Matterhorn said. "Parachutes, climbing gear, night vision visors. Where do you get the money to buy all this gear?"

"There's a bank account Travelers can access with a special credit card," the Baron said. "I buy the equipment I need off the Internet and store it at my workshop in the Propylon."

"Where does the money come from?"

"Former Travelers mostly."

"Former Travelers?"

The Baron smiled. "Time travel is hard on the body. People can't do it forever."

"So what happens to them?" Matterhorn asked.

"They go on with their lives," the Baron said. "Get married, raise families, find careers, whatever." The Baron scrounged through his pack while he spoke. "They still stay involved with First Realm, looking for new recruits when needed, investing in the Traveler's Fund."

"What should Matterhorn and I do while you're gone tomorrow?" Jewel asked.

"Get the Bigfoot to work together on clearing the exit tunnel," Nate said.

"Not likely," Matterhorn snorted. "The Browns would have killed Seymour and us if Jewel hadn't saved the day. I can't see the two tribes cooperating."

"They're not that different," Jewel said, "except for their fur coats."

"There's more genetic variation within races than between them," Nate pointed out. "Still, color's a big divider. Jewel's people were herded onto reservations because of it. In my country, black babies were sometimes taken from their parents to be raised by 'civilized' whites."

Jewel nodded. Even though humans were more advanced than Sasquatch, they hadn't learned to be color-blind. From South Africa to North America people were persecuted for simply being a few shades different from their neighbors. "Perhaps the threat of extinction will be enough to get them to work together."

"I hope so," the Baron said. "But save the Sasquatch or not, we have to remember why we're here."

"To get the Band of Justice," Matterhorn said.

"What are you saying?" Jewel asked.

"If all else fails," the Baron replied, "we'll have to snatch the Band from Seymour and take it to the Queen."

"Can't you use the Traveler's Cube to take the Sasquatch outside?" Matterhorn asked.

"No. The Cube can only be used by Travelers. That's a cardinal rule."

"Why?"

"Because well-meaning Travelers would use it to save lives and avert disasters."

"What's wrong with that?"

"It would change history, and that's one thing First Realm will absolutely not allow."

Jewel and Nate nodded in confirmation of the Baron's words.

"If the Praetorians found out I'd done such a thing," Aaron continued, "no matter how noble the reason, the Talis would be revoked and our traveling careers would be over."

It was quiet for a long time after this. Finally, the Baron checked his side. Not finding a rash, he roasted some yellow seeds. They reminded Matterhorn of artichoke hearts.

"These taste like candle wax," the Baron complained.

Nate produced some dried mountain pepper leaves, ground them between his fingers, and sprinkled them on the Baron's food. After one large bite, Aaron's nose began watering and the tips of his ears turned red. Sweat beaded on the back of his neck. The tiny flecks felt like acid on his tongue. The heat radiated upward and cleaned out his sinuses. "Aahhgg!" he cried, groping desperately for his water bottle.

Matterhorn's interest perked up at this reaction and he asked for a dose of the spice. To his more experienced taste buds, the pepper rated somewhere between serrano and cayenne. Not as potent as insanity sauce, but intense enough to make his own head sweat—just the way he liked it. "Have you ever heard of Scoville units?" he asked Nate.

The bushman shook his head.

"It's the heat index used to rate the capsaicin level in peppers. Bell peppers have zero. Habaneros, the hottest peppers on earth, can pack more than 350,000 Scoville units. That's hot enough to melt the enamel off your teeth."

"Why not just swig gasoline and set your tongue on fire?" the Baron said.

Matterhorn rolled his eyes and reached for another pod.

Blown Assignment

The campers were awakened by a faraway shout. Nate's small face—haloed by light blue sky—shone down from above. A yellow strand of Kevlar rope reached partway down the inside of the volcano from the vent hole where he perched. The route up the inner wall to the rope went from steep to vertical and beyond.

"How in the world . . .," Matterhorn began.

The Baron knew it had to do with Nate's Sandals, but he didn't take time to explain. Instead he got up and started stuffing items into his pockets, including a pair of gloves and some energy bars. He donned his red corduroy cap and clipped a water bottle to his belt. "Take care of my gear," he told Matterhorn as he headed out.

Scooting upslope to where the mountain wall steepened, the Baron considered how far he would have to free-climb to reach the rope, dangling what seemed like miles overhead. He chided himself for not bringing another coil, but when he'd left home his pack weighed over sixty pounds. At least he didn't have to heave it up this rock face.

Through the skillful use of cracks and bumps, he made it to the end of the line in a stressful half hour. From here the rope was anchored to pitons driven into fissures every twenty feet. It took the Baron another ten minutes to hand-over-hand climb his way to the vent. His arms ached, his neck and shoulders screamed, but it felt good to be outside.

Nate squatted on his haunches and watched Aaron crawl like an ant out of its hill. "You climb like a girl," he said.

"Don't let Jewel hear you say that," the Baron rasped. "She'll zip up here and challenge you to a duel. Besides, you cheated. Let's trade shoes and see who's faster."

"No time, mate. This volcanic slag will get slicker'n elephant snot on bamboo if it rains."

"You mean when it rains," the Baron said. "This is the Pacific Northwest."

The rocky slope was tricky and took all their concentration to navigate. But when they made it to gentler terrain, they fell into easy conversation. From their previous trip together, the Baron knew that Nate had been a Traveler since he was ten years old. While on a spiritual quest to Uluru, a stranger had appeared to him who turned out to be a Praetorian. He explained about First Realm and traveling and showed Nate a special cave that housed a portal.

Curious about what Nate did when he wasn't traveling, the Baron asked him.

"Always traveling," Nate replied.

"Even when you're not portal hopping?"

Nate nodded. "Aboriginals don't build cities. We move with the seasons."

"What about school?"

"Half my year's spent in the outback, half at a mission school. My family taught me to read nature; the missionaries taught me to read books."

The Baron stooped to pick up a branch for a walking stick and got a good look at Nate's Sandals. "When did you get those?"

"A few months back."

Nate didn't offer any more information and the Baron didn't press.

When they stopped for lunch by a friendly stream, Nate went fishing. Instead of using a line and hook, he found a supple branch and tied one end to the other to form a loop. He draped his tank top over this to make a net and quickly bagged two large trout.

"That's not very sporting," the Baron said.

"Aboriginals are into survival, not sport."

The Baron built a fire and roasted the fish. Nate made stone tea by filling his animal-bladder canteen and adding a mixture of leaves and herbs. Using his shirt as a hot pad, he picked flat stones from the coals, dropped them into the bladder and let it simmer.

"Ummm, this is good," the Baron pronounced after his first sip. "You might say this drink really rocks."

"Please, don't," Nate groaned.

Walking away from the spot a few minutes later, Nate paused and looked back. "See anything?" he asked.

The Baron scrutinized the area and shook his head. They had left no ashes, no whiff of smoke, no rock out of place. Nate had seen to that.

"Leaving nature undisturbed shows respect for creation," the bushman said. "It also gives an enemy no path to walk."

They reached the base of the waterfall by mid-afternoon. The pool was shallower than when the Baron had last seen it. That's because the river water was now pouring into the hidden alcove and down the tunnel.

From a vantage point off to one side, they peered through the mist at the rock formation behind the thundering waters. "Can you set a charge to drop that overhang to block the tunnel?" Nate yelled above the din.

The Baron pointed his stick at the ledge and shouted, "Can't tell! We'll have to find a natural crack to exploit! Ready to get wet?"

They made their way around the falls and into the alcove. The Baron climbed on Nate's shoulders and scanned the ceiling. He spotted a crevice running across the roof about five feet from the entrance. Something closer to the edge would be better, but this would have to do.

The Baron rolled his C-4 into a snake and stuck a wireless detonator in one end. He stuffed it into the crack, then he and Nate moved back outside. From a fair distance away he said, "If this works, that slab of rock should drop straight down."

"Use enough explosives?"

The Baron shrugged. "That's all I have." With that, he touched the stud on his belt.

The blast could barely be heard over the noise of the waterfall. The rock overhang shuddered, then creaked downward, as if hinged to the side of the mountain. A moment later the huge slab broke free and jabbed edge-first into the cavern floor. It toppled forward into the pool instead of backward into the alcove.

"Oops," the Baron moaned.

There was a loud crack as more chunks peeled like dead skin off the granite face and splashed into the water. Rather than blocking the tunnel, the rocks now deflected even more water down into the bowels of the mountain.

Nate slapped the Baron on the back. "Aim's a bit off, mate. Best get back and get our friends out."

The uphill climb and an afternoon downpour slowed their return trip. It was well after dark by the time they reached the vent hole and slid down the rope like spiders on silk. The Baron went first. He secured himself at the end of the line while Nate undid the rope from the top and free-climbed to his partner. They repeated this leapfrogging descent all the way to the cavern floor.

Last night's campsite was submerged.

Matterhorn and Jewel were gone.

Ambush

Earlier that morning, after Nate and the Baron had gone to shut off the water, Matterhorn and Jewel planned their day over a breakfast of seeds. The chamber floor below them was flooding faster than expected. Broad bushes and stunted trees downhill from the Green village poked through the glassy surface like tropical islands.

"At this rate," Matterhorn said, "we won't be able to reach the Browns after today without swimming."

"And that's something the Sasquatch aren't good at," Jewel said. "Me either for that matter."

"Did you know what you were getting into when you agreed to become a Traveler?" Matterhorn asked.

"Not really," Jewel said, stirring her tea. "How could I? How could any of us? Traveling didn't used to be this risky. We watched and reported and didn't interfere. But since the trouble in First Realm we've become Talis hunters with dark spirits shadowing us."

At the mention of wraiths, Matterhorn felt the old wound in his thigh begin to throb. He rubbed his broken arm above the air splint and experienced a flashback of his tumble down the tunnel. "Traveling is definitely hazardous to one's health," he said. "You could have told the Queen you didn't want to come."

Jewel stiffened at this. "Just because it's gotten hazardous doesn't mean I want out."

"I didn't—"

"Everyone has a destiny," Jewel said over the top of his protest, "something we're meant to discover and do. When I was given the chance to Travel, to do what most people can't even imagine, I felt so blessed. So chosen. And if I checked out during the hard parts, I would be cheating my calling." She softened her tone when she realized she was preaching to the choir. Matterhorn had obviously made his own decision to obey his calling, a calling more direct and dangerous than that of other Travelers.

"I didn't mean to raise my voice," she apologized.

"That's okay," Matterhorn said. "I know what you're feeling. I was almost killed on my first trip but I was glad when I got the summons here. I swore an oath to carry the Sword and serve the Maker. What is it they say at weddings? 'For better or for worse, in sickness and in health, till death do us part.'"

Jewel laughed. "I trust it won't come to that."

"I believe we are protected until our work is done," Matterhorn went on. "I was scared spitless when I jumped off the falls, but I didn't die. And I don't expect to croak in this volcano." He patted the quote book in his hip pocket and added, "Davy Crockett once said, 'If a fella's born to be hung, he'll never be drowned.'"

Having finished breakfast, they put on their U-Trans—the units were fully functional now—and went to find Seymour. He was busy with a group of Bigfoot, the village elders, Matterhorn guessed. Jewel went over and stood next to the seated chief. She rested her hand on his arm and thus tuned in to the discussion. It was twenty minutes before Seymour called a halt and stood up. He looked tired as he walked past Matterhorn and started across the cavern.

"Seymour's exhausted," Jewel said, falling in step with Matterhorn. "He and most of the Greens spent last night trying to dam up the tunnels. It didn't work. The current's too swift. He thinks if the Browns help they might be able to do it. That's what he wants to talk to Bertha about."

"It's too late," Matterhorn said, glancing over his shoulder. "The tunnels are almost underwater by now."

"You have a better plan?"

"Yes. But it involves Sara and I don't know where she is."

The path to the Brown village was knee-deep in water that made for slow going. Near the Brown village they were met by a patrol as they had been yesterday. This one was not so obliging. Two hulking Browns blocked the way and refused to move despite Seymour's insistence.

Jewel's animal sense went to red alert. "These aren't the same Sasquatch as before," she told Matterhorn as three Browns circled around to close the trap. "We're in trouble."

Matterhorn turned and drew his Sword one-handed. The light within the diamond blade gleamed as he faced the towering trio.

"If you kill them, we'll never get the Browns to trust us," Jewel said.

Before Matterhorn could reply, Seymour collared the closest Brown and flung him downhill into deeper water. Another Bigfoot bear-hugged Seymour from behind and jerked him off the ground. The Browns in the back moved to join the action, expecting to sweep the puny humans out of their way like toddlers.

Matterhorn had a different idea. It was called shikake waza, the kendo attack technique where a fighter strikes first. Heating his blade at the speed of thought, he swept it broadside on the Bigfoot like rattling a hot poker along a picket fence. He landed several scorching blows while darting beneath their wildly swinging arms.

The startled Sasquatch howled in pain and retreated. They beat at their smoldering fur and splashed water on their burns.

Matterhorn spun to help Seymour, but the chief didn't need any. He had flipped his attacker over his head and somersaulted onto the poor creature's chest. The blow cracked a few ribs and ended the ambush.

Or so it seemed until Bertha and a second squad of Browns appeared on the path ahead.

eymour began fishing in the water at his feet for rocks to hurl when Jewel ran past him toward the Browns. She sensed that Bertha had not come to finish them off but to rescue them. The Brown chief had not ordered the attack and was even angrier than Seymour that her tribe had broken the promise of safety she had given yesterday. Bertha had the bushwhackers hauled away and personally escorted Seymour's party toward the tribal circle.

"It seems some Browns don't want anything to do with us," Matterhorn said, pausing to wash the burnt hair off his blade and to dry it on his pant leg. Now that the fight was over his hands were shaking, even the one in the sling.

"You're pretty good with that," Jewel said.

"I've been practicing," Matterhorn said. "What now?"

"The two chiefs have to talk."

Matterhorn frowned. "We can't waste another day gabbing. Time is getting shorter with the rising tide. Can you think of any way to speed things up?"

Jewel laced her fingers together and cracked them in a series of pops. "Now that you mention it, I can." They had reached the village and Jewel grabbed Seymour's massive hand. She led him to where Bertha was just sitting down in her usual place. Nudging a scowling male aside, Jewel positioned the two chiefs together. Then she plopped between them and rested her hairless arms on their shaggy knees. In effect she was forming an empathic link allowing both Bigfoot to benefit from the Talis on Seymour's head. Instead of words and gestures they could now share thoughts and feelings and come to a meeting of the minds much sooner.

The sensation was overwhelming for all three participants. Images strobed through the shared minds in panoramic 3-D. Neural pathways overloaded as sensations crashed into each other like bumper cars gone berserk. Nerve endings throughout their bodies tingled in what amounted to virtual reality.

Jewel then began asking questions to focus the mental trialogue. Would the tribes put aside their differences during this crisis?

Both Bigfoot were skeptical, yet knew they needed each other's help.

Could they work together to stop the flooding?

Not all Browns or Greens could be trusted in close quarters with their enemies. Some would seek revenge for past wrongs. The chiefs would have to handpick the work crews.

Would it be easier to stop the flooding or unblock the escape tunnel?

The water was so high in the Green tunnels by now that their only option might be to clear the Brown tunnel.

Were there any other ways out of the mountain?

A fleeting picture in Bertha's mind caused her to jump up and break connection with Jewel and Seymour. She stomped off, leaving a broken circle of bewildered Bigfoot.

Jewel understood what had upset the Brown chief. The image that Bertha did not want anyone to see was of a long, low passage snaking through porous rock. One end of the tunnel was concealed in a sprawling thicket on the backside of the mountain; the other end lay somewhere east of the Brown village.

This tunnel was how the Browns had first found their way inside. Its location was their most closely guarded secret. It was their emergency escape route if the Greens ever became strong enough to destroy them.

Jewel had managed to pick up an even more vital piece of information before Bertha broke away. Her tribe had decided to use this tunnel to sneak out of the volcano—and leave the Greens to drown! With their enemies dead, the Browns would have the whole territory to themselves.

Seymour had seen only a portion of a murky image before Bertha had disconnected. It was not enough to locate the tunnel or to pick up the Brown evacuation plan. He stood and rubbed at the headache behind his eyes.

Jewel got up and went after Bertha. "Don't let Seymour leave," she told Matterhorn.

"Where are you going?" he yelled after her, but she didn't answer.

Jewel found Bertha behind a boulder near the sleeping niches. She squatted with her forearms on her knees and surveyed the sea that would soon engulf her village. The relentless waters would drive them from paradise. She did not move when the human came up and put those soft, tiny hands on her shoulders. She had nothing to fear from the Small Ones. This one called Jewel had saved her son's life. Jewel was a friend.

The unspoken bond between them gave Jewel something to work with. She knew that Bertha had no remorse about leaving the Greens to die. Survival of the fittest was the way of things. If Bertha helped the Greens escape, the fighting between the tribes would go on till one destroyed the other. Better to let the mountain swallow the Greens.

Jewel scooted around to face Bertha. When they were eye to eye, Jewel thought and said the word, "Mother."

Bertha smiled at the small, childlike tone of voice. She played with Jewel's braid and repeated the word. "Mother."

"Will you leave me to die with the Greens?"

Bertha shook her head emphatically. Of course she would not leave Jewel. Her plan was to send Seymour away with the promise of help while asking the Small One to stay. Tonight, under cover of darkness, they would sneak outside and seal the tunnel.

"Can my friends come, too?" Jewel asked, her eyes not leaving Bertha's.

Bertha paused a moment and then nodded. "Friends."

What Jewel did next changed the course of Sasquatch history.

Friendly Persuasion

ewel pulled on Bertha's arms like a child dragging a reluctant adult off the couch. "Come," Jewel said. "I have something important to show you."

The Brown let herself be led back to the meeting circle. Matterhorn was entertaining the Bigfoot with his harmonica. He even let Seymour try the mouth harp to keep the Green chief occupied until Jewel returned. Seymour's fat lips fluttered as he blew wet air through the instrument. It filled with thick saliva and sounded like a kazoo being played underwater.

"It's about time," Matterhorn said when Jewel and Bertha arrived.

Rather than put the two chiefs together again, Jewel dropped Bertha's hands and walked to Seymour. She wrapped both arms as far around his thick waist as she could. "Friend!" she said with passion. "Friend!"

Bertha shook her head. "No Greens!"

"Friend," Jewel said again, tightening her grip to make it clear that she wouldn't go without him.

Bertha's features clouded in anguish. She did not want her new friend to drown. She also did not want to betray her tribe. The instinct to protect her own was strong. But so was her gratitude. Confused, she turned her back on the group and sat down. She hugged her knees and rocked sideways like the pendulum of a grandfather clock.

In the long silence that followed, Matterhorn slipped up next to Jewel and asked under his breath, "What's this all about?"

The Princess let go of the Sasquatch and pointed to the edge of the clearing. Once away from the Bigfoot, she explained about the secret tunnel and her gamble to use the concept of friendship to save the Greens.

Matterhorn gave a low whistle. Jewel's quick thinking impressed him, but he didn't think her ultimatum would sway Bertha. "If Bertha doesn't volunteer to show us the tunnel," he said, "we'll have to use force."

"Don't be such a Neanderthal!" Jewel snapped. "Trying to grab something from someone only makes them hold it tighter. Better to ask in love and hope for love in return."

"And if it doesn't work?"

"That's the risk love takes."

"If the Browns leave the Greens, would you really stay with them?"

The question surprised Jewel. "Yes, wouldn't you?"

Matterhorn thought for a moment. "I suppose so. Queen Bea ordered me to retrieve the Band of Justice and to protect you. As long as you're both here, I'm not going anywhere." With that, he went down to the water to wash out his harmonica.

Jewel returned to Seymour, who was anxious to go home. She explained that Bertha was struggling with whether or not to cooperate with the Greens, and they had to give her time to decide. She did not tell him about the tunnel.

By the time Matterhorn got back, the clearing was empty except for Jewel and Bertha. Seymour had refused to wait. Bertha had sent the Browns away to prepare for their evening exodus.

Matterhorn sat with Jewel and wondered if she wasn't expecting too much from the Bigfoot. Could they look to the future instead of the past? Could they understand and respond to friendship that went deeper than color? He sighed as he recalled that humans hadn't done very well at it. Why hadn't the Maker made all His creatures color-blind? That would have saved a lot of grief.

Across the way, Bertha rocked back and forth and wrestled with her thoughts. From Jewel she had caught a glimmer of a future that could be different from the past: cooperation instead of killing. Her higher instincts were stirred and something akin to hope sprouted in her heart like spring grass. If nature could start over every year, why couldn't Sasquatch? She would offer to share the secret of the tunnel in exchange for Seymour's promise to stop the fighting.

When Bertha came over and smiled her decision, Jewel jumped up and hugged her, crying with happiness in the Bigfoot's fur. Bertha hugged back, careful not to squish the Princess. Then she held Jewel at arm's length and pronounced Seymour's name.

"She wants to see Seymour," Jewel told Matterhorn.

"Then let's take her," Matterhorn replied.

"You have to come alone," Jewel said to Bertha. "No bodyguards."

The Brown chief understood this. As they walked downhill she ordered away the males who came to argue or accompany her on such a dangerous journey. It was a sign of their respect that they obeyed and let her go.

At the low point of the eastward trip the water lapped at Bertha's knees, Matterhorn's waist, and Jewel's chest. It felt as cold as the melted snow that was its source. Matterhorn and Jewel were half frozen by the time they reached the Green village. Matterhorn went to check on their gear, which they had stowed in one of the empty sleeping niches. Jewel and Bertha waited for Seymour under the watchful gaze of wary sentries.

When the Green chief arrived, he extended his hospitality as Bertha had done the day before. He called a circle of counsel and waited to hear what she had to say. As before, Jewel sat between the two chiefs and established an empathic link. The experience wasn't as jarring the second time.

Bertha thought right to the point. She imagined the secret cave and the Sasquatch flowing upward through it to safety. In her vision, the refugees were both Brown and Green. She was offering Seymour a way to save his tribe. But she wanted something in return. She was taking a great risk, one that many in her tribe would not understand. They would think she had betrayed them. Some might even attack when she brought the Greens back with her, as she planned to do. She had to know that Seymour would work with her toward peace and that things would be different on the outside—no more fighting.

Jewel understood that Bertha was doing more than saving the Greens. She was gambling on a better future for all Bigfoot. Her ante in this high-stakes game of survival was her tribe's most prized possession. Was Seymour willing to match her bet? That's what Bertha wanted to know as she stared at him over the top of Jewel's head.

It was Seymour's turn to count the cost of peace. "Sees More" had been so named for a reason. Wearing the Thinking Stone had amplified his natural intelligence. He had grown in his ability to acquire knowledge and to understand what was best for his tribe. Here was a chance to end the bloodshed and start over with the Browns.

Bertha had made the first bold move toward peace.

He would answer in kind.

Peace Offering

Seymour slid around Jewel to face Bertha knee to knee. Then he did something he never thought he would do. Slowly he took off the Thinking Stone and placed it on her head, combing her bangs around the ruby. The Greens around the circle went ape over this amazing turn of events. They began yelling and thumping their chests. Some threw dust in the air and flailed their neighbors with windmill arms. The sacred artifact that made them the superior Sasquatch had just been given to their foes. The symbol of ultimate authority now rested on a Brown forehead.

Jewel and Matterhorn looked on in stunned silence. Seymour had matched Bertha's courageous act of leadership. Would the Greens understand he was trying to save them from certain death by submitting to her?

Bertha touched the smooth gem and her eyes lit up. All Bigfoot regardless of color knew about the Thinking Stone. Its powers had given the Greens a great advantage in their struggle against the more numerous Browns. She even knew the legend of the Giver and his solemn charge to safeguard the Stone until his return. Before today Seymour would have died defending what he had just freely given her. Looking into his stern face Bertha knew he would still protect the treasure with his life. She rubbed the smooth area on his forehead where the band had rested for so many years. "Thank you," she said. "Thank you."

"Stone for safety," Seymour said. "Fair trade." Then he rose and began shouting and motioning to the gathering throng of Greens. They were to collect the children and wounded and follow Bertha back to Brown territory. There she would show them a new way outside. Greens and Browns would leave together and live together once all were safe. The old hatreds would stay inside the mountain.

Seymour made it clear that Bertha would lead, pointing to the Thinking Stone. Anyone who did not want to follow her could stay here and drown. Anyone who came along but caused trouble would wish they had drowned by the time Seymour got done with them.

The Sasquatch that the Baron had named Thrower began loudly reinforcing Seymour's instructions. He broke up a small knot of grumblers by banging two heads together and kicking a third protester in the rump.

There would have been a stronger revolt against Seymour's actions if not for the floodwaters swirling nearby. Bigfoot didn't even like rain, so the prospect of drowning was unimaginably horrible. Cooperating with the Browns was the lesser of two evils.

"Seymour did a very wise thing," Jewel said as Matterhorn helped her up with his good arm. "This is a great day for all Bigfoot."

"But not so great for us," Matterhorn said.

"What do you mean?"

"It would have been hard enough to talk Seymour out of the Band of Justice. No way is Bertha going to hand over her new symbol of authority."

"Let's worry about that once we're outside," Jewel replied. "Right now we need to get to the Brown village before the water gets any higher." She had no way of knowing that the volume of river water pumping through the tunnels had doubled due to the Baron's failed blocking maneuver.

By the time the Greens started their pilgrimage east a half hour later, the path was six feet underwater in places. Children were hoisted to parental shoulders. Jewel accepted a ride from Seymour. Matterhorn perched on Thrower like an overgrown parrot on a pirate. The Bigfoot had no neck to straddle; his sloped shoulders started at the ear and angled down into muscular arms. Matterhorn had to loop his right arm around Thrower's head to hold on.

The coarse fur felt supple, yet scratchy, through Matterhorn's clothes. Thrower's breath was surprisingly fresh compared to his body odor. He was eating a yellow pod like those Nate had discovered yesterday and offered one to Matterhorn.

Without a free hand, Matterhorn could only shake his head.

Thrower understood and raised the snack to Matterhorn's mouth. He took a bite of the pod and chewed. The juice from the seeds was refreshing, but the husk was like chewing Styrofoam. When he eventually had to spit out the yellow cud, Thrower burst into laughter that almost pitched Matterhorn into the water.

"Careful big fella!" Matterhorn cried. He wished he had Jewel's empathic powers so he could tell what was going on inside Thrower's giant green noggin. But he didn't, so he adjusted the throat patch of his U-Tran and began talking. The Sasquatch cooperated with the learning exercise and the chatter continued for the rest of the trip.

When the Green parade reached Bertha's village the Browns were ready to rumble, rocks and clubs in hand. Bertha bellowed for quiet and got it. The Thinking Stone on her head and Seymour by her side made it evident that she wasn't a prisoner. Far from it, she was in charge. She told of the new alliance required by their shared danger. The Greens would be going with the Browns to the tunnel. They had agreed to abide by her authority; she expected her own tribe to do the same.

Matterhorn waited with the Greens while Jewel went with Bertha and the Browns to make final arrangements for the exodus. It didn't take long as they had been preparing to leave all day. Soon Bertha was back with her young son in her arms. He was awake and alert, but still too weak to walk. Before setting out, she appointed two large Browns to help Seymour and Thrower keep order.

Standing on a rock ledge by Thrower and watching the furry brown and green caterpillar crawl away, Matterhorn prayed that the uneasy truce would hold. The procession climbed as far as it could up the inside wall of the cavern where the vegetation was sparser. Even here the cold water splashed to Matterhorn's thighs. Jewel put her belt around her neck.

The farther from the center of the cavern they traveled, the darker it got. Matterhorn and Jewel relied on their night visors to see. The Sasquatch were used to the darkness, but not to the water. The stink of fear added to their noxious odor. The only thing smellier than a dry Sasquatch was a soggy, scared one. Matterhorn's nose clogged with the moist, liquid stench and he begged Jewel for more mountain mint leaves.

The last traces of sunlight had disappeared by the time they reached the escape tunnel. It was hidden by a clump of tall, prickly shrubs that resembled holly, except the berries were white. Since the need for secrecy was past, Bertha had the bushes torn away to reveal what looked like a keyhole in a huge granite door.

The narrowness of the passage meant they would have to proceed single file. Bertha decided that a string of Browns would go first, followed by a group of Greens, then another bunch of Browns, and so on until everyone was outside. Jewel would go with Bertha in the lead. Matterhorn would join Seymour in the second group. Thrower and his Brown counterpart would bring up the rear.

While the Sasquatch were busy sorting themselves into the right pattern, two shapes glided through the black water toward them as quietly as crocodiles. Matterhorn caught the movement and drew his Sword.

he "crocodiles" surfaced as Nate and the Baron. "Got room for two more on this expedition?" the Baron said as he sloshed up to Matterhorn.

"I think we can squeeze you in," Matterhorn said, putting away his Sword. "Do you prefer the Green section or the Brown?"

Thrower greeted the Baron with a loud grunt and a clap on the shoulder that knocked him back into the water.

Matterhorn laughed and helped his partner up, "Were you able to stop the flooding?"

"Just the opposite," the Baron admitted. He explained how his strategy to block the tunnel had backfired. "The Green village is underwater," he added. "So is the path between villages."

"How did you find us, then?"

Nate tapped his nose.

"Even I could smell it," the Baron said.

"This tunnel go topside?" Nate asked.

Matterhorn scratched his stubbly cheek and nodded. "It's the Brown's top secret passage." He pointed to where Jewel was changing the leafy dressing on Bertha's son. "The Princess arranged a peace plan that involved Bertha showing us the tunnel. Seymour sealed the deal by giving Bertha the Band of Justice."

"He did what!" the Baron cried.

"Gave away the Talis," Matterhorn repeated. "I'm not sure we can take it from her without starting another war, but that's not our most pressing concern. We've got a lot of big bodies to get through that small hole. I wonder why we haven't started yet."

The problem was with the wounded. Bertha didn't know how to get her son and the other infirm Bigfoot through the long passage. The Sasquatch would have to crawl, which meant they couldn't carry the injured in their arms. The ceiling was too low for the wounded to be hauled piggyback and Bertha refused to let them be dragged.

Some Greens wanted to abandon those who couldn't make it on their own and an argument broke out. Matterhorn, Nate, and the Baron shoved their way to Bertha and Jewel, while Seymour made it quite clear no one would be left behind.

"That's what has them jumpier than a mob of joeys?" Nate said. "No worries." He waded into the gloom and returned with several large, leafy branches. He showed Jewel and the Baron how to knot these into litters and started Matterhorn and Thrower stripping bark to serve as straps before going after more lumber.

When there were enough litters and harnesses to go around, Bertha dropped on all fours and entered the tunnel. A Brown male pulling her son was next, followed by Jewel and a Brown female.

Seymour was leading the first group of Greens into the passage when the air above the Baron shimmered and solidified. Sara glared down at him and demanded, "Were you going to leave without me?"

"Sara! You're alive!"

"Last time I checked," she said, pinching her cheeks.

"Where have you been?"

"Under a rock."

"No, seriously," the Baron pressed. "Where have you been?"

"Seriously, under a rock," Sara said. "I was working on my ice wall when the big quake hit. A slab of ceiling fell and trapped me in a shallow recess in the floor." She patted the bill of his cap. "You would be about this size if you had been there."

"How'd you get out?" Matterhorn asked.

"A great surge of water hit the stone and shifted it just enough for me to escape."

Nate poked the Baron and said, "Seems your blast did some good after all."

"I rode the wave into the cavern," Sara went on. "This place is filling fast. You air breathers are in trouble."

"I'd ask you to go back and freeze the tunnels shut," the Baron said, "but it's not important now. We're on our way topside." He found Sara's vial and removed the stopper. "In you go."

Sara crossed her arms in protest. "I want to stay out and help."

The Baron remembered not being able to find her when Matterhorn was missing at the falls. He thought about the last few days when no one knew her whereabouts. He knew nothing about the tunnel he was about to crawl into. He shook his head. "It's too risky. I don't want to lose you again."

Sara pouted, then dissolved like a genie into her bottle.

There was a commotion at the mouth of the cave and the humans went to investigate. Thrower would not let any Sasquatch in until Matterhorn took his spot behind Seymour. Matterhorn apologized for the delay and ducked in. While the Bigfoot were forced to their knees in the corridor, Matterhorn could get by with a crouch. There were sections where he could almost stand. The floor was steeper than the entrance tunnel, which gave him hope that the way out would be shorter than the way in. The walls were rough and veined with minerals, so this wasn't a lava tube.

Time passed in a straight line. There were no twists, bends or forks to slow things up. It was as if the way had been bored by a giant drill. Matterhorn's night vision visor and headlamp helped him avoid jutting rocks. He didn't need to light up his Sword, but his mind was on the blade and his plan to take it home with him.

Soon they would be above ground. Jewel could charm the Band of Justice from Bertha and their mission would be over. Perhaps Queen Bea would show up like she had in Ireland to collect the Talis. Or maybe they would take it to her in First Realm. Either way Matterhorn wanted to keep the Sword the way the Baron got to keep the Cube.

He had already made preparations for the Sword's arrival. When his Great Aunt had died earlier that year, she left $5,000 to each of her nieces and nephews. Matterhorn put most of his money in the bank for college, but he talked his parents into letting him use some to start a sword collection. So far he'd bought a samurai sword of fine Japanese steel, a replica of a cavalry officer's saber from the Old West, and an English broadsword. They hung on the wall above his bed and would provide a natural setting for the Sword of Truth. He figured having the Talis with him would make it easier to be called into service at a moment's notice.

Matterhorn got so engrossed in making up a history of the Sword to tell his parents that he didn't notice the glimmer of light ahead. He didn't see Bertha crawl out of the hole on the side of a hill—or hear the crunching sound when a large rock cracked her skull.

Ensnared

Bertha's unconscious bulk was dragged into the bushes before the Sasquatch pulling her son came into the moonlight. He gave an exultant yelp at seeing the starry sky overhead. A moment later he saw a different kind of star as a tree branch broke across his forehead.

Jewel heard both the yelp and the crack and knew something was wrong. She approached the opening and peered out at the ghostly landscape. While not being able to see beyond the surrounding shrubbery, she could make out the drag marks on the soft ground. She stuck her neck out a bit farther—and was yanked upward by her collar.

The green Sasquatch holding her was nine feet tall. He was one of the two stealth creatures that had been tracking the humans for the past week. His leathery face wrinkled into a snarl as he said, "About time." Using his arm like a crane he swung her away from the tunnel and dropped her beside the unmoving Bertha.

Before she could scramble to her feet a second Bigfoot shoved her face-first into the dirt and snaked a thick vine around her hands and feet. Her capture had taken less than ten seconds.

The Brown female who came out next was ready for trouble. She dodged the first blow and charged her attacker, head-butting him in the chest. He clapped his cupped hands on her ears with enough force to rupture her eardrums. She let out a terrible scream and passed out from the pain.

The score was five to nothing in favor of the visiting team, with only Jewel and Bertha's son still conscious. Seymour was next up. Being chief of a tribe of Sasquatch was not an honorary position. He was a shrewd fighter whose natural instincts had been sharpened by the Thinking Stone. He rocked back on his haunches and blasted out of the cave like an enraged bull. The heavy branch meant for his head hit the ground behind him. Seymour somersaulted to his feet and took off downhill. Not because he was afraid of his enemies, but because he wanted to draw them away from the others.

If they had been Sasquatch, they would have chased him.

They weren't.

They didn't.

Seymour had no idea what a wraith was, and the wraiths had no idea what a Sasquatch was until just before their trip through the portal. They had assumed their hairy disguises to track the Travelers, which they had done until the unpredictable humans had jumped off a cliff. By the time the Sasquatch-wraiths made it down to the base of the waterfall and discovered the secret tunnel, it was already flooding because of the quake. That might have been the end of it if not for the chance sighting of a Bigfoot foraging for food. They followed the unsuspecting Brown to this tunnel on the backside of the mountain and set their snare.

Instead of going after Seymour, the wraiths turned to the shaft of light glowing by the tunnel opening and the man who held it—the Sword of Truth and Matterhorn the Brave.

Matterhorn knew what was happening as soon as he stepped outside. So this is where the wraiths had been, waiting for the rabbits to leave the hutch. He yelled down the passage, "We've got company! Everyone's been caught except Seymour. He ran off!"

The thought of facing two wraiths made Matterhorn's liver quiver. But he willed his body to act on what his mind believed; the Sword would protect him. He couldn't swing it with much force one-handed, but he didn't have to. One touch would destroy the dark spirits.

They knew it, too, which is why they kept away from the glowing shaft. The taller of the two picked up Bertha's son and splayed his massive hand on the youth's head, ready to unscrew it like a light bulb. "Stay where you are," he ordered Matterhorn.

Nate and the Baron squeezed past the Bigfoot ahead of them and came out on either side of Matterhorn. Instinctively the three formed a triangle with their backs and moved forward cautiously.

Tightening his grip, the Sasquatch warned, "Stop, or I will twist his head off."

The Travelers froze, except for the Baron's wrist, which snapped a Chinese throwing star at the Bigfoot's face. The creature swatted the chrome blade away as though slapping a mosquito. "Save your toys," he said with disdain. "I will take your Talis, however." His large red eyes moved from the Baron to Nate to Matterhorn to the unconscious Bertha. "I came for one and will leave with four. That makes this stinking skin more than worth wearing."

"Don't count your Talis before they're snatched," Matterhorn said, raising his Sword.

Suddenly, a loud grunt erupted behind him and Matterhorn spun in time to see the second Sasquatch jerk a small log from beneath the edge of a huge round stone. The rock rolled along a gouge and came to rest over the mouth of the tunnel. With that, the final piece of the well-laid trap was in place.

"You have two options," said the first wraith in a voice loud enough to regain everyone's attention. "You can resist, in which case we will kill you and them." He nodded to the wounded Sasquatch. "We will also leave the tunnel blocked and all the Bigfoot will drown." He made a gurgling sound in his throat and put on a mocking frown. "Or, you can come with us to the portal."

The wraiths would have already tried to kill them, Matterhorn knew, except that they needed the humans to carry the Talis. Being dark spirits they couldn't touch the Maker's handiwork. "Can't handle the Talis, can you?" Matterhorn taunted. "Light and darkness don't mix. Truth and lies—"

A heart-stopping scream interrupted Matterhorn's smug speech as the wraith holding Bertha's son snapped the youth's arm in two.

Matterhorn had never wanted to hurt anyone before, but had he been a few feet closer, he would have cut the wraith's head off and used it for a soccer ball. He was too angry to speak and it was Nate who finally said, "Leave the Sasquatch alone. We'll go to the portal."

The second wraith untied Jewel and ordered her to take the Band of Justice off Bertha and put it in her pack. After doing so she joined the others as the first wraith said, "Each of you must swear on the Sword not to fight or flee. Your oath will bind you as servants of . . ." He couldn't say the Maker's name.

"Will you swear on the Sword to move the stone if we do?" the Baron asked.

The wraith scoffed at the obvious trick. "You are wasting time," he said above the wails of the injured youth in his arms.

"We can't let others suffer because of the Talis," Jewel said. She put her hand on the Sword. "I swear by the Maker that I will not fight or flee, but will go with you to the portal."

Nate and the Baron followed suit.

From his quote book Matterhorn recalled the advice of Napoleon, "The best way to keep one's word is not to give it." But he could see no other choice. "I swear by the Maker that I will not fight or flee," he repeated.

"Good," said the wraith. He dropped his hostage carelessly on the ground.

"And I also swear," Matterhorn continued in a steel-edged tone, "that if you do any more harm to the Bigfoot, or try to hurt us, I'll—"

The wraith's animal laughter rang through the trees. "Big words for one so small."

"It's not my size you have to worry about," Matterhorn said. "I've seen what this does to your kind." The blade in his hand flashed, then went dark.

Jewel rushed toward the young Sasquatch even as his mother groaned from the bushes. Matterhorn removed his air sling and gave it to Jewel, who applied it after aligning the broken bone.

"We do not have time for that," the wraith scowled.

"Go stuff yourself," Jewel snapped. She gave the youth some willow bark to chew on and helped Nate carry him to his mother's side. Shielding her actions from the wraiths with her body, she took the replica of the Band of Justice that Queen Bea had given her and placed it near Bertha. The copy didn't have the power of the real Talis, but it would help Bertha and Seymour make peace between their tribes.

"Enough," the Sasquatch said. "Let us go."

"Move the rock first," Matterhorn said, adjusting his aching arm in the yellow sling.

Indicating the crest of a nearby hill, the Sasquatch said, "When we are up there." He started toward the spot while the other wraith piled the victims of the ambush in front of the tunnel. The idea was that the freed Bigfoot would be more concerned with their injured than with chasing after the humans. The wraith then shouldered the boulder aside just enough to open a small gap. And when the first Green male tried to squeeze through, the wraith smashed the creature's knee sideways, breaking his leg and clogging the opening.

The wraith bounded up the hill more like a gazelle than the 1,200-pound gorilla he was. In no time the humans were being hurried through red cedars and ponderosa pines toward the sunrise. The lead Sasquatch set a grueling pace with his long strides. The Baron, who was behind him, had to dodge bristly branches as they swished violently in the Bigfoot's wake. Nate and Jewel jogged side by side. Matterhorn trailed them and the second Sasquatch used a switch to make sure he kept up.

Topping a gentle ridge, they reached a sparsely forested area awash in flat yellow light. Matterhorn's flesh and spirit were flagging. His arm throbbed. His legs throbbed. His head throbbed. He knew they had done the right thing by surrendering in order to save the Bigfoot, but he hated giving the Talis to the Queen's enemies. There had to be something they could do short of breaking their oath.

Finally Matterhorn's sleep-deprived body gave out. He stumbled, lost his balance, and fell. The Baron circled back to his fallen partner and propped him against a fallen tree. "We've got to rest," he told the wraiths.

Either Sasquatch could have tossed Matterhorn over his shoulder like a blanket and never slowed down. But neither wanted to get close to the Sword. The lead wraith spat on Matterhorn in disgust. "What the royals see in humans I will never understand. Such a weak species."

"Ever hear of scorpions?" Nate asked, sliding between the Sasquatch and Matterhorn. "Small but lethal critters you don't want to cross."

This obvious challenge angered the wraith. "I do what I want!" he bellowed, then made a lightning jab at Nate's head.

The furry fist caught nothing but empty air. Nate dropped to the ground and rolled between the Bigfoot's legs and sprang up like a jack-in-the-box, lifting the brute off the ground and dumping him on his back. Nate had a rope around the creature's ankles before his head bounced the second time on the hard ground.

The other Sasquatch was also caught off guard by Nate's feat of strength. He knew what the flashing emeralds in the bushman's sandals meant, but he was determined to kill the human. Before he could gather himself to lunge at Nate, the Sword of Truth flashed in his face.

Matterhorn was on his feet and staring up into the fiery eyes of his worst fear. At that moment he experienced what in kendo is known as *take kurabe to iu koto*, "the comparison of height," when a warrior sizes up the situation to see if he has the spirit to become taller than his foe. A determined spirit is more important than physical size and Matterhorn was determined to protect Nate, even though it meant fighting a nine-foot wraith.

One slash and it would all be over, yet Matterhorn didn't strike because of his oath.

The wraith had no such reservations about killing Matterhorn and Nate. There would still be two humans left to carry the Talis. And while he had great respect for the Sword, he had none for the one-armed man who held it. He tore a large, gnarled branch from a nearby tree and swung at Matterhorn's head.

Every nerve in Matterhorn's body wanted to jump at once: sideways, backwards, anywhere away from the savage blow. Instead, he braced himself and swung his Sword to meet the branch. What had Queen Bea said back at the portal: "All things are possible to those who believe." He believed the Sword was more powerful than the wraith.

He was either right—or dead.

Self-Defense

There was a sharp fsssst when the branch hit the blade and just the briefest flash of laser brilliance as the wood vaporized. The momentum of the swing twisted the Bigfoot completely around. The palms of his hands steamed and swelled with instant heat blisters. His eyes shot sparks of molten hatred at Matterhorn.

Meanwhile, the grounded Sasquatch had come to his senses. He sat up and grabbed Nate around the waist. He lifted the bushman over his head, careful to keep away from the Sandals. Matterhorn heard Nate's grunt and spun with such precise control that his blade stopped an inch from the Bigfoot's throat.

Once again he kept himself from killing a wraith, even as he wondered why he should honor his word to a dark spirit with Nate's life at stake.

Because it was given to me, said a voice Matterhorn instantly recognized. He did not bother to glance about for the speaker but formed a clear thought in response to the divine presence. Now that you're here, you can take care of these awful wraiths.

What makes you think I just arrived?

If you'd seen what they did to the Sasquatch—Matterhorn brought to mind the sights and sounds of cracked skulls and broken arms—you could have prevented it.

I see all the evil that goes on in creation.

And you don't stop it?

For the time being, I limit it.

Limit it? How?

The Sword of Truth flashed and the voice vanished.

The Talis existed as tangible expressions of the Maker's character and power, Matterhorn realized. They were weapons that could defeat evil if wielded honorably. He held the blade motionless and ordered the

279

wraith to release Nate. "We swore not to fight but we said nothing about defending ourselves. Try to harm any of us again and you're smoke."

The Bigfoot tossed Nate to one side. These humans were more trouble than expected. Best to get the Talis to the Realm as soon as possible. Then there would be time to make them pay for their insolence. He stood and snapped the rope from his ankles. Without a word, he walked back the way they had come to make sure they weren't being followed. That would give him time to cool down.

"You have ten minutes to rest, no more," the other wraith said. He licked his sore palms and backed himself against a tree to scratch.

Matterhorn slumped down beside a mossy rock, exhausted and exhilarated by what had just happened.

"Our fearless foe has fleas," the Baron said under his breath.

"I hope they give him the plague," Jewel said.

The Baron removed the lid from a water bottle and handed it to Matterhorn. "You may be onto something," he said. "If we provoke the wraiths into striking first, we can defend ourselves without breaking our word."

"Don't push that too far," Nate cautioned. "The wraiths only need one porter. Three of us are expendable."

"Not if I can help it," Matterhorn said with more confidence than he felt. He took a long drink then poured the rest of the water on his head.

"What happened back there?" Aaron asked. "I thought you were going to kill that wraith."

"I wanted to," Matterhorn muttered, so tired now that the words dribbled down his chin. He didn't have the strength to speak of what the voice had said.

"Try these." Nate offered Matterhorn some round brown berries from a worn leather bag. "Thanks for covering my back."

The berries were so bitter that Matterhorn spat them out.

Nate grinned. "Forgot how rough these taste." Handing over a few more he suggested sucking instead of chewing. He also gave berries to the Baron and Jewel.

"Coffee beans," the Baron guessed after a few minutes. "They've got quite a kick."

"They've been, er, chemically enhanced."

"How?"

"Don't ask."

"Is it a family secret?"

"Only if you're a weasel."

Jewel winked at the Baron. "Leave well enough alone."

But he kept pressing until Nate finally said, "They've been coated with enzymes from a Luwak."

"A what?"

"Luwak. Member of the weasel family."

"You mean . . ."

"We're not the first ones to eat these beans," Jewel said. "I told you not to ask."

Matterhorn thought about ejecting his second batch of berries but decided against it. He felt new energy stirring in his rubbery limbs and didn't care where it came from. He adjusted his sling and leaned toward the Baron. "Can you use your Cube to get us out of here? We're all Travelers so it won't violate the rules."

Aaron shook his head. "I could only transport two of us. It takes an incredible amount of energy to uncoil a dimension and hold it open long enough for matter to slide through. And the Cube needs time to recharge between uses."

"Okay," Jewel replied. "You and Matterhorn take the Talis to safety. That's all that matters."

"And leave you and Nate behind? No way."

"We can outrun these brutes," she said, fingering her onyx earring.

"You're the one who told us Bigfoot are faster than horses," the Baron reminded her. "And these are super Sasquatch."

"We swore we wouldn't run," Matterhorn said with an authority that ended the discussion. "We'll stand by our word and by each other." A moment later he added, "That is if someone will help me get up."

Forced March

he Bigfoot that Nate had toppled returned from his walk and announced, "Time to go. I do not want to stay in this skin any longer."

Falling in line, the group set off. Matterhorn double-timed next to the Baron and quietly said, "The wraiths don't need their Bigfoot disguises now. Why not shed them?"

The Baron shrugged. "Maybe they can choose whatever form they want when traveling, but can't change back until they return to First Realm. Just like we can't revert to our natural ages."

"Is that where they're taking us?" Jewel asked. "First Realm?"

"Not to the Propylon," the Baron replied. "The Praetorians control that. There must be a portal in heretic hands somewhere."

"There are more things in heretic hands than you imagine," sneered the wraith behind them.

"Best keep our thoughts to ourselves," Nate advised the others.

For several foot-weary hours the wraiths drove them toward the portal cave like cattle to slaughter. Under different circumstances, Matterhorn would have enjoyed the scenery. Intense volcanic activity and ice age glaciers had shaped this rugged terrain. Rainbows of delicate wildflowers painted the basalt terraces along the hillsides and scented the brisk air. Ferns grew to prehistoric size. Lush moss draped trees of every shape and size.

All afternoon they hiked under the sharp-eyed gaze of mountain goats and big horn sheep. Overhead, bald eagles surfed the coastal winds between jagged peaks that wore snowcaps on their green heads. Since the escape tunnel came out on the backside of the volcano, the trek to the portal was much shorter than the Travelers' original route. This geographical fact, plus their unflagging speed, brought them within sight of their destination before dusk.

The wraiths showed no signs of fatigue but the humans were spent. It had been nearly two days since any of them had slept. The caffeine effect of the Luwak berries had worn off long ago.

The Baron's lungs hadn't fully recovered from his recent bout with pneumonia and Nate had been supporting him the last half hour. Matterhorn was almost too exhausted to care what happened anymore. A quote from his book kept running through his brain: "Being defeated is temporary; giving up is what makes it permanent." Still, he was ready to quit. Only a miracle could save them now.

Jewel and Nate weren't so gloomy. Both knew they were being tracked by real Bigfoot. Jewel sensed Seymour and others nearby. Nate had picked up telltale signs his captors had missed. Within sight of the portal he stopped and told the wraiths, "I need a bathroom break."

"Me, too," Jewel chimed in.

They weren't thinking about their bladders; they wanted to give their would-be rescuers a chance to act.

But the wraiths were too close to home to tolerate any more delays. "No!" barked the one in the lead. "I do not care if—"

The rock swooshed in hard and struck him in the right temple with a sickening crack. Blood and hair splattered everywhere and the stunned creature crashed to the ground.

Seymour stood beside a massive spruce and thumped his chest in triumph. He gave a loud yell and a dozen other Green and Brown Sasquatch appeared from their hiding places. All held rocks at the ready.

The chief of the Greens had not forgotten the humans, especially the smallest one who had shared his mind. When the false Sasquatch had refused to follow him into the woods, Seymour had doubled back and watched them lead away their captives. After making sure Bertha and the other injured would be all right, he set out with several Sasquatch to rescue the humans.

The Bigfoot posse had no trouble staying unseen while they tracked their prey. This land had been their home for generations. They knew every tree and bush, every rock and ravine. Seymour realized too late that the chase would lead to the one cave in the entire region the

Bigfoot never entered. If the false Sasquatch took their captives into that strange and sinister place, all was lost.

Seymour wanted to wait until dark before attacking since Bigfoot hunted and fought best at night. But with the sacred cave only a few yards away he had to do something. So he cast the first stone.

The Baron punched the air with his fist and shouted, "Yes!" over the fallen wraith. But his joy quickly vanished when the wounded Bigfoot shook his head and lurched to his feet. The oozing gash closed as if by reverse motion photography. All that remained of what should have been a fatal injury was a streak of blood in the beast's fur.

"He's still alive!" Jewel gasped.

This resurrection didn't shock Matterhorn. Dark spirits had supernatural strength, so why not miraculous healing power? He knew of only one thing that could kill a wraith—and he had sworn not to use it.

Emergency Exit

If they had not been so close to the portal, the wraiths would have fought the Sasquatch and enjoyed killing them one at a time. But delivering the Talis took priority over personal pleasure. The wraith closest to Jewel roughly grabbed her with one hand and Nate with the other. He crouched behind the human shields and began backing uphill toward the portal. The wraith with the disappearing wound seized Matterhorn and the Baron and did the same.

Seymour was stunned by the recovery of the false Sasquatch. These evil creatures could not be stopped.

But not all the Bigfoot were paralyzed with awe. Thrower was perched on an outcrop above the cave as still as a gargoyle. When the wraith dragging the Baron got close, Thrower jumped. He landed like a rockslide on the wraith's back, knocking him down and jarring the humans loose.

The startled wraith spun and grabbed Thrower and the two became a blur of flying fur.

"Stop!" yelled the other wraith. He lifted Jewel by her braid like a puppeteer as he strode toward the fight.

Jewel reacted quickly to save her scalp by twisting herself around the Bigfoot's arm like a snake around a branch. Why did bullies always go for the hair, she wondered. She bit down hard on his thumb and kicked at his eyes.

The wraith stumbled and almost fell, more annoyed than hurt. He shook Jewel off and lifted a huge foot to crush her only to find the point of Matterhorn's Sword ready to make him a new navel.

"Come on and die!" Matterhorn threatened.

The beast backed off just as Thrower screamed.

Out of the corner of his eye, Matterhorn saw the Sasquatch fly through the air and splat headfirst into the rocks from which he had jumped. His eyes rolled back and he crumpled to the ground.

The Baron rushed to Thrower's side as the wraith scooped up a large stone and moved in to finish the job.

"Enough!" shouted the lead wraith. "Get the humans into the portal!" he commanded. "Now!"

His companion growled and hurled his rock an inch above Thrower's head. Stone chips sprayed everywhere, cutting the Baron's face.

The wraiths herded their hostages into the cave's open maw. Outside the Sasquatch watched in frustration. Seymour howled with rage at being unable to help those who had helped him. He scrambled upward to see if Thrower was dead or alive.

The wraiths answered with a howl of their own, a howl of triumph! Another few seconds and they would be out of this dreadful place.

The Sword in Matterhorn's hands grew brighter in the enveloping darkness.

"Put that out!" one of the wraiths cried.

"I'm not doing it," Matterhorn argued, taking advantage of the light to scope out the cave. The floor was smooth, the walls were scalloped with rough stones, and the ceiling was double-arched with a ridge down the middle. The wide passage doglegged left and Matterhorn was shoved into it. A few yards around the bend, he stopped.

"I can't go any farther," he said.

"Quit stalling!" the wraith screamed from behind.

"I'm not stalling. Someone's in my way."

"That's impossible!" the wraith fumed.

"I'm afraid not," said the man planted tree-like in the passage. He was tall, well built and completely bald. His amber eyes had a deadly gleam.

"Who are you?" the wraith demanded. Without waiting for an answer, he pushed Matterhorn aside and charged the stranger, who dodged with the footwork of a boxer.

"You will have to do better than that," he chided, snapping a straight-fingered jab at his attacker's throat.

The Sasquatch jerked back with a partially crushed larynx.

The other wraith circled to the right of the unexpected intruder and motioned his injured companion to the left. He hated this animal body and was fed up with all these problems. This last delay on a mission that had already taken too long was the most disturbing. Where had this stranger come from? Did he know about the Talis?

The Bigfoot were now on opposite sides of the unmoving figure. At a nod they pounced in perfect unison, one lunging for the head while the other rolled into the feet.

The man didn't crumple under the onslaught; he vanished!

Jewel sensed there was someone behind them, and she spun to see the man standing by a niche in the wall. "This way!" he cried.

The other Travelers heard it, too, and raced toward the man. "In here," he said, waving then into the niche.

Jewel and Matterhorn skidded to a halt in confusion. The shallow recess was only a foot deep. The Baron kept going—right through solid rock.

The wraiths untangled themselves and rushed after the fleeing humans.

"Move it!" Nate yelled as he shoved Jewel and Matterhorn into the wall.

Epilogue

Matterhorn didn't have time to protect his face from being smashed into the stone. But instead of hard rock, he felt a tightening slick surface as if he were being shrink-wrapped in plastic.

He could not move.

He could not breathe.

He was trapped between moments, suspended in time.

Is this what it feels like to be dead, he wondered? A light show danced across the outside of his clear envelope. There was no sense of motion inside. Then everything faded to deep black and he heard rustling. A wave of heat dried the sweat on his face. The darkness became a shade lighter.

"Where are we?" Jewel asked in a shaky voice.

Good, Matterhorn thought. He wasn't alone. And he probably wasn't dead. Before he could say anything, he heard the Baron reply, "I don't know. Wherever it is, let's hope the wraiths can't follow us. Matterhorn, are you okay?"

"I think so. Where's Nate?"

The question rang in the void like an unanswered phone.

As Matterhorn's eyes adjusted, he made out two shapes. There should have been three. Had Nate missed the magic exit? Had the wraiths grabbed him?

"What happened?" Jewel wanted to know. "Who was that stranger?"

"My name is Elok," came an unexpected response.

A shrouded shape glided in front of the Travelers. The man's smooth head and bull neck reminded Matterhorn of a brass bullet.

His movement raised a cloud of dust. Jewel coughed and said, "I have a feeling we're not in Kansas anymore."

Elok smiled. "Not even close."

Matterhorn was in no mood for guessing games. The harrowing events of the last week had made an omelet of his emotions. He had barely escaped drowning in a flooding volcano only to be captured by wraiths and forced to march for a day. His broken arm hurt like crazy. His nerves were shot. He had just been shoved through a rock wall. "Where are we?" he demanded, raising his Sword. "Is this First Realm?"

"If it were," Elok replied, "you would be dead and that would be lost." He pointed at Matterhorn's Talis.

"How do you know that?" the Baron challenged as he stepped forward, switchwhip in hand.

"There is no cause for alarm," Elok said. His gaze moved from the Sword to the whip while his body remained relaxed. "I serve the Maker and the royals of the Realm. As to your present location, you are still on Earth. In Egypt to be precise."

Matterhorn let out a sigh and lowered the weapon. It remained lit and formed a halo around them.

"Thank you for saving us," Jewel said. She reached her right hand toward him in a Traveler's salute while concealing something in her left hand.

Elok leaned away and warned, "Do not be so quick to use the Band of Justice, especially on one who has given no cause for mistrust."

Jewel blushed at the exposure of her secret intent.

"Talis are not to be used lightly," Elok said. "Put the Band away and use your common sense. What does it tell you?"

Jewel did so and stared up into Elok's unblinking amber eyes. "You saved our lives," she sighed after a bit. "I suppose that's enough for now."

The Baron put away his switchwhip and shed his pack. "If you used a portal, then we're either in the Great Pyramid at Giza or in the Valley of the Kings. What time period?"

"We are in the Valley," Elok said. "1325 B.C., local time."

"What are we doing here?"

"Please sit," Elok motioned to a pile of dusty furniture. "I will explain."

"Not until I know what happened to Nate," Matterhorn said, splashing Sword-light this way and that. They were in a vaulted storeroom with what appeared to be life-size comics on the walls. Odd pieces of furniture and household items were piled everywhere, including clay pots full of decaying foodstuffs and reed hampers crammed with clothes.

"Calm down," Elok said. "Your companion has been watching from the shadows to see what I will do. Is that not so, Nate?"

"Maybe." Nate followed his voice into the light—and tripped on a carpet.

Elok caught the stumbling bushman. "Your caution is wise," he said.

Nate regained his feet and smiled. "Didn't have a chance to look before we leaped. Why Egypt?"

"My master and I are here on the business of the Realm," Elok said. "Business for which the Band of Justice would be of great help. Because we knew where it had been hidden I went to retrieve it."

"How did you know to show up when you did?" Matterhorn asked.

Elok ran a hand over his smooth scalp and admitted, "The timing was a divine coincidence. I did not foresee your arrival at the portal, or your need of rescue."

Matterhorn pondered this as he sat down against an elaborately carved trunk. The Talis were safe; that was the important thing for now.

But what was he doing in Egypt?

And how would he get home?

The End

Matterhorn the Brave

www.MatterhornTheBrave.com

When heretics murder the king of First Realm—a mirror world of Earth—his daughter, Queen Bea, recruits twelve-year-old Matthew Horn and others to find the Ten Talis. The heretics need these sacred objects for their scheme to take over the world by rewriting its history.

Each book in this epic adventure is set in a different place and time and features a colorful cast of unique characters.

DOUBLE-DIP BOOKS IN THE SERIES:

Book 1
The Sword and the Flute – Ireland, AD 700
Talis Hunters – Pacific Northwest, 10k BC

Book 2
Pyramid Scheme – Egypt, 1325 BC
Jewel Heist – Bermuda Triangle, AD 1292

Book 3
Dragon's Tale – China, 246 BC
Rylan the Renegade – Greenland, AD 985

Book 4
Tunguska Event – Siberia, AD 1908 & Asia, 160 BC
The Book of Stories – Chicago, AD 1983

TLC - The Lighthouse Company

www.TLCstories.com

BOOKS IN THE SERIES:

UFO on the Rez - Zack Fox has seen a UFO—and he has proof! But while hunting for more clues, he and JJ stumble upon Juan, a young migrant worker who needs to find his missing uncle before Miguel, the evil crew boss, finds Juan. TLC is also hired by Angus Keaton to catch the burglar who keeps breaking into his cabin.

Bezer's Billions - Did Old Man Bezer leave behind a secret treasure when he died? Will the skeleton key JJ finds in the basement lead to untold riches for TLC or unexpected trouble? Meanwhile, the arrival of shotgun-toting eagle poachers creates a more pressing—and dangerous—situation.

The Long Walk Home - One morning, JJ and Zack are blown out to sea by a freak storm. When the Coast Guard finds their empty canoe, the search is on to rescue the boys before the dangers in the Olympic forest put a tragic end to their long walk home.

Zack's Cavern - Is there any truth to the legend of pirate treasure on the Makah reservation? Does Spanish gold lie hidden in the sea caves at Cape Flattery? And what would make all the members of TLC jump off the lighthouse tower? Crack the pages of this fourth book in the TLC series to find out.

The Green Bees - My cousin Eli has started his own club in Colorado Springs. They call themselves The Green Bees. Saving the environment is their thing, but when I show up they get drawn into the shadowy world of government conspiracies to change the world.

About Mike Hamel

Mike Hamel is a seasoned storyteller who first told the adventures of Matterhorn to his four children—Aaron, Nate, Matthew and Julie—as bedtime stories. The children have grown, and so has the series. He is also the author of the TLC series and several books for adults. He and his wife, Cindy, live in Colorado Springs.